Praise for Dawn McClure's *Asmodeus*

Rating: 5 Stars "Paranormal Romance has a new champion and her name is Dawn McClure! I'm delighted to say that ASMODEUS was every bit the five star novel I've come to expect from this incredible new author. I loved everything from her characters to the enthralling paranormal setting she's created. Believe me when I say Asmodeus is a must read for romance fans everywhere!"

~ *Crave More Romance*

"ASMODEUS is a wonderful ride through the land of witches, vampires, angels, Nephilim, demons and fallen angels. Dawn McClure writes a very engaging story of these different types of creatures and how they all live in our world. ...This is a story I would highly recommend to all lovers of paranormal romance."

~ *ParaNormal Romance*

Look for these titles by

Dawn McClure

Now Available:

Fallen Angels Series

Azazel

Asmodeus

Samhain Publishing, Ltd.
577 Mulberry Street, Suite 1520
Macon, GA 31201
www.samhainpublishing.com

Asmodeus

Print ISBN: 978-1-60504-433-0
Digital ISBN: 978-1-60504-357-9

Editing by Sasha Knight
Cover by Angela Waters

First Samhain Publishing, Ltd. electronic publication: January 2009
First Samhain Publishing, Ltd. print publication: November 2009

Dedication

Mom, this book is for you. Thank you for your encouragement and support. Asmodeus is all yours.

A big thank you to my editor, Sasha Knight, who has the patience of a saint and the skills to make my writing shine.

Chapter One

Brianna sat on her bed and held the spell book to her chest, paralyzed by fear. A bright flash of light had burst through her house only seconds before, accompanied by a sound that had her reciting the Lord's Prayer. Her light yellow curtains tangled with the rush of wind sweeping through her bedroom, fanning out like wisps of ghosts. Family photos fell from their place on her dresser, and her television made a loud popping noise just before going blank. Gray smoke poured from the top of it, filling her room with an acidic stench.

From now on she was going to listen to her inner voice. The very same voice that had told her not to cast any spell that lay within the leather-bound pages she cradled in her arms.

The power contained in the book had called to her the moment she had touched it. Dark and compelling. That should have been her first indication not to play with the spells contained within. In retrospect, it was more than likely the reason she had purchased it. The rare ancient language sparked an academic interest. Deciphering the language posed a challenge.

A whisper of darkness slid through her, a steadfast warning that hadn't affected her as it should have.

She ought to have known something like this would happen. She was pushing herself to become a witch, focusing all her energy on spells and her obscure success at casting them. It was safe to say she was out of her league in this ambition. How long would she torment herself with powers she had no hope of mastering?

Now, after years of casting and studying spells, she knew what true darkness felt like. And it was currently in her house.

In the hallway.

Moaning such as she'd never heard nor imagined came from just beyond her opened bedroom door in the darkness that lay outside the circle of light cast by her bedside lamp. The question wasn't *if* something was in her house, it was a question of *what.*

Her psychic abilities were failing her. The only truth she could discern was whatever lay ten feet away wasn't human, and it certainly wasn't virtuous. She was unable to control her emotions long enough to concentrate on the entity, another one of her Achilles' heels. She needed meditation for her psychic visions to come to her. It was safe to say her skills concerning psychic capacity were sorely lacking.

The moaning coming from the hallway slowly gave way to silence. She closed her eyes and prayed the situation wasn't as bad as she was making it out to be. She hadn't merely made a blunder with a spell; she'd done something terribly worse. Something she may have no control over.

She listened for movement as her house once again grew silent.

Perhaps whatever she had summoned had died. That thought, though tantalizing, didn't leave her with a comfortable feeling. Whatever condition this creature was currently in, the simple fact it was in her house remained.

She put the book on her nightstand and crawled out of bed. She couldn't ignore what had happened, nor could she leave whatever it was in her hallway, possibly dying. This had happened because of a spell she had cast, and now it was her responsibility to rid her house of her mistake.

She grabbed her old, tattered spell book off her dresser and flipped to page forty, to her Oops Spell, as she liked to call it. It was a retraction spell.

Unfortunately she used it quite often.

She tiptoed to her door and summoned the courage to face what she had called forth. The house was so damned quiet she could hear her refrigerator humming in the kitchen. She took a deep breath and forced herself to peek around the corner.

There was a naked man lying on her floor. A rather large, *unconscious*, naked man sprawled in her hallway.

Had she yanked someone from a different time? A different dimension?

She tiptoed to his side, close enough to poke his leg with her foot. Years of watching horror flicks had her imagining all kinds of things. Him jumping up and snarling at her, brandishing a knife and a mask. His face contorting into a vampiric nightmare, fangs extended, claws tearing at her skin.

"Are you alive?" she whispered. She nudged his side with her bare foot.

He moaned.

She stepped back so fast she tripped over her own feet, fell against her bedroom doorframe and landed in a heap on the carpet.

She scooted against the wall and opened her book to page forty again. Her hands shook so badly it was difficult to turn the delicate pages. To hell with this. Whoever it was had to go back to where he came from.

She fumbled with her spell book, glancing up when the man, a mere silhouette of shadow in the darkness, moved. "Sorry for yanking you from wherever it is you're from, but I'm sending you back. Don't worry," she muttered as she scanned the familiar spell.

There was just enough light coming from her bedroom for her to see the words on the page. It wasn't as if she needed the spell book. She practically had this spell memorized. Still, she always followed a spell with painstaking accuracy. Even one missing word could cause a terrible disaster. A disaster such as the one lying before her.

Why she'd uttered a spell in a different language, which brought this being into her house, she had no idea. It was a stupid blunder on her part, and far beyond anything she had done before.

She gathered her courage and focused on the energy emanating from the Earth surrounding her. The natural energy provided the fuel she needed for her words to take on a greater power. "Tainted words escaped, a bad mistake, to make it right—"

"No!"

Her head snapped up at the rough command torn from the man's throat. She hit the back of her head against the wall.

The man pushed himself up, and if it was at all possible, he seemed larger. His long, blond hair fell around his face, shielding his features. The light from her bedroom danced along the contours of the muscles in his back as he slowly twisted to face her.

"Listen," she said, running a hand over the back of her head to ease the ache. "I'm sorry I snatched you from wherever you were, but I'll send you back."

She took a deep breath and began her spell again. "Tainted words escaped, a bad mista—"

"No," he growled, rising to snatch the book from her hands. For someone so close to death, he sure could move his ass when provoked. One second he was three feet away, moaning and in obvious pain, the next he was on her like a deranged madman. She yelped, scrambling away from him. He made it quite difficult when he grabbed her by her hair.

He flipped her onto her back and yanked the book from her hands, displaying strength and speed beyond that of a human.

With the book in hand he fell against the same wall she had just launched herself from. His hair was still a tangled mess around his face, reminding her of a wild animal. He was gasping for breath and holding his side.

"No. Going back. No."

Whispering those few words seemed to tap whatever strength he had left. He began to writhe against the wall, clutching his chest while straining against some unseen force.

She wasn't in the business of killing people. She crawled to him, her fear *of* him diminishing in light of her fear *for* him. She couldn't let him die. This was her fault. By performing a spell she hadn't understood, she had created this problem for him. It was her duty to fix it.

She held her hand just out of reach of his body, for the first time realizing how physically perfect he was. Absolutely perfect.

His jaw, barely visible underneath his golden hair, was square and smooth. Full lips pulled back to reveal perfect teeth, white and even. His shoulders were rounded with muscle, arms and chest ripped.

He couldn't be from too far in the past, because the man obviously liked to get waxed. Other than the hair on his head, and the bit at his, *ahem*, he was bare and golden, if not a bit flushed. The muscles on his body were taut, perfectly sculpted, not a bulging vein to be seen. He had very few blemishes on his skin. Those she saw looked like blisters.

She slowly reached out, as one would to a stray dog, placing a reluctant hand on his chest. His skin was scalding. She snatched her hand away, forced to withdraw before she burned herself. Leaning forward, she noted the blisters were forming, then in the blink of an eye they were healing.

Oh my God...

She had never wanted to hurt anyone with her spells. In fact, she had always tried to help others with her knowledge. It made her sick to think she may be the cause of the man's pain.

She had no choice but to help him. "Hold on. I'll be right back."

She ran down the hall and flipped the light switch on in her kitchen. Stumbling to the oven, she ripped off the dishtowel hanging on the handle. Trying to control her shaking, she told herself this problem would work itself out. The man would be okay. He had to be.

She took the towel to the sink and wet it with cold water. This was all her fault. What business did she have casting spells? None.

Twisting the towel, she wrung out the excess water and turned to run back into the hallway.

He was now sitting up, no longer writhing in pain, his head back against the wall and his eyes closed. His hair had fallen back, revealing his face. The muscles in his jaw were clenched. He had to be struggling against some serious pain.

She knelt in front of him and put the towel against his chest. He sucked in his breath and grabbed her wrist, causing her to stumble forward onto his lap, their faces only inches apart. He opened his eyes and looked at her for the first time.

His eyes were black. Liquid tar. No whites, no color, just one big, dark pool of black.

"What did you do?" he demanded.

She opened her mouth but the only thing that came out was a squeak. The hand holding her wrist was burning her. Everywhere her skin touched his she burned.

Her mind could process only one thing—she'd summoned a demon.

He shook her. "How did you free me?"

"From Hell?" Had she sprung a demon from Hell? This was not good. Not good at all. She highly doubted her Oops Spell would do anything for that. But then, she had thought demons' eyes were red. That's what she had read in her studies of the species. *What the hell had black eyes*?

He let her go, his head falling back against the wall again. She pushed herself away from him, unable to bear the heat. Sweat beaded on his forehead, poured down the sides of his face and chest. "Hell...I wish. The Abyss. That is where I was." His obsidian gaze met hers. "I will not allow you to send me back."

Brianna sat back, shocked. The Abyss was in Heaven. She'd read about the Abyss in one of the missing books of the bible, in the scroll known as the Book of Enoch. The Abyss was a place rumored to contain the worst of the fallen angels, set aside for those angels who had been reprimanded for terrible crimes, sentenced to eternal torture and damnation.

So he *was* a demon.

He started shaking as his body once again grew tense. She put her fingertips against his chest. He was still burning hot.

No matter what he was or where he came from, it was her responsibility to help him. She couldn't stand to see anyone hurting, and if she could help she would.

She drew her hand away. "I'll run a shower. You need to cool down."

She pushed herself up, trying to shut out his pain as she went to the bathroom and turned on the shower. She made the water hot, figuring he could turn it down as his body temperature cooled down. She couldn't put him in a cold shower in his current condition. It might send him into shock.

She tested the temperature once more, snatching her hand back from the scorching water. This wasn't exactly the way she had envisioned her evening. A little late-night reading, a snack—but cooling down a demon? Not so much. She stood and turned to get him.

She bumped into him, not realizing he had been behind her.

He leaned heavily against her sink, intense and quiet. He was solid muscle, and even hunched over she could tell he was well over six feet tall. His presence in her small bathroom prevented her from getting out. She fought down her panic when he collapsed against the sink, reminding her that he wasn't in a state to cause her harm.

Would he hurt her once she helped him?

Again, his obvious pain pushed thoughts of fear away. He was literally steaming her mirror.

"Here, let me help you." She tried putting her hand under his elbow to help him but had to draw away again. His skin was practically sizzling.

He shuffled to the shower, holding onto the walls. He pushed the shower curtain aside and stepped into the tub. When he got under the showerhead he sucked in his breath.

"Crap, is it too hot? I can cool it down." She bent to turn

the faucet.

"Cold. It's cold," he whispered.

She withdrew her hand and watched as he shivered under the flowing water.

The water was blistering hot. Steam began filling the bathroom as the water rolled off him, bubbling as if it was past the boiling point.

If she hadn't seen it with her own eyes, she would have never believed it. How could someone survive this?

Because he's not human, a terrified voice reminded her. *He's a demon!*

Demon or not, she felt awful for him. His eyes were closed and his breathing was labored. There wasn't a whole lot more she could do for him. Taking him to the hospital was out of the question.

For the second time in the last few minutes she couldn't help but notice how perfect he was. Well, other than the fact he was a virtual furnace.

She let her gaze wander down the length of his golden, drenched body.

Hot damn and damned hot. Literally. If she'd known demons had bodies like this she might have called one up sooner. Talk about an instant pick me up. The steam emanating from his skin could be overlooked with a body such as his.

Her gaze slid down a little farther.

Whoa. That thing should come with an instruction manual.

"Colder."

Her head snapped up to meet his liquid-black eyes.

"I'm sorry?"

"Make it colder."

"Oh. Colder, yeah. Sorry." Jeez, she'd been caught staring at his wanker. Hopefully he was too feverish to realize she'd been peeping.

She turned the knob upward. The water would be

lukewarm now. At least her idea was working and his body was cooling down.

She stepped back, keeping her gaze averted this time. Here he was in agonizing pain and she had been checking out his package.

"You speak English. What country is this?"

She glanced at him, trying to place his unique accent. Or was it a lack of accent entirely? God, she was losing her mind. "The United States of America."

He put his hand against the wall of the shower and dipped his head, letting the water run down his back. "The year?"

The muscles in his arms flexed as he moved. He seemed to be gaining control, his mind working, his body rebuilding strength. She cleared her throat. "Two thousand nine."

He gave a curt nod. "I now know how to work the equipment. You may leave."

She gave him a once-over, surprised at his dismissal, then quickly turned to do as he ordered. She was quite sure he could have told her to jump up and down on one leg and she would have complied.

"Or you can join me, if that is your preference."

She paused mid-stride, not sure if she had heard him correctly. "I-I beg your pardon?"

"You may join me in the water."

She almost snorted. Almost. Talk about too hot to handle. "I think I'm going to pass."

The sight of his magnificent body flashed through her mind. Firm, rippling muscle covered his entire length. Lord, when was the last time she'd had an offer like this? She paused in the bathroom, her hand on the doorknob.

What was she thinking? Was she *insane*? The man was a demon. He was practically on fire.

She shook her head and left the bathroom. She had to start thinking of a way to send him back.

Demon or not, could she, with a clear conscience, send him

back to such torment? Was it for her to decide?

Would an angel come for him and take him back?

Her mind went in a thousand different directions. She couldn't do this by herself. She needed reinforcements.

Scurrying to the phone in her bedroom, she yanked it off the receiver. She dialed her friend Kelly's number. Kelly Pendleton, psychic to the stars, famous tarot reader and witch extraordinaire. Kelly would know what to do. Kelly was the one with the inherited power, the extensive knowledge of witchcraft she had honed over twenty years.

She had gone to Kelly to get a reading, which was how they'd met. Kelly had seemed surprised by Brianna's reading, telling Brianna she had powers inside of her that remained untapped. She still didn't know why she felt compelled to be a witch, other than the tarot reading which foretold of great power.

Great power. Ha! Before this, the only spell she'd performed right had been to locate someone's missing dog.

"Hello?"

"Kelly, it's Brianna. I've got a slight problem." She paced in her bedroom, listening to the shower run in the other room. She tried to get the image of him standing naked in the shower out of her mind. Focusing on his perfect form wasn't going to help the situation.

"Something your Oops Spell can't fix?"

This was so beyond an Oops Spell it wasn't even funny. Brianna stopped pacing and closed her eyes. "Have you ever summoned a demon before?"

Kelly had the gall to laugh.

"It's not funny. I'm *serious.*"

The line fell silent. Kelly cleared her throat. "You really summoned a demon?"

"Yes." Brianna recognized the hint of disbelief in Kelly's voice. It was hard not to display a sense of misplaced pride in her accomplishment.

"Wow. Well, actually I have summoned a demon once before. But sending him back depends on the demon you summoned, what type of demon they are and how badly they want to stay in this realm. Who did you summon? Do you know his name?"

Knowing his name would give her power over him, but because of the chaos involving his appearance she hadn't thought to ask. "No, I don't know his name. The only thing I know about him is that he has black eyes and he came from the Abyss."

"Get out of your house. Now."

Kelly's demand brought her pacing to a quick stop. Brianna took Kelly's reaction as a bad sign. "Why?"

"First of all, if he has black eyes he's not a demon. He's an angel, and those are beings you *never* want to mess with. Demons' eyes are a light green and yellow mix, though when they are in a highly emotional state their eyes turn red, not black. Archangels, Warrior Angels, Virtues—their eyes turn black when highly emotional. The black color shows they have more power. Those with red eyes have less supremacy. Does he have any color to his eyes at all? Perhaps his eyes are just dark green. It's a rare color for a demon, though not unheard of."

Brianna shook her head, even though Kelly couldn't see her. How did Kelly know so much about demons? "No. All black."

"Then he's an angel."

"But he said I took him from the Abyss."

"Hmmm. Perhaps you took one of the angels who are in charge of torturing the Fallen Ones, which would explain why his eyes are black. Brianna, if his eyes are black then he's an angel."

When the shower turned off, Brianna looked out the open door of her bedroom. She whispered frantically, "Kelly, he's a demon. He wasn't in the Abyss as an angel, I'm sure of it. He says he doesn't want to go back. When I asked him if I'd summoned him from Hell he actually laughed and said, 'I wish.'

Now, what do I do?"

"If a demon wants to stay in this dimension there's not much you can do. You can perform an exorcism on a demonic spirit, but not an actual physical demon. I can try and contact Father Henry and pose a few questions to him."

Brianna felt like jumping up and down like a two-year-old throwing a tantrum. Was Kelly not listening to her? "What do I do *now*? The demon is in my shower, Kelly. Are you even listening to me?"

"Is he violent?"

How the hell did she know? Weren't all demons violent? "Probably." She recalled his invitation.

You may join me in the water...

"Where did you say he was? In your shower? What next, dinner and a movie?"

Before Brianna could respond to Kelly's flippant attitude, a bright flash of light illuminated her bedroom and she held her hand over the receiver. Shit, not again. No wind had come through her house as it had done earlier. The lights hadn't flickered. Had he gone back?

She walked into the hall and noticed the door to the bathroom remained closed, the light shining underneath the doorframe. She heard talking in her living room. She went past the bathroom, farther down the hall until she reached the sound of voices.

Standing in the middle of the living room were three men, all dressed in casual attire that looked ridiculous on them. They were wearing jeans and T-shirts, completing their look with combat boots. There was not a piece of clothing in all of Los Angeles that could make these three inconspicuous. All stood well over six feet tall with long blond hair that shined as though touched by the sun. They glowed with an otherworldly aura that framed their bodies. She'd never seen anything like it.

And each had obsidian eyes.

She brought the phone back to her ear as she backed up into the hallway. "I think I'm looking at your angels. Do you think they're here for him?" They had their eyes trained on her as if she was the prey and they were the hunters. As they followed her with their eyes she went weak in the knees. "And if they are, what do I do?"

"Get out of their way. *Now.* Angels are not the sweet, compassionate beings we've come to know through religion. They can be terrible, and sometimes worse than any demon has *ever* aspired to be. They are probably there for the demon. Get the hell out of there."

Chapter Two

Brianna bolted back to her room, panic rising through her body like bile. When she arrived at her bedroom door she came to an abrupt stop. The demon held the brown leather spell book on his lap as he lounged against the pillows on her bed. His long, blond hair, still wet from the shower, fell around his face.

He calmly thumbed through the spell book she had used to summon him, a bright yellow towel around his waist, as three angels stood in her living room ready to take him back to his damnation.

He looked up at her thoughtfully, his tar-black eyes resting in the general area where she stood. "Interesting. How did you read this? It's in the demonic tongue, which I have not yet heard you speak."

She wasn't sure who she was more afraid of—a half-naked demon lounging on her bed conversing with her, or three angels currently residing inside her house. "Are you aware there are three—?"

"I am aware. They are here to take me back." He turned his attention back to the book and smiled. "Let them try."

Was he *insane*? He had to be. Even if he was as powerful as the beings in the living room he had to understand there were three of them and only one of him.

Could he be that confident in his abilities?

A presence approached, as profound and horrifying as the entity stretched out on her mattress. She quickly shuffled to the other side of the room, searching for a place to hide, leaving the demon to fend for himself.

To hell with him. Literally.

She'd be the first to admit this was partly her problem. But the last thing she was going to do was put herself between a demon and three angels sent to apprehend him.

He glanced at her as she settled herself against the far wall.

"Sorry, but you're on your own, dude." Common sense told her the space of a small bedroom was not enough to keep her safe as a demon and three angels went toe to toe.

He smiled as if amused by her actions. "You have no need to concern yourself. I am out of their imprisonment with no intentions on returning."

Like she cared about *his* issues at the moment. Let them take him. It would save her the trouble of having to find a way to send him back. All she wanted was to stay in one piece as they did so.

He laid the spell book on the bed and stood, stretching. "You will not be reprimanded for breaking me out. I will take care of this problem."

An enormous steel sword materialized in his hands. His skin began to sizzle, cracking and sparkling as though he'd been dipped in electrified glitter. The muscles in his arm bunched under the weight of his sword as he braced his legs apart and stood before the door to her room.

In a yellow towel, no less.

She slid down the wall and sat on her butt, wrapping her arms around her legs, fully prepared to kiss her own ass goodbye. It was official. The demon was a psychopath, and he was about to get his ass handed to him.

The angels now stood in front of the demon, looking about as pleased as an irate mother with a switch.

"Asmodeus, as leader and commander of the Second Angelic Revolt, which resulted in the birth of the Nephilim and the purifying Flood thereafter, you will accompany us back to the Abyss, wherein you will continue serving a sentence for the aforementioned trespasses."

The demon only raised his sword as he faced the angels filling her hallway.

The angel continued, ignoring the three-foot steel blade presently pointed at his head. "If you decide to disobey the direct order of the archangel in charge of your current apprehending, we will be forced to extend your sentence and impart on you the highest persecution known in the Abyss. Your conduct in regards to your compliance or disobedience in this matter will be noted and recorded for future reference. We understand you were summoned, therefore we will not hold you responsible for your current fall. We will take care of that matter separately."

The demon turned around to look at her. His lips twisted into a smirk as if he found this situation highly entertaining. Had the angels been talking about her part in Asmodeus's summoning? What matter were they going to take care of?

Holy hell.

The demon turned back to the angels and answered them by raising his left hand. Sparks flew down the hall, a roar of glitter-fire that scattered the jean-clad angels like windblown ashes. It was like the Fourth of July at her house, only it was August, and she wasn't waving an American flag. It was just as awe inspiring, however, and she found herself low-crawling toward her door, like she was a soldier in a battle, as the demon calmly walked out of her bedroom and down the hall.

There was no confusion over who was in charge of this situation as the demon Asmodeus attacked again. He cupped his left hand, bringing with it a frigid wind that knocked the pictures off the wall in her hallway, and raised his arm toward the ceiling.

Before the angels could regain their footing from his first attack, Asmodeus brought his hand down. The three angels hit the wall in her living room, crumpling to the beige carpet in a tangled mess of arms and legs.

One of the angels thrust his hand toward Asmodeus. The air snapped to life as heat engulfed the room. For a few seconds she could hardly breathe, and she couldn't help but wonder what Asmodeus was experiencing, as the heat had been concentrated on him. Moving so quickly she barely caught the gesture, he brought both arms up and his sword shot into the air.

He lost his towel in the process.

Damn. His backend was as nice as his front.

Asmodeus uttered words she had never heard spoken before, pulling her out of her hot, hormone-induced stupor.

One of the angels disappeared, leaving behind a deflated T-shirt and jeans.

The other two materialized behind Asmodeus, only a few feet from where she was hunkered down on all fours. Asmodeus turned and thrust his sword through one angel. She backed away when the tip of the sword emerged from the back of the white T-shirt, now stained black. The angel disappeared.

The last angel stood tall as he faced Asmodeus.

"You have no purpose, Asmodeus. There is nothing for you here in this realm."

Asmodeus's face revealed no emotion. "Freedom from the echelon. That was all I had asked for in the beginning. To receive the same small freedoms the humans were given. If these liberties will not be given unto me, then I shall take them."

The angel clasped his hands behind his back and took a step toward Asmodeus. "Tread carefully, my fallen brother. The choices you make in the near future will not only affect you, they will determine the fates of others. There will come a time when you will beg entrance to that which you have departed, and it will not be given to beings such as yourself."

The angel faded away, leaving her and Asmodeus in the hallway. He scarcely moved his head, but she was distinctly aware the second he turned his attention to her.

She caught sight of the phone that lay only a few feet out of her grasp. She had dropped it when retreating from the angels.

Who was she kidding? Who could she call? This demon had just defeated three archangels single-handedly. Kelly couldn't help her now, and what kind of friend would she be to drag Kelly into this disaster?

She was up the proverbial creek without a paddle. Hell, she wasn't even in a rowboat at this point.

"What do you have for food, witch?"

She slowly pulled herself up off the floor, balancing her hands against the wall for support. The demon didn't seem rattled by what had just happened in her living room. She, on the other hand, had difficulty standing. "You're hungry?"

He was still naked. She kept her eyes glued to his face, but peripheral vision was a bitch. Though she wasn't looking at any part of his body other than his face, she saw more than enough. She'd thought him perfect earlier. Perfect didn't properly describe him. Delectable. Irresistible. *Demonic.*

"Ravenous is more apropos." He waved his hand over his torso and a brown robe materialized on his body. "Prepare the food for travel."

"Where are you going?" She fought down the panic threatening to take over. His presence was her responsibility. She had to figure out how to keep him from leaving and corrupting...whatever it was he would corrupt. She couldn't let a demon loose on the populace. She was sure there was some form of unwritten rule about that.

His sword disappeared. "More appropriately, where are *we* going? First I will locate a brother of mine. You will travel with me. Then you will summon Michael for me, allowing me access to kill the bastard."

Who the hell was Michael? "I can't summon people. I don't even know how I summoned you. In retrospect I wouldn't have—" She stopped herself there, figuring telling him she wished she hadn't summoned him from his torment might not be a great idea. "I'm not a witch." Not a good one, anyway.

"Witch or not, you contain the power to summon beings. Get the food, woman. We must leave this place."

His presence made her living room seem tiny. His close proximity unnerved her. It made her realize that though he was a demon, he was also a man.

A man who held power of which she could only imagine.

He turned slightly, letting his dark gaze travel around her home. "Do you own an automobile?"

"I own a car, yes."

"Good. If you will, get the food and let us be on our way. I can feel Naberius close by."

She had to stop this before it went any further. She wasn't going anywhere, and she needed to keep him here as well. "I'm not a witch. I mess up half the spells I try to cast." She pulled her hands inside the sleeves of her pajamas and bunched the material into her fists. "I also don't know who this Michael is, and even if I did I don't think I can help you locate him."

He quit assessing her house and focused his attention on her again. "Michael the archangel. During my prior visit to this realm most humans knew of his existence."

Was he *serious*? He looked serious. "You want to kill the archangel Michael?" she asked in disbelief.

"I'm *going* to kill him," he corrected her.

She pushed past him and began pacing her living room. "Well, good luck with that, but I'm not going to help you. That's just ridiculous. You think you're in trouble now, go try to kill Michael and see what happens." Talk about the point of no return. There was no way in *hell* she was summoning one of the greatest angels in all of history so a demented demon could attempt to eradicate him. "If you want to leave, by all means, go right ahead. I can't stop you. But I can't help you with Michael. I won't."

She quit her pacing to gauge his reaction, surprised at her own outburst. His eyes were changing color to a light green, yellow mix. His pupils were not round like a human's, or even vertical like a cat's. They were horizontal. He leveled those disturbing eyes on her.

"What will you do when the angels come for you?" He folded his arms across his chest as he waited for an answer.

"Come for *me*?"

"You commanded my presence from the Abyss, shortening the sentence they had given to me. There will be repercussions. If you like, you can face such sentencing alone, or you can come with me for the time being and avoid all such scenarios. Unless you believe you contain the strength to defeat them."

What a damned choice he was giving her. Go with a demon who offered protection from the inevitable, or stay and accept the sentencing from angels who represented the fury and authority of the highest.

The thought of angels coming after her with punishment in mind didn't leave her with a comfortable feeling. "You still hungry? I'll pack the food."

"Wise choice."

She shot him a dirty look before heading into her kitchen. She was making a mistake, yet she could not determine another course of action. Nonetheless, this situation was going to get worse and worse the longer she remained in the demon's company. If she could just find a way to send him back she might avoid whatever those angels had in mind for her.

She grabbed a healthy choice of chips and a Coke. Her mind was cluttered with thoughts of spells and repercussions as she walked back to him and handed him the chips.

He took the chips, studying the bag with interest. She opened the bag for him.

"What are these?" He leaned down to smell the contents.

"They're chips."

He pulled a chip from the bag and studied it. "What are they made of?"

She shrugged. "Potatoes."

He gave her a look that made her feel two inches tall. "These are not potatoes." He put the chip in his mouth and chewed slowly. After a moment of seeming to savor the taste, he smiled. "They are inherently better than potatoes."

She waved a dismissive hand at his midnight snack. "Whatever. I want to know what consequences you think those angels have in mind for me."

If this wasn't a lesson in preventive spell mistakes, she didn't know what was.

"You will summon Michael."

Nice way to avoid the question. Didn't he hear her when she told him she wasn't a witch? "I don't know how. I have very few psychic abilities, and I don't contain the knowledge of how to control the abilities I do have."

He closed the bag. "Then it looks like you will be doing some research. You obviously contain the power to summon or I would not be standing before you. One way or the other, you will be coming with me."

She resisted the urge to argue with him. She didn't think it wise, not after what she had seen him do to the angels. "I guess I'll go change."

"You will want to pack some clothing. I do not know how long I will need you."

She bit back the remark that came to mind and turned to go to her bedroom. Kelly had warned her about dark magic and taught her how to keep away from it. She had always been jealous of Kelly's powers, of her ability to cast spells and read palms. Because of Brianna's psychic abilities, Kelly had told her she could learn the art of witchcraft. Some were born with it, and others, like Brianna, could learn and practice it.

So much for practicing it, she thought as she grabbed a small tote bag from her closet. She put the can of Coke on her dresser, opened her dresser drawers and filled her bag with clothes. When she was finished she picked out a pair of shorts and a T-shirt.

She was through with spell books and tarot cards. She'd still sell them at her store, but she'd be damned if she picked one up again. She was through with palm reading as well. If you read someone's future wrong, the power of suggestion could change the true predestination of a person's future.

Yes, she was finished with this art. She'd leave it to those who were truly gifted, like Kelly.

First she had to figure out how to get rid of Asmodeus

without him finding out what she was trying to do. The last thing she wanted was to go toe to toe with that man, but she had no choice but to send him back to the Abyss.

As she slipped into her shorts she caught sight of him walking into her bedroom. Her foot caught on the waistband and she went tumbling to the floor. Lying in a heap, she yanked her shorts on and pushed herself off the floor, swinging her hair from her face. “A little privacy, please?”

He stood just inside her bedroom door, ignoring her chagrin as he held up her most prized possession.

“Explain this to me, witch.”

Chapter Three

Asmodeus waited impatiently as the human looked at the dagger in his hand, emotions tearing across her face as she tried to think of a lie. Did the woman take him for a fool?

The hilt of the dagger was pure ivory, with three rubies encrusted at the top, representing the Son, the Father and the Holy Ghost. Michael's name was embedded in the Angelic tongue in the steel of the blade, which was as sharp as it had been millennia before. He should know. The damned thing had been used on him on more than one occasion.

"Do not stand before me and lie, witch. You told me you could not summon Michael, yet you have his dagger. Explain yourself."

She shook her head, her dark hair cascading around her shoulders. Her blue eyes rounded in feigned innocence. "It's a dagger. Someone pawned it in my shop and I liked it enough to take it home."

She lied. She was well aware this was no ordinary dagger. As a witch she would be able to feel the power emanating from it.

She had known how to speak the demonic tongue to summon him. He could not fathom why she wouldn't know the Angelic language, and if she had not been able to comprehend the writing when she had acquired the dagger, he was positive a witch such as herself would have done some research.

He had sensed her possessiveness toward the dagger the moment he revealed it. A slight shift in her gaze, the small, tense lift of her shoulders just before she masked her surprise. It was obvious the dagger meant a great deal to her. "You know more about this dagger than you are willing to admit. Keeping that information from me is not a wise course of action."

"I-I don't know anything about the dagger."

He had found the dagger mounted on her living room wall and below it a leather casing. She'd taken great care with this possession. He was certain it was not merely an object intended for decoration. In his current condition he did not feel like arguing with her.

"Finish dressing," he said as he left the room. He went to where the dagger had been mounted and took the leather casing down, carefully placing the dagger in its sheath.

Summoning Michael would not pose him any difficulties now. As long as the witch had a decent summoning spell, this dagger would ensure she summoned the right person. It had belonged to Michael for centuries; therefore it would call to him immediately.

He heard footsteps in the hallway and turned as the witch walked into the main room. She wore very little clothing. Her shirt clung to every curve and her pants were cut off mid-thigh, revealing too much smooth, golden skin. She had pulled her hair back from her face and secured it with a band.

His body reacted to her presence with the speed of lightning. Her current state of undress made his sex hard, a forgotten reaction to the feminine species. He'd been in the Abyss for so long, without pleasure, without female companionship, the excitement came as a surprise. The arousal could not be mistaken.

The witch before him stood tall for a human female. Likely five-ten or five-eleven. The perfect height for someone of his size. The shape of her body was built to entice, and he grew harder knowing she would fit well lying beside him. Under him.

The woman had suddenly become a temptation. Sleek and strong, she would be an exotic assault on his resolutions. He couldn't recall the last time he had lost himself in the arms of a woman.

Yes, he was attracted to the witch, yet look where lust had cast him? Centuries locked away in the Abyss. He had learned his lesson. He would keep well away from humans and all of the punishments a relationship with one of them would entail, no matter how tempting they may be.

"What are you doing with that?" she asked, dropping her bag on the floor next to her.

He gripped the sheath in his right hand, willing away the effect she had on him. "I am keeping the dagger for now. We will need it soon."

He managed to keep the smile from his face as he watched her barely control her anger. She had irritated him with her lies earlier, though her actions were now becoming somewhat humorous.

She put her hands on her hips, her eyes revealing her defiance. "It was a gift. I'd appreciate it if you put it back where you found it."

Moments before the witch had displayed a very sensible amount of fear where he was concerned. Now her anger seemed to outweigh her trepidation. Shifting her weight from one foot to the other, she tugged her shirt down, causing the material to stretch tighter across her breasts. He forced himself to meet her gaze. "You told me you brought it home from your shop."

Her eyes rounded slightly. She realized she'd been caught.

"Okay, it was a gift. Now put it back."

He smiled. The truth kept inching closer, though she tried so hard to convince him the dagger held no great importance other than personal interest. "I've no intention of doing any such thing. Gather your things so we may leave."

She didn't argue as she picked up her belongings, the muscles in her legs flexing as she bent her knees.

"Where are we going?" she snapped.

He ignored her outburst as he headed toward the front of the house. He had to remain focused on his mission. Appreciating the witch and the beauty she possessed seemed a fool's game.

"Will you please tell me where we are going? You're in my home, you have my dagger, you've called me a liar and now you're demanding I go to some unknown destination with you. Why can't you just tell me? It's not as though I'm not going to find out anyway."

Why did she care when he gave her no choice in the matter? "I'll know when we get there."

"So, you're a demon? You don't sound like one."

Her incessant questions were causing his head to ache. "As compared to?" When she didn't answer him he continued. "In the late fifties I spent a few months in New York."

She stormed by him, pivoting just inside the front door to face him. She dropped her bag and put her hands on her hips, drawing his attention to her small waist and lack of clothing. "Okay fine. I'm going to drop that line of thought and focus on the issue at hand. How are we going to get where you want to go if you don't know where that is?"

He walked up to her, stopping only when he could feel her heat. "When we get in your vehicle I will sense which way we need to go."

He could tell the witch wanted to back away, though she kept her ground. Instead of putting space between them she brought a gray contraption out of her back pocket and held it in front of her.

"What's this guy's name again?"

What was the witch angling for? Names carried power, especially when it came to demons. Giving away his brother's name could be a mistake, but she would learn his name in time anyway. "Why?"

She flipped the gray object open. "If you give me his name I can probably locate him a hell of a lot faster than you can. So, what's his name?"

He had no idea what she was holding in her hand. He didn't sense it was a weapon, but he wouldn't put it past her. "What is that?"

"It's a cell phone. You can call and talk to people on it."

He'd run into this problem in the nineteen fifties when Naberius had broken him out of the Abyss. There had been advances in the human realm that bordered on the powers the angels held. Vehicles had been new to him, along with electricity and many other devices that made life much more complicated. Could this help them locate Naberius faster? "His name is Naberius."

She tapped the cell phone with her thumb. "Last name?"

"He doesn't have a last name that I am aware of."

She put the phone against her ear. "Is he in the general area?"

He could feel Naberius's proximity. "Within twenty miles, give or take."

She looked unconvinced. "Are you sure?"

"Unlike you I do not doubt my powers."

The witch said nothing, turning away from him. "Los Angeles, California. Yes, can I have a listing for Naberius? Residential, please. No. No last name."

He waited, wondering what it was she was attempting to do. Could she locate Naberius with just one call, a question posed to an available source? He'd been aware of phones in the nineteen fifties, but none such as this. It had no grounding, no cord attached to it.

"Okay. It's ringing."

She handed him the phone. He turned it around in his hands, looking at the lights on it and hearing a distant ringing.

She took the phone from his hands and put it against his ear as she rolled her eyes. Their proximity no longer seemed to bother her as her breasts brushed against his chest. Now he was the one to grow uncomfortable with their closeness. To feel another's touch after so many years in the Abyss, it was difficult not to pull her into his arms.

The top of her head nearly came to his shoulders. She was tilting her head back as she looked directly into his eyes. Of course his eyes would make her curious, as they were not like her own. A soft scent wafted up to him that he couldn't place. It reminded him of the flowers that had once grown wild around his home. Sweet and potent.

Her obvious assessment of his eyes and her earlier appreciation of his body told him she was the worst kind of enticement. What would it feel like to bury himself between her—?

"Hello?"

The voice ripped him from his thoughts. Asmodeus put his hand over the witch's, steadying the phone as an annoyed female voice barked in his ear.

"Hello?" he said.

He heard a sigh. "It's past midnight. Talk fast." The sharp sting of the female's voice grated on his nerves.

"Is Naberius available?"

"Just a sec."

It couldn't be that easy to locate Naberius. The witch smiled and stepped away, her hand falling from his. She seemed more than pleased she had proven him wrong.

"What is it?"

Asmodeus couldn't help but smile as a voice he hadn't heard in years came through the device. "Naberius, how are you faring, brother?"

There was a silence. Asmodeus could hear the woman in the background asking who was on the phone.

"Asmoday? Holy shit! Where the hell are you? You served your sentence?"

Asmodeus doubted if he would ever be finished serving his sentence. During his imprisonment the subject of release never came up. "I did not."

"Oh shit. So you broke out?"

"In a manner of speaking, but not literally. Do you have time to see me tonight? I have access to a vehicle and we are in the area."

"We?"

He looked down at the witch. "I'm bringing a witch with me."

She straightened her back. "My name is Brianna, and I'm not—"

"Brianna the Witch." He watched as the witch threw her hands up in the air and turned away, muttering something under her breath. "Speaking of others, who answered your phone?"

Naberius was silent for a moment. "My girlfriend."

Asmodeus could barely control the urge to crush the phone with his hand. Had Naberius learned nothing? Had the Rebels continued mating with the humans after everything they had been through? He kept his voice level as he addressed his brother. "You are with a human?"

Asmodeus caught sight of the expression on the witch's face. His eyes had likely changed back to black, causing her to become concerned. He would have tried to alleviate her fear, but her silence served him well. Perhaps she had finally figured out exactly who she had summoned.

"No." Naberius sighed. "It's a long story, but don't concern yourself. I have handled the situation and the echelon is not ignorant of the circumstances. We can discuss it when you get here."

Asmodeus held his hand out in gesture for Brianna to leave. She opened the door and he followed. The air fell against his skin, warm and refreshing as he stepped out of the house. A half-moon hung in a sky with very few stars surrounding it. The city he was currently in seemed to light the night sky, making it difficult to see the cosmic wonders.

"So she is not a human?" he asked, unwilling to let the matter drop.

"Listen, Asmoday. Valencia is a vampire. She's unable to get pregnant."

Asmodeus stopped just as he reached for the handle to the car. "A vampire?"

"It's a long story."

"Well—"

Asmodeus jumped when a sharp sound came from the vehicle. He bent down and looked inside the window to see the witch with her hand on the steering device.

"You can get in and talk on the phone at the same time, you know," she yelled at him.

"Woman," he warned. Truth be told, he was surprised to find that he liked the defiance in her much better than the fear he'd sensed from her earlier.

When he settled in his seat he tensed as the witch leaned across him, laying her body over his.

"It's easier to buckle you than explain the process."

Her hair tickled his face. Her wildflower scent wafted up to him. The feel of her body pressed against his ignited a hunger he hadn't experienced in centuries. This feeling went far beyond his appraisal of her earlier. The arousal. All he had to do was wrap his arms around her to keep her body against his.

She finished strapping him in with a long piece of material.

"It's the law. You have to wear this when riding in a vehicle."

Naberius spoke. "Do you want me to give her directions?"

"Yes." He handed the phone to her and began tugging at the strap that lay across his chest.

"Yeah, I know where that is. Okay. Sure will." She snapped the phone shut.

The constrictions of the strap she placed around him didn't seem necessary, and it set him on edge. For so long he had been forced to endure all measures of torture, and though this paled in comparison, he felt controlled, as though he had no choice in the matter. He needed to take his mind off the restraints. "Your fear faded quickly."

She turned in her seat and started backing the vehicle up. "I plan on dropping you off and coming back home, now that you know someone in the area. I'll face whatever consequences pertain to my summoning, but I want my knife back."

Her defiance was becoming less and less amusing. "You will summon Michael first. Then if you are successful I will release you and return your dagger."

The muscles in her jaw moved under her skin and anger pulsed off her. Like him, she did not tolerate being controlled. "Fine."

He settled back in his seat as much as the small space would allow. His body still ached from the Abyss. He was starting to feel cold and weary. The foreign feeling did not settle well underneath his skin. It would take some time to decompress in this realm. The pain was a far cry from what he had grown accustomed to, but the ache in his joints and muscles nagged him.

The stop and go of the vehicle made him ill, though her control of the vehicle made the strap he was wearing understandable. More than once he had to put his hand on the door to the vehicle to keep his body upright.

His stomach objected to the food she had given him, though he had not eaten much. Different colored lights coming from overhead metal, lights from other vehicles coming and going, all added to his sense of unease. He closed his eyes, convincing himself they would arrive at Naberius's soon.

In the Abyss he hadn't slept as it had not been an option available to him. No matter how tired you became, no matter if you thought you couldn't take the pain any longer, relief was always denied.

Pleasure forbidden.

He allowed the vehicle to lull him, seduce him to give in to sleep. In this realm he could do as he pleased. He now had the free will the Angelic host lacked.

He accepted the light feeling that came over his body, unable to withstand the sweet caress of slumber.

Brianna knew the second Asmodeus was truly asleep. His mouth had gone slack and a soft snore filled the car.

She needed to get away from him, *now*. Far away. The

longer she waited to distance herself, the harder it would become. The consequences of summoning a demon from the Abyss were one thing, but she was sure if she summoned Michael, and Asmodeus had the strength to kill him, they might not overlook her part.

Besides, the bastard had stolen her magical knife.

Kelly had given her that knife. Brianna hadn't lied when she had told Asmodeus a man had pawned the knife. Someone *had* pawned the knife—in Kelly's shop. Kelly had told her the knife had tremendous power emanating from it. Powers that could help in casting spells. Being a practicing witch who needed all the help she could get, the knife meant everything to her.

She'd been thinking of a plan to escape him while he had teetered on the verge of sleep, but nothing had come to her. It was nearing one o'clock in the morning and the streets were deserted in her small neighborhood.

As she pulled to a stop at a red light she eyed the dark streets with longing. How easy would it be to slip out of the car right here and now? She could go home, find a spell to send him back, and since she had the directions to his friend's house she could locate him later. Better yet, she could go to Kelly's. He wouldn't look for her there—and he would look for her.

No. She couldn't drag Kelly into this. She'd have to do this on her own.

The sight of him asleep, vulnerable in every way, made him look like any other man. Any other man who also happened to be the sexiest, most delicious man she'd ever seen. Her senses were telling her he was never truly vulnerable. If she attacked him right now, with all her strength and a weapon of her choice, he would still come out on top.

Which had everything to do with her flight response. She had to get the hell away from him or she was going straight to Hell with him, and that thought wasn't particularly pleasing.

Allowing herself no more time to think, she slowly pulled to the curb and put the car in park. She carefully slipped the dagger from his limp hand, stuck it in her bra, opened the door and took off.

The red light turned to green, reflecting its light off the wet pavement as she ran to the Circle K parking lot across the street, jogged toward the back of the store and kept going. When she came to a six-foot-tall fence she whistled to see if the owners had a dog. When none came slobbering up to the fence she pulled herself up and over.

Fence after fence came into view, and she snaked over each one. After a while her hands began to burn from the wood fences. Her legs had several scrapes on them, but the security the backyards gave her made her keep going.

Her legs and back hurt from her exertions. Feeling confident he couldn't drive and wasn't going to come running after her, she took a small reprieve and walked down a sidewalk. She had to take a break and catch her breath. Her lungs were burning from her exertion. A runner she was not.

Her cell started to ring and she quickly fished it out of her pocket. The ID let her know it was Kelly.

She stopped to adjust the knife in her bra and answered the cell. The leather sheath was sticking out of her shirt. "Hey, I am *so* glad you called. I need a huge favor. Do you have a protection spell I can put over my whole house to ward off demon entry?"

She had to get home as fast as possible, ward her house and then find a spell to send him back. The spell book that summoned him should contain something to send him back. All she had to do was get to it in one piece.

"Hold on, let me look. Actually, I think I do. Are you all right? I tried calling you back earlier. What the hell happened?"

Brianna let out a pent-up breath. The darkness that surrounded her, lit with the occasional front porch light, felt like a physical weight. Every sound had her twitching, every shadow had her looking over her shoulder. She started walking again. "I'm all right for now. It's just a lot of crap happened, and all of it is my fault. Listen, I'll be home in a few minutes, and

I'm sure that demonic bastard—"

A car turned down the street, and she squinted as the bright headlights hit her in the face. She thought about flagging the car down, but decided against it. If Asmodeus did come after her she didn't want to involve anyone.

She kept walking until the car passed under a street lamp, then she stumbled to a stop.

Damned if it wasn't Asmodeus driving her car.

"Fuck." She lowered the phone from her ear and took off in a dead sprint, her heart slamming against her rib cage. She ran through a nicely manicured front lawn and tore across a makeshift garden, petals flying in every direction.

Tripping over a garden hose that hadn't been put away sent her tumbling into a tomato plant.

She managed to regain her balance, terrified to look behind her and find Asmodeus hot on her heels.

How the hell did you run from a demon?

She didn't have the answer to that, and she sure as hell didn't have the time to contemplate it. She practically vaulted over the first fence she came to, not bothering to whistle, knowing good and well she'd rather face a slobbering rottweiler than a demon.

She bolted through the backyard and flew over another fence. A sharp pain shot through her thigh. She fell the five feet to the ground on the other side of the fence. It took her too long to regain her breath, and every second that went by she imagined Asmodeus flying over the fence to apprehend her.

She tried to get up and winced as a fresh wave of pain raked her body. She glanced down to where the pain was coming from.

"*Sonofabitch.*" She'd scraped the whole left side of her leg on the fence.

She attempted to survey the damage before getting back to her feet. She couldn't see very well in the dark, so she gave up on her leg and pushed herself up. Through the sting of the cuts she started jogging again, her teeth clenched against the pain.

Only one house away from the next street, and she tasted sweet freedom. She was nearly home. All she had to do was get to her house and slap up a protection spell to keep him out.

Had he stayed in the car? If he had, then most likely he would be waiting for her on that street. If not, wouldn't he have caught her by now?

She skidded to a stop and decided to go in the opposite direction. She doubted he would think of that. Unfortunately she would be running away from where she wanted to be, but she had no choice. The change in direction might throw him off. She had no idea if he could locate her with his powers or not.

When she made it over another fence she had her answer.

Asmodeus stood in the middle of the goddamned yard looking smug and clearly in better shape than she was currently in.

Out of breath and unmistakably defeated, she put her hands on her thighs, careful not to hurt her injured leg, and bent over in attempt to catch her breath. Nearing late August the air was still considerably warm, and a fine sheen of sweat covered her body.

So much for her grand escape.

"Not a bad first try." He walked over to her and snatched the dagger out of her shirt.

She jumped when his hand lightly brushed her breast. He didn't yell at her or physically harm her, and for some odd reason she had known he wouldn't. He merely took her by the arm and led her through the gate and to her car that sat in the middle of the road.

She felt quite calm considering the circumstances. "Didn't know...you could drive," she said between breaths.

"I have too much invested in your current task to let you go. I'm depending on your powers. Please keep that in mind the next time you attempt to leave. I will not be so lenient in the future."

He opened the passenger door for her, and she fell into the seat. He shut the door. She eyed him as he walked in front of the car to the other side, the headlights illuminating him. As she looked at his physique, which the brown robe couldn't conceal, she wondered at why she had thought she could escape him. Add his powers to his physique and she had been a goner from the beginning.

She carefully ran a hand down her thigh as he opened his door and sat down. The wood from the fence had left a jagged cut on her upper left thigh. It wasn't bleeding much, but it did hurt like hell.

He shut his door and turned to her. He moved her hand and replaced it with his own. "What happened?"

She brushed his hand away, embarrassed. "Nothing."

He ignored her, replacing his hand on her thigh. "Hold still."

He looked down at her leg with an intense expression on his face. She flinched when a terrible stinging sensation ricocheted through her leg. It was as though she had dropped a hot curling iron on her thigh.

"Ouch!" She tried shoving him off her, the burn causing her eyes to tear up. As she pushed against him, the pain melted away. When he removed his hand her leg was smooth, completely healed.

"How did you do that?"

"I healed your wound," he said as he put the car in drive. He didn't speak as he drove out of the neighborhood.

Attempting to control her breathing, she focused on the street. She'd heard some beings had healing powers, but what shocked her was he had healed her at all after the trouble she had given him. Then again, she was integral to summoning Michael, so of course he would want her in tiptop shape.

She turned and studied his profile in the dim light of the car. The handsome ridges of his face were lined with exhaustion. Asmodeus came to the place where she had ditched him, and she started feeling guilty she had run off.

"Your running is absolutely pathetic."

The soft timbre of his voice in the small confines of the car rattled her. She forced a laugh as she gazed out of the passenger-side window. "*What*?"

"Your running. I felt as though I were chasing an errant toddler."

She was unable to answer him right away, completely confused as to why he was acting so...snarky. Demons weren't supposed to be snarky, nice or conversational. They were evil, malicious beings. "You wouldn't know the first thing about running after a toddler. They're quicker than you think."

She turned to gauge his expression, surprised when she noticed he looked angry. She hadn't done or said anything that would anger him. What a moody sonofabitch.

He ignored her as they drove down Naberius's street. His house was in a nice neighborhood. Most of the houses on the block were two- and three-story brick Victorians. A few stood off the main road, with only a brick mailbox at the end of a lonely driveway.

"Hey, how do you know where you're going?"

He didn't look at her as he kept his eyes on the road. "I told you. I can feel his presence."

"Yeah, but there were a few turns you made—"

"Silence."

She let it go and looked for the address Naberius had given her. When she caught sight of the number on a mailbox she waited to see if Asmodeus turned into the drive.

He did.

Naberius's home was the only dwelling with a black iron gate surrounding the property. Large pine trees stood just within the gate, obstructing the view of his house from the road. But one thing was obvious.

Naberius was loaded.

She couldn't help but wonder why he had a virtual fortress for a home, but his number was listed in the directory.

They waited only seconds before the massive gates began to open. A black camera mounted at the corner of the gates pointed at them as they passed. Apparently this man put security high on his list.

What was worse were the two giant bushes just outside of the gate. Each bush was shaped into a winged, demonic creature. Though the fangs and wings were made from harmless leaves, the creatures looked as though they could come to life.

As Asmodeus drove down the winding driveway, two men came out of the three-story brick house. Both men were tall, broad and looked like they matched the demon bill quite nicely.

"I'll be damned," Asmodeus muttered.

"Pssht. You already are, dumbass."

He cast her a dirty look before he turned back to the men and stopped the car.

She peered at the men who were now only a few feet from the car. One was tall and blond, much like Asmodeus. His hair was shorter, cut in a stylish fashion that allowed his bangs to fall in his eyes. The other had long black hair and looked about as frightening as Satan himself. Even though he wore a smile, he seemed to have a darker aura than the blond. "Do you know both of them?"

"The blond is Raum, and the dark-haired man is Naberius. Both fell with me."

She snorted. "Certainly something to brag about."

Before he got out of the car, he turned to whisper to her, "I think I liked you more when you were a frightened little witch."

Her gaze fell to his lips. Full, inviting, and only inches from her own.

He's a demon. A demon! She forced herself to look into his eyes, which were now a green and yellow mix. "Will frightened get me released?"

He shook his head, those perfect lips rising slightly into a lopsided grin. "Not a chance in Hell."

What a play on words. "Then wicked witch it is," she said brightly.

His smile faded. “And that will get you killed.”

She deflated a little. “A dead witch can’t summon Michael.”

“I never said how long it will take to kill you.”

Was this playful bantering, or was he really threatening her? “You’re a killjoy, you know that?”

He opened the car door. “I’ve been called worse.”

She bet he had.

She had to move to plan B. Plan A: Get Thy Ass Gone, hadn’t worked so well. Plan B had to have a better outcome, because if she didn’t relieve herself of Asmodeus’s company soon, she’d probably be joining him in his damnation. Somehow she doubted they served nonfat, grande mochas in the Abyss.

Chapter Four

Asmodeus settled in his chair, ignoring the heat that lingered in his chest from the Abyss, and glanced across the kitchen table at his fallen comrades. Their clothes, their language and their surroundings had changed considerably, but their mannerisms remained the same.

Raum had on jeans and a white T-shirt, his hair a bit shorter than the last time he had seen his friend. He fit perfectly in the contemporary setting, and perhaps he was attempting that very thing.

In the years following their fall from grace, each Rebel had done their best to conform to the ideals of the populace. Using their powers they effectively masked the differences of their eyes, the spark of power that caused the air around them to pulse and the aura that surrounded their bodies. What they had never succeeded at concealing was the immortality each possessed.

Naberius, on the other hand, looked every bit the ancient demon. His black hair was long, past his shoulders, and the black stubble on his face was most definitely a change from his usual clean-shaven look. He had on jeans which were loose and faded with a few holes in them. He had yet to discern why Naberius's home spoke of wealth, though his clothing reeked of poverty.

"You have a nice home, Naberius." Asmodeus scratched his thigh, the denim making him itchy. Naberius had loaned him a pair of jeans, though Asmodeus had forgone the shirt that had been offered, instead wanting to feel the cool air on his skin.

"Cut the shit, Asmoday, how the fuck did you get out?" Naberius leaned forward, his elbows resting on the table. He lit a cigarette. The offending smoke drifted across the table and caused Asmodeus's eyes to water.

Ignoring the smoke, Asmodeus adjusted himself, thinking the jeans were a form of torture unto themselves. "The witch summoned me out earlier this evening. It took me a while to get my bearings. Three archangels have already attempted to apprehend me."

Raum's eyebrows shot up. "And?"

"And I sent them back."

Naberius whistled, settling back in his chair. "They'll be back."

"I am quite aware." His thoughts drifted to the dark-haired witch, Brianna. As much as she annoyed him, he wasn't going to allow the bastards to hurt her, which was half the reason he forced her to come with him. She could summon Michael and he could keep her safe from whatever fate the angels had in mind for her.

"If you want I can start calling around, getting available resources willing to fight should the need arise."

Asmodeus eyed Raum. Yes, his brothers would offer their services to keep him out of the Abyss, though he didn't want to go that route. It would mean imprisonment for everyone involved, and hadn't he already been down that road and learned his lesson?

When Naberius broke him out of the Abyss in the early fifties he had spent nearly a year on the run, forcing Raum and Naberius to do the same. In the end it hadn't mattered. Michael had taken him back to the Abyss, catching him unaware and with his fallen comrades. He would keep in mind the repercussions that disaster had entailed. Raum and Naberius had been sent back to the first tier of the Abyss for a decade. At least this time they weren't responsible for his release. The witch was.

Hell, just his being here could endanger the two he was closest to. "Let's wait and see what they do before you call in the troops. How many are there, anyway?"

Naberius drank from his steaming mug of coffee laced with Bailey's. "About a hundred and eighty. All would be willing to fight."

Which was the problem. He'd already damned his brothers once. He would not do so again. Each of the Rebels fell of their own accord, though he felt personally responsible for their decision to fall. He had been the instigator. "So, who is this Valencia?"

Raum raised his mug. "A total rotten bitch as far as I'm concerned."

Naberius rolled his eyes. "Raum doesn't like her."

"That's obvious. What about you?" Asmodeus was still finding it hard to believe Naberius had taken up with a vampire. Then again, vampires couldn't get pregnant, and that alone made them acceptable for a demon mate.

Naberius shrugged. "She's a good lay."

He was already having a problem with the language barrier. In the late fifties he'd had to figure out what "cool babe" and "daddy-o" meant. He'd thought fitting in had been bad after the original fall. It was nothing compared to conforming to the modern world. Before the first fall he had watched the humans. It had been his job. He'd come to this realm with a good idea of what to expect. Between his last two ventures to this realm he had been locked away in the Abyss, ignorant of the advances of the human realm.

He glanced at Naberius. "A good what?"

"A good lay means she's good in bed. Get it? He's *laying* with her." Raum got up to refill his cup. He poured straight Bailey's inside the mug, forgoing the coffee.

Asmodeus looked down at his own coffee. "I thought you two liked vodka." Of course he knew their answer before they uttered a word. Things changed. People changed. Except for him, as he had been imprisoned for the better half of his life.

"Bailey's doesn't incapacitate us, whereas vodka has a tendency to knock us on our asses every now and again." Naberius tilted his drink back, emptying the contents. "We rotate our schedules, so we don't work every night, but on the nights we do work we've been known to drink Bailey's."

Now *this* was something he could relate to. Demons had to report to the angels every quarter with Neph numbers. It was their sole purpose in this realm. "What are the Nephilim numbers like in this area? The city seems to be decently populated. Where do they hide themselves during the day?"

Raum shrugged, leaning against the counter. "Actually, the numbers aren't very high here. Nephs like to stay in the wooded areas. There are few parks around this area they stick to, but like I said, the numbers are pretty low. Those that do inhabit this area remain mostly in the sewers and storm drains. They keep a low profile."

Pain settled in his chest as they discussed Nephs. A Nephilim was a nasty creature with no conscience or reasoning for right or wrong. They were purely animalistic, and they knew they needed blood for survival. Where the blood came from was of little consequence. The fact that the Nephs were beginning to reason, staying hidden for self-preservation, spoke of evolvement, though he was damned certain they couldn't reproduce.

The archangels had put out the order that demons from the second fall were required to keep the Neph numbers down or face the Abyss once again. It was a never-ending cycle. It was no secret that human women appealed to demons. Lust was a powerful driving force which threatened even the strongest of resolves, and for that reason the Nephilim problem would never go away.

"Do the Rebels work for money, as they did in the fifties?"

Raum shook his head. "Most of us have learned investing techniques, and our money makes money. Others work out of boredom, or they may suck at handling money. Fucking Samael worked at an accounting firm for a few years."

Naberius nodded, laughing. "We busted his balls for years

after that."

Asmodeus cupped himself. "Sounds painful."

Raum barely kept the smile off his face. "Nah, busting balls just means we gave him hell for the job he was working."

Asmodeus sighed, putting his mug down. Exhaustion wrapped around him and it wouldn't be long before his eyes closed of their own accord. "I'm going to check on the witch. I'll be right back."

"It's too bad she's human. She's hot."

He turned back to Raum. "Hot?"

Raum and Naberius laughed. Naberius quit smirking long enough to say, "Hot, as in good looking. But then again, there's always condoms."

When Raum and Naberius started laughing again Asmodeus shook his head and left the kitchen.

Learning the new language wasn't the issue. It was staying around long enough to learn the new language they were speaking that posed the biggest problem.

When he stepped into the living room he paused by the entrance. Brianna was on the couch, curled into a ball, her hair fanning over the pillow. He wasn't anywhere near her, yet his body was already reacting to her presence. The itchy denim restricted the hardness of his cock, a dull reminder he shouldn't be reacting to her at all.

No, it wasn't the language barrier that posed the biggest problem in his life.

First thing tomorrow morning he would have her summon Michael. The last thing he needed to do was take her as his body demanded. He had only brought her with him to complete the summoning and possibly keep her safe from the angels.

It had nothing to do with lust.

The couch in Naberius's living room was probably the most comfortable piece of furniture Brianna had ever had the pleasure of laying on. The plush beige dream wasn't the cause of her inability to sleep, far from it. In fact, she wished Valencia, Naberius's insanely attractive girlfriend, had given her a cot on the floor instead. Perhaps she would win the battle to stay awake if she were uncomfortable. How could she go to sleep in a house full of demons?

Asmodeus, Naberius and Raum had disappeared into the dining room shortly after they had arrived, leaving herself and Valencia to sit in the living room in awkward silence. After ten minutes of said silence, Valencia had indicated she needed sleep.

Brianna was covered in a cashmere blanket, lying on a sofa that likely cost more than her car, unable to keep her sleep-laden eyes closed.

It was too bad her plan to break free from Asmodeus had failed. Slipping away from one demon had to be easier than slipping away from three. She also had to call Kelly back, knowing her friend would be in hysterics by now.

Unfortunately for her, Asmodickhead had confiscated her phone. And the knife.

Without a phone, the knife or her spell book she was completely hopeless. Or, as her grandmother would put it, shit out of luck.

There had to be a way to send him back. Surely the book she had used to summon him would have a spell that contained the power to counteract her mistake.

She attempted to close her eyes again. The second she did the vision of Asmodeus popped in her head. She forced her eyes open again. If only he weren't a demon, a chauvinist, or...hell, who was she kidding? None of those realities kept her from thinking he was, hands down, the most handsome man she had ever had the pleasure of setting eyes on.

It didn't matter. He was a demon. And she was human. A very plain-looking human. As hard as it was to admit to herself, it was obvious there were no men, demon or not, pounding down her door. Besides, she was too busy with her bookstore to become involved with anyone. As Kelly would put it, she was career-oriented. Men just didn't fit into the picture.

She glanced at the grandfather clock in the corner of the family room, which was letting out a god-awful chiming. Three o'clock in the morning. Who was going to open up her bookstore in five hours?

She turned on her side and tried to close her eyes as the grandfather clock's chimes reverberated through the house. As soon as the clock quieted down, thunderous, rowdy laughter filled the house. She pulled a fluffy red pillow over her head.

What the hell did demons have to laugh about?

She switched back to her other side and locked eyes with Asmodeus, who was standing just inside the living room. Great.

"Are you comfortable? Do you need anything?"

As if he cared. "How about my freedom?"

He grinned. A sudden vision of him in her shower, water dripping down his torso, flashed though her mind. She shook the vision away. She was only thinking about that because he wasn't wearing a shirt. Someone had given him a pair of jeans, which Asmodeus obviously thought was enough clothing. Which was just as well. Now that his skin was no longer blistering, he was the epitome of perfection. She tried imagining him as an angel, pure and beautiful. Powerful. He held the secrets to the afterlife, and that alone was intriguing.

"Soon enough, Brianna," he promised.

To hear her name come from his lips, soft and melodic, chipped at the barrier she had set up between them. She was surprised he even recalled her name. She had figured he would just keep calling her witch. "I have to open up my shop at eight in the morning."

A look of confusion crossed his features before he masked it. "Is there anyone else you can call to replace you?"

Yeah, but she wasn't going to tell him that. "No."

He shrugged. "Then it stays closed."

She sat up, clutching the red pillow in her fists. That wasn't what she had wanted to hear. "What?"

"I have already told you. You will summon Michael."

He turned and left her in the family room. She wanted to throw something hard and breakable at his head. Instead of attempting suicide she lay back down. There wasn't much she could do to help the situation, and pulling some stupid stunt would ensure she had three demons hot on her ass.

Asmodeus hadn't harmed her, though common sense made her realize he could do so easily if she provoked him enough. Strange he hadn't been furious when she tried to escape.

Just as she settled back and closed her eyes, intending to give in to sleep, she heard a rapping sound coming from the other room.

Jeez. What the hell were they doing now?

She had to get some sleep, but the noise kept her from doing so. What were they up to? She didn't want to wake up as a virgin sacrifice or something.

Well, a sacrifice anyway.

The rapping slowly turned into a pounding. She sat up on the couch again, trying to figure out just where the noise was coming from. Her gaze wandered over to the front window.

There, just on the other side of the glass, stood Kelly. She was cupping her hands over the glass, peeping in at her and knocking against the windowpane.

Brianna almost passed out. What was Kelly thinking to come here?

She jumped off the couch, arms flailing back and forth. *Go back*, she mouthed to Kelly, coming up to the window.

Kelly threw her arm up in a show of helplessness.

"Damn it, go home," she snapped. Brianna could feel Asmodeus's presence as he walked into the living area. The air behind her became energized.

"Invite her in."

It figured. Of course he had heard them. Kelly would have known these demons could sense her as well. Why would she risk them both getting caught?

Brianna shuffled to the front door, turned the locks and opened it. A wave of cool air hit her, ruffling her T-shirt. "What are you doing?"

Kelly came out from the bushes, picking leaves off her black sweater. "I was worried. It's obvious you need my help."

"How exactly are you going to help now?"

Brianna waited as Kelly stood speechless.

"Well?" Brianna prodded.

Kelly threw her hands in the air. "Hell, I don't know. I just couldn't ignore the situation and let you face the demon alone."

Try *three*. "How did you find me?"

Kelly gave her a "duh" look as she picked a leaf out of her short blonde hair. "A spell. I stopped at your house and grabbed your hairbrush. Then I did a simple locating spell, and poof, I knew where you were. I tried to summon you, but for some reason it didn't work." Kelly looked around and gave an appreciative nod. "High-end neighborhood. Classy."

Brianna ignored Kelly's appraisal. Didn't Kelly realize the danger she had put herself in?

Asmodeus leaned against the doorframe, brushing her backside with his body. She stumbled forward from the intimate touch, her body instantly warming.

"Why don't you two come inside? You can introduce me to your trespassing friend, Brianna."

"Great," Brianna muttered. She glared at Kelly.

"He doesn't seem so bad," Kelly whispered to her as they walked through the door past Asmodeus. He didn't give them very much room. "I expected much worse."

Brianna leaned into Kelly to whisper, "You're basing his worth on his looks. Just wait until he starts talking."

"Enough," he barked.

Brianna raised a brow at her friend. "See what I mean?"

He gave her a look and she zipped her mouth shut. She wasn't quite sure what he would do, and until she knew, she wasn't going to push him to find out. Well, to a degree, anyway.

Kelly, on the other hand, came in on a mission—to bust her out. She didn't hesitate to try and accomplish that goal, either.

Kelly grabbed her arm. "Stars are out, moon half mast, let our exit be swift and fast."

A tingling traveled through her body, but it quickly faded. They were still standing in the family room, only now they had a pissed-off demon staring at them.

"Why didn't that work?" Kelly asked no one in particular.

Brianna shrugged. As humans they wouldn't have been able to teleport anyway. She wasn't sure what Kelly had been trying to accomplish with that spell. It would be useless for beings such as themselves. Humans could be summoned, but they couldn't teleport themselves with their own powers. The energy of the earth didn't work that way.

"Because of the necklace you now wear, more commonly known as a blocker."

Brianna looked at Kelly's neck. A silver necklace with a dark rock at the end lay against her collarbone. Brianna reached out and touched it, instantly feeling a pull against her own limited powers. A negative energy source.

"What is that?" she asked.

Asmodeus started walking out of the room. "A grounding stone."

Kelly growled, "A grounding stone? When did you put this meteorite around my neck? How?"

He stopped by the hallway. "No amount of tugging or spell casting will remove that from your neck. Only the one who put it on you can take it off, and that's not something I plan on doing in the near future."

Brianna couldn't believe it. Kelly was the strongest witch she knew. Then again, Kelly's powers came from the energy of the earth. A meteorite had a way of neutralizing those powers, making it impossible to draw up on the energy the earth provided. To put it in laymen's terms, it rendered Kelly's powers useless. To put it in Brianna's terms, she was screwed.

She briefly wondered if she should try the teleporting spell herself, but it was an impossible hope.

Asmodeus inclined his head. "Now, I'm going to get some sleep. Being in this realm is tiring. You two can sleep down here. Don't try leaving. Just ask Brianna. It will not get you far."

"How did you know I was a witch?"

He cocked a brow at Kelly. "I could sense it."

He turned to leave, and for a few seconds Brianna thought Kelly was going to hurl a lamp at him. Funny, she had wanted to throw something at him earlier.

As he sauntered away she watched the muscles of his back move, and the way his broad shoulders melted into a thick waist. She had the urge to ask him where he slept.

She gave herself a mental slap. What the hell was wrong with her?

When he was gone she put a hand on Kelly's shoulder. "Thanks."

"For nothing," Kelly spat. Her short hair was in disarray, her face without its usual makeup. Kelly had always looked the part of palm reader slash witch. Though older, she had the spirit of someone half her age.

"Kelly, you didn't have to come. Actually, you shouldn't have come, but that's beside the point. Thanks for being here." Brianna and Kelly had known each other for only a few short years, but in that time they had grown as close as sisters.

Kelly fingered the necklace with her red nails, a thoughtful expression on her face. "We'll figure something out. A damned moon rock won't get in the way. I won't allow it."

Brianna didn't share the same optimism with Kelly. She didn't want to seem too downtrodden either. "Now it's two witches against three demons. At least we're evening up the odds. Who knows what tomorrow will bring?"

Actually, she did know. She just didn't want to tell Kelly about Asmodeus's insistence she summon Michael. She didn't want Kelly to stress about it. When Asmodeus learned she couldn't summon the archangel, shit was going to hit the fan.

More than likely Asmodeus would turn to Kelly, an experienced witch, when Brianna failed.

What concerned her was what would happen should they both fail.

If she could only get rid of him before any of that took place.

Kelly sighed. "Three demons?"

"Well, four at the moment. Asmodeus, the one you just met, and his friends—Raum, Naberius and Valencia."

"Great."

"Do you know any spells that will send him back?"

Kelly walked over to the couch. "His power is greater than ours. He would merely counteract it."

"Yes, but he said he couldn't use the energy the earth provided, so how could he counteract that type of force? Not only that, if we sent him back we could make sure he wasn't aware his departure was imminent. The book I used to summon him should contain a retraction spell." Brianna refused to think her only plan was doomed to fail.

"Sorry, doesn't work that way. Besides, I didn't bring any spells with me. Not to mention this damned necklace. I'm not sure you contain enough power to work one of those spells anyway."

That stung. "Well, I got him here, didn't I?"

Brianna sat next to Kelly. She looked down at the grounding necklace that sat against Kelly's collarbone. Was it hateful to be somewhat smug that Kelly had no powers at the moment? Asmodeus had become aware of Kelly's powers before Kelly had even stepped into the house.

And it was painfully obvious he didn't find her powers a threat because he hadn't placed a grounding necklace on her.

"I didn't mean any offense by what I said. I've told you before, I wouldn't let you be my apprentice if I didn't think you had the power and talent for it."

Kelly felt sorry for her. That was the reason she was Kelly's understudy. "There has to be a way to send him back." She refused to believe otherwise. "Didn't you say you had summoned a demon? How did you send him back?"

Kelly became interested in the seam on the armrest. "I didn't. Brianna, some things don't have an explanation. They just happen for a reason. Maybe he was meant to be here."

Brianna saw a shadow of a man on the hallway wall, just beyond the stairs. It disappeared quickly. She lowered her voice. "I think he can hear us."

"Oh, I know he can." Kelly turned her attention back to her. "Here's the thing, Brianna. You brought him here, but you can't force him to leave. Not unless he allows it. And from what I've gathered, that's not likely to happen."

Chapter Five

"Coffee?" Asmodeus asked.

Brianna stumbled into the kitchen, eyes half open. She had caught a whiff of freshly brewed coffee as it wafted into the family room. The aroma was too much for her to pass up. Demons be damned, she'd brave Satan himself to get some caffeine in the morning.

She nodded at Asmodeus as he rose from the table. "Yes, please." He pulled out a chair for her and she thanked him as she sat, still in a sleepy haze. He wore jeans and a blue collared shirt. Both were too tight on him, but she was quickly learning he looked good in anything he wore.

Naberius and Valencia sat across from her. Valencia's dark, auburn hair was perfect and shiny, her face clear, her disposition cheerful. Brianna tried smoothing her hair, raking her fingers through the long tresses in a pathetic attempt to look civilized.

"You take your coffee black?" Asmodeus stood posed with the coffeepot over a red porcelain cup. She was being thrown off her game with this domesticated scene.

Hell, who was she kidding? She didn't have game.

"Yes, black. I can't stand the taste of sugar and cream in my coffee. Makes it taste like syrup."

Asmodeus poured the coffee and brought her the steaming mug. She wrapped her hands around the warm designer mug and took a small sip of the dark liquid. Looking across the table she noticed Valencia's cup was frothy.

Valencia smiled sweetly. "I made a cappuccino. I like the taste of sugar in the morning."

Brianna resisted the urge to sneer at the demonic Barbie doll. What a disheveled mess she must look like sitting across from Valencia. Jealousy had never been a trait of hers, but she felt the claws of the green monster nonetheless.

"Would you like me to make you something for breakfast?"

Oh, so she was gorgeous, sweet *and* she could cook. Bitch. "No thanks."

Brianna heard footsteps padding into the kitchen. She glanced over her shoulder as Kelly walked into the room.

Kelly looked rough. At the age of thirty-eight, Kelly could pass for a woman in her late twenties. She was a health food fanatic, and she exercised daily, so it surprised her when Kelly went straight for the coffeepot. She waved a dismissive hand when Asmodeus stood up from the kitchen table. Asmodeus sat back down when it became obvious Kelly didn't want his assistance.

After making her own cup of coffee Kelly came to the table and sat to Brianna's right. Kelly mumbled something about spells, but Brianna didn't catch it. Good thing, that. Kelly had a penchant for being reckless, last night being a good example. Brianna just hoped her friend would ride the wave as they had discussed just before falling asleep last night. No point in breaking free when it was so easy for one of the demons to apprehend them. It would only serve to piss them off.

"Sorry we didn't meet last night. I'm Valencia."

Kelly eyed the hand Valencia offered, her brows raised. It was clear Kelly didn't give a shit who Valencia was, and she let the whole table know.

Valencia withdrew her hand. "Okaaay."

Asmodeus glared at Kelly. "There is no need to be discourteous to your host."

"My host?" Kelly leaned across Brianna, practically snarling at Asmodeus. "I'm not here enjoying brunch as a guest. I'm here because you're holding my friend against her will." She sat back and mumbled, “Host my ass. A gilded cage is a cage nonetheless.”

Brianna sat back and offered an apologetic smile to Valencia. Yes, they were being held against their will, but she realized these demons didn’t have to give them such inviting accommodations. Things could be a whole lot worse, and might be, if Kelly didn’t learn a little diplomacy.

The table fell into an uncomfortable silence. Asmodeus touched her arm and Brianna instinctively pulled back. He slowly drew his hand away as if her action surprised him. If she didn’t know any better, she would have thought she had offended him. Too bad for him that like Kelly, a cup of coffee wouldn’t make her forget she was nothing more than a prisoner, held against her will. A domesticated kitchen scene with fresh bagels on the table—*ohhh, bagels*—couldn’t take away from that simple fact.

He pushed his chair back and stood. “Brianna, come with me.”

Knowing protesting wouldn’t get her very far, she wrapped a hand around the warm coffee mug and stood to leave.

As they were walking out of the kitchen Asmodeus stopped abruptly. She nearly bumped into him, spilling her coffee. He turned back to look in the kitchen.

“You stay,” he said to Kelly, who had left the table to go with them.

“But—”

“Stay.”

Kelly’s face grew red. She didn’t say any more as she sat back down at the table, which surprised Brianna. Docile was not a word one could associate with Kelly.

“Are you still going out hunting tonight?” Naberius asked, leaning back in his chair. His eyes were black and yellow, his expression peaceful as he brought his left arm around his girlfriend’s shoulders.

He freaked her the hell out.

“Yes. Call Raum if you like.”

"Will do."

Asmodeus turned to leave and she followed behind him. She covered the rim of the coffee cup as they ascended the stairs. Spilling coffee this early in the morning was a sin, not to mention the carpet looked damned expensive.

"So, what are you doing tonight? For some reason I don't see you as the clubbing type."

"Clubbing?"

She glanced up at Asmodeus. His hair shone like that of the angels' on the previous night. At times he could pass for an ordinary man, though she was beginning to believe he did that intentionally. When the time warranted, he made her aware of the power he possessed.

Naberius *always* looked the part of an immortal demon. His eyes had an ethereal glow to them, his aura consistently deadly. Asmodeus, on the other hand, chose when to display these attributes.

The imp in her surfaced. "Yes. We club each other around with ancient weapons just for shits and giggles."

They stopped at the top of the steps. Asmodeus smiled over the rim of his coffee cup. "I prefer swords," he said, taking a sip.

"I'm sure you do." She thought about the ancient weapon he had wielded in her shower. The length had been impressive, and she had been mesmerized by the droplets of water falling from the tip. She cleared her throat, forcing the image away. "So, where are you going tonight?"

A dark look crossed his features. He turned and led the way down the hall. "Naberius, Raum and I will be hunting Nephilim."

"Nephilim? There are Nephilim in the area?" She had been under the impression that Nephilim no longer existed.

He held a door open for her. "Are you familiar with the creatures?"

She slipped past him, ignoring the rush she felt as her body brushed against his, and found herself in a library. As with the rest of the house, the shelves that adorned the walls from floor to ceiling were made of oak. A vast array of books lined every inch of the shelves, and a huge oak desk sat at the end of the room. Behind the desk was a grand window which bathed everything in a soft light.

She kept taking in her surroundings, trying to focus on anything other than the man she was speaking with. "I remember reading about Nephilim in the Book of Enoch. They are the offspring created when a demon mates with a human."

He walked by her and picked up a book off the desk. "You study the ancient texts?"

She set her coffee on a coaster, glancing at the object he held in his hands. "Yes, I'm a bore. I thought the text mentioned the Flood had killed them all off."

He flipped the book open and leaned against the desk. "It did."

"Well then...oh." The flood had destroyed all of the Nephilim, but apparently he and his friends had created more. Perhaps that was why he was damned to the Abyss. "What happened? Did you and those who fell with you make more?"

Once again his normal visage melted away, leaving something profoundly disturbing in its place. He looked at her with eyes that seemed brighter than the morning sun. His pupils went from being round and normal, to horizontal slits. His skin held a dark illumination. "I made no more of those children."

She refused to allow his ethereal stunt to frighten her. "Children? The way the Book of Enoch describes them they seemed more beast than cherub."

He pushed from the desk with a rage that seemed barely contained, though his actions were slow and calculated. His strange pupils melted into black pools, engulfing the color of his eyes. "I will forgive you that, for you were not there. The book does not describe what they were like as young beings."

Okay. She'd hit a sore spot with that one. What exactly was he trying to convince her of? "So, if you didn't create any more, why are you responsible for terminating the remainder of the

Nephilim?"

"I'm not. The other rebels are. I have no responsibility in this realm. No purpose."

She had witnessed a sadness lurking in Asmodeus's eyes the day before, and she read the same emotion now. She had yet to master control with her psychic abilities, though sometimes her powers came through with such clarity other's emotions left a mark on her soul. Just as Asmodeus's emptiness was now doing. She felt desolate and alone, as though her enemies had spared nothing in their vengeance, leaving her cold and helpless. Were these Asmodeus's emotions?

Looking at him one would never use the word vulnerable, but that's what he felt right here and now. Hopeless and alone.

"When do you think the angels will come after you again?" she asked quietly.

He turned his attention back to the book. "Soon."

"Are you willing to live a life like that? Always waiting for another angel to come and take you—"

"Quit asking me your endless questions. I am here. I am breathing. There is nothing more I need at the moment."

Again, a feeling of hopelessness settled itself into her core. She feigned interest in the books lining the wall, picking one off a bookshelf and flipping through it. Nowhere had she read that demons were good or righteous. He did bad things in his past, and now he suffered from the guilt. Why should she let his emotions wreak havoc on her?

Then again, she had never thought demons would feel guilt. Did that make him more human in her eyes?

Before she could contemplate that thought she began feeling weak and dizzy. The assault came on suddenly, with a ferociousness that caused her heart to race. The bookshelf in front of her tilted, the books lining the oak shelves blurring.

Within seconds the dizziness brought her to her knees. She laid her hands flat on the floor, putting her forehead on top of them. She fought the wave of vertigo. Taking deep breaths, she realized the library had lost the musky, leather scent. The air smelled like nothing. It was cold and invigorating, still as death.

A white mist replaced the hardwood floor, and though she didn't fall she felt nothing beneath her. She called out for Asmodeus as she tried to find something with which to balance herself. Nothing but air surrounded her.

She waited to feel strong arms steady her, though none were forthcoming. Finally the dizziness faded away, and she was able to right herself when she felt a hard surface underneath her. She sat back on her heels. All she could see was fog beneath her.

Instead of facing a line of bookshelves, four angels now stood before her, though they didn't resemble the three who had been in her house the night before. Only the black pools of their eyes incited recognition.

They were bigger. Much bigger. Battle gear covered their massive forms, and each wore helmets resembling what the Romans wore in ancient times. An angel standing in the middle held a flaming dagger, and she could feel its heat from where she kneeled.

The other angels stood with their hands behind their backs, only their torsos visible through the mist. She slowly stood to face them. Asmodeus had told her he would protect her from the angels' wrath. He had been sorely mistaken.

"We embody the Powers of Heaven, the select few of the angels who represent Destruction, Punishment, Vengeance and Death."

Well, this didn't look good.

"Through your actions you have released the leader of the Rebel Watchers from his imprisonment in the Abyss."

The angel to the right of the speaker held up a golden scroll. "Asmodeus, formerly an archangel, fell from grace of his own devices, bringing with him two hundred Holy Watchers. His deceit and lechery caused the Second Angelic Revolt, for which he was sentenced three millennia imprisoned in the Abyss to atone for his actions."

The angel lowered the scroll. The angel who spoke first stepped forward. "There are two choices given unto you this day. One—a millennium imprisoned in the Abyss, of which you would report to immediately. Two—the death of Asmodeus by your hand, therefore eliminating the possible war his opposition may create."

"War?" she choked.

"A contingent of angels lies in a state of readiness to apprehend the Rebel." He opened his palm and raised his arm. Behind him the mist lifted, revealing a group of angels in full battle gear. Rows upon rows of them.

"The resistance the rebel has shown leads us to believe he retains his powers bestowed upon him in this realm. Together, with his fallen comrades, he can lead a force to which we have already begun to prepare. If you decide to report to the Abyss we shall be forced to go to your realm en masse to apprehend him and any others who would resist us."

Who? As in Naberius and Raum? Who were they kidding? Asmodeus hadn't had time to gain a force that could effectively go up against those who stood before her.

She wasn't sure she should address them with that bit of inside information, though.

"Inform us of your decision."

The sound of the angel's voice resonated deep within her chest. Her senses were being attacked, bombarded. She fought the urge to run from their company screaming.

What choice were they giving her? Kill Asmodeus or face the Abyss? She'd witnessed Asmodeus emerge from the Abyss practically on *fire*. She didn't want to go there.

On the other hand, how could she kill a demon three archangels could not kill? How could they possibly expect that of her? It was ludicrous.

She had to convince these angels the mission they were giving her was doomed to fail. "His powers make a mockery of mine, which are precarious to say the least. How can I kill him?"

"Obtain his trust. Rely on your realm's powers as you did when you summoned him."

Obtain his trust...

She was so far out of her league she couldn't begin to comprehend it. To put it simply, it was her or him. She wished she had never laid eyes on that book. What had possessed her to utter a spell she couldn't understand? Look where it had gotten her.

A strong urge to just tell them he was in the library came over her, but she realized they would know that simple truth. "Why didn't you just summon him? It would seem the most logical—"

"You are being given the opportunity to remedy the problem you have created. We give you this mission as a chance for you to redeem yourself. Inform us of your decision."

Well, when he put it that way... There was only one choice. "I'll try to do as you ask."

"If you do not complete the mission you will be subject to the fire from which you summoned the Rebel."

The pain in her chest tightened to an agonizing degree. So this was what a heart attack felt like. She was damned if she did and damned if she didn't. "I understand."

"You have one week in your realm to complete this mission."

One week?

Before she could voice her shock at the period of time they had allotted her, she found herself looking at a bookshelf. She stood in the library, as she had been before the dizziness had brought her to her knees.

She turned to find Asmodeus thumbing through the book as though he had not sensed her absence at all.

Dismayed and more than a bit shaken, she made her way to one of the plush chairs in the room. The book she had taken off the shelf before her summoning was still in her hand.

She sat and pretended to flip through the book, but she couldn't focus on the pages. How did one kill a demon? What was she supposed to do about Michael, and Asmodeus's insistence she summon him? The angels had made no mention of that. Would that put her in even more trouble?

Hell yes it would!

She caught Asmodeus walking toward her and she hid her wariness. Now what?

He handed her the book and she placed it on top of the other one on her lap. He then handed her the dagger.

"On page thirty-four you will find a strong summoning spell, and you have Michael's dagger before you."

He stepped away from her, his aura bright, his eyes shimmering. His face was set in cold determination as he held out his hand and a long sword materialized within his grip.

"Summon him."

Chapter Six

Before the Flood

The sun had no effect on the frigid air that surrounded Asmodeus and his sons. An unforgiving wind blew in from the north, picking up speed and intensity. Soon the sun would set, forcing him and his sons to find shelter. He had already found an alcove that would block the wind, a perfect place for them to bed down for the night.

Jorian, his oldest son, only came to his chest. Bael, his youngest, reached his waist. Both had a head of blond, unruly hair and vivid green eyes.

Jorian kneeled next to him, holding the bow in his capable hands, pulling the arrow's feathers back to the top of his ear, just like he had been taught. Jorian waited for the rabbit to come closer. Precision killing.

The forest grew quiet, save for the chirps of the birds and the snap of an occasional twig from a small animal. The timing was perfect. The rabbit was close, the wind had died down...

"Father!" Bael cried out, bouncing toward him and Jorian. Jorian's arrow flew from his hands, striking a tree and becoming embedded in the bark. The rabbit stood on its hind legs, twitched its pink nose and turned and fled.

"Bael! Look what you have done!" Jorian stood, tossing the bow to the ground. He folded his arms over his chest and glared at his younger brother.

Bael looked devastated. He worshipped his older brother, and he had only been trying to help. In his small hands he clutched various twigs for the fire they would soon be building. The twigs fell from his grasp.

Asmodeus placed a hand on his thigh and pushed himself from the ground. He wanted this time with his sons, had looked forward to it for a long while. "Bael, you will have to become more aware of your surroundings." He found it difficult not to smile. Both boys were trying so hard to become men. They did their best to impress upon him their worth.

"What will we eat now? We will go hungry," Jorian complained.

"We have enough light left in the day to catch prey. Hunting takes patience, Jorian." That was the one skill his oldest son lacked. Patience. He believed things came easy for a man, that a man did not make mistakes. What he needed to learn was being a man meant you learned from your mistakes, grew from them. Which inevitably led to fewer blunders. However, as he had come to learn himself, there always seemed to be something else to learn. Mistakes had created the man he was.

His oldest picked up his bow with one last glare cast at his brother.

Asmodeus walked over to Bael and hoisted him onto his shoulders. "While your brother finds us our meal we shall build a grand fire."

Bael squealed. "I'm helping Father build a fire!"

Jorian huffed and moved farther into the woods. His oldest was learning the value of tolerance, thanks to his younger brother. The boys would come into their own in time. Soon they would be men, leaders among their peers.

They had taught him his greatest lesson—ultimate love, the sacrifice one made for others. Until Jorian and Bael had been born he had not known what love truly was. He had witnessed humans displaying this emotion from Heaven, and he had ached to feel love for himself. Having experienced what unconditional love felt like, he realized the responsibility that came with that emotion. He was responsible for their safety and well-being.

He had every confidence in their abilities and the honor he was instilling in them. They would grow to be so much more than their father had ever been...

"Asmodeus, I can't. I-I don't want to."

Asmodeus let the reality of his past fade away, though the sense of loss and failure never left him completely. He concentrated on what he was here to do. Avenge his brothers and take his revenge on the man who had forced him to do the unthinkable.

As he looked at Brianna he could see the fear etched on her face. He could feel her unease as if it were his own. He needed her. If he contained the power to command the energy of the earth he would summon Michael himself. Unfortunately his powers, though extensive, didn't extend that far. He had the power to heal, materialize what belongings were left to him, move with adequate speed, but he could not command the energy the earth provided. Only humans could summon angelic beings.

"Sometimes we are forced to do that which we do not want." If anyone knew the truth of that statement, it was he.

Jorian's face swept through his mind's eye again. After all these years he could recall what his children looked like. He remembered the innocence his young face had held before he turned into a Nephilim.

It wasn't Jorian who haunted his dreams. It was Bael. Bael had never turned, but Michael had enforced the command that all children made by demons be killed, whether they had turned or not. Asmodeus had been forced to end Bael's life. He'd tried telling himself Bael would have turned into one of those monsters, but that conclusion had never settled in his heart or given him peace.

The vision reminded him of his mission. He was going to kill the bastard who hid behind a façade of righteousness. He was going to do to him what he had been forced to do to his sons so many years before.

He tightened his grip on the hilt of his sword. He stepped closer to Brianna, fury causing his vision to blur. “Summon him.”

She jumped, the dagger falling from her lap. For a fleeting second he saw his wife’s face the day he had been taken to the Abyss. The paralyzing fear that had crossed her features as he had completed his duty and been taken away by Michael. It was the last time he had seen her. He never knew what fate had befallen her. How she had responded to her husband killing their children.

She hadn’t suffered long. The Flood had ensured that.

He lowered his sword and turned away. Conflicting emotions tore him between duty and honor. He did not want to hurt someone again. He did not want to lower himself to Michael’s level.

Damn it all. How else could he avenge all those who had perished those many years before? All the souls who had been thrown into the Abyss? Michael held the key to the Abyss, still, after all these years. And where had the souls of the children gone? The Nephilim? Would he ever know?

Why did the faces of the fallen still haunt him so?

Because he was the reason for the fall. He was the reason the Nephilim had been created. Because of his dream of love and acceptance on the earth, his compelling argument on how the angels could really live if they were only given the chance. He had convinced the angels a fall would lead them to fulfillment.

The fall had only led to pain and death.

Indecision, such as he faced now, had never been a part of his vision. He had made it through the Abyss with two things in mind—escape and Michael’s demise. He had never considered what it would take to accomplish those goals, and in truth he had never cared. He had always used whatever means necessary to achieve the end result.

He was no better than Michael.

That realization crept up his spine with cold accuracy. He turned back to face Brianna. She sat in fear, awaiting his next move. Her eyes were round, her knuckles white as they grasped the book.

How had he repaid her for releasing him from that hell? He had taken her from her home and kept her against her will. He had hunted her down when she had tried to escape, threatening her into submission.

He reached a decision. He would deal with Michael on his own. This was his battle, his personal vendetta. He couldn't expect her to do any more than she already had.

"You are free to leave." He let the sword evaporate from his grip, just as he wished the pain of the past would disappear. He doubted it ever would.

"Leave?"

"All I ask is that you call me should you have any trouble in regards to your summoning me." He took the book from her hands. He wouldn't take her dagger. It belonged to her, therefore it was not his to take. Picking it up off the floor, he handed it to her. "You have Naberius's number. He programmed it into your phone. Your keys are in the hallway on the table by the front door, along with your phone."

"I—"

"Thank you, Brianna." He left her sitting in the library as he took the spell book to his temporary room, leaving quickly so his emotions could not take over his actions. He couldn't explain why, but he felt her departure even though she still sat in bewilderment, his chest cold and empty. Brianna was a good woman. More the reason to send her away. Everything he touched he ended up corrupting. His fellow angels, his wife, his sons.

He would not allow himself to hurt another person. The farther Brianna was from him, the better.

Brianna sat in the plush chair, eyes locked on the open door Asmodeus had just walked through.

Now what? His sudden change sure put a kink in her mission. How could she gain his trust if he forced her to leave? How could she not garner suspicion if she asked to stay?

She pushed herself out of the chair and left the library, dagger in hand. She had to calm her nerves and figure out the best course of action. Being threatened with the Abyss by angels of death wasn't exactly the highlight of her life, but she had to concentrate on a way out of this mess. Basically it came down to her or Asmodeus, and as much as she hated to admit it, she was going to pick herself.

She stopped at the top of the stairs, trying to calm her nerves long enough to form a coherent thought. She had to figure out what she should do first to keep her ass out of the Abyss.

Long-term goal—kill Asmodeus. Short-term goal—earn his trust so she could kill him.

Killing wasn't exactly something she had done before, and she wasn't sure she could go through with it. Could she effectively carry out her mission? How did the angels expect her, an aspiring witch, to kill an ancient demon?

Then again, if she didn't complete her mission, burning for all eternity didn't sound so appealing.

Killing it was.

The first thing she needed to do was get Kelly out of the house, go home and regroup.

One step at a time, she told herself as she went down the stairs. Once she secured Kelly she would come up with a reason to come back to Naberius's house. She had to be around Asmodeus to gain his trust.

But the question remained, how would she gain access to him once she left?

Before she reached the kitchen she heard raised voices. One of those voices was none other than Kelly's.

"Then you would be up there, or he would be down here. Drop the subject, Raum. You're bad, Gabriel's good. End of story."

Brianna peeked around the kitchen door. A tall blond man stood in front of Kelly, who was backed against the kitchen counter, entrapped by the man's arms. Both of his hands were resting on the counter behind Kelly, their faces only inches apart. Brianna recognized him as the man she had met last night. Raum.

"You speak of Gabriel yet you know nothing about him. He fell in the sixth century, much for the same reason I did. Even the Catholics stripped him of his divine status, and more than one rumor traveled through our circles about him. They were saying he was either gay or a woman, for someone saw him being intimate with a man. Do you know why he fell?"

Kelly sucked in her cheeks and pursed her lips. "Doesn't matter, does it? He's back in Heaven where he belongs, and you're stuck here, where you belong. I'd say that speaks for itself."

"Woman, did you hear nothing I just said to you? I *want* to be here. I've no interest in going back to Heaven."

Kelly snorted. "Like I believe that for a second."

"Kelly?" Brianna wouldn't look at Raum. He wasn't as scary as Naberius, but there was something uncontrollable in his character, and she didn't trust him. "Um, it's time to go."

It took a moment for Kelly to comprehend what she had said. "As in free to go? We can leave?"

Brianna quickly nodded. "You ready?"

Kelly smacked at one of Raum's arms. "Move." Kelly ducked under Raum's arms when it became apparent she couldn't budge him. "Let's get the *hell* out of here."

Brianna waited for Kelly, and she blanched when Kelly turned back to Raum. Christ, why couldn't Kelly just leave well enough alone?

"I'm curious. Why *did* Gabriel fall? Because of the intimate act?"

Raum settled his light green, luminous eyes on Kelly. "Because he killed a know-it-all, annoying blonde woman."

Kelly hissed at him. Actually hissed like a cat. Brianna

grabbed Kelly's arm and pulled her in the direction of the front door. She picked up her keys and cell from the table by the door, balancing the dagger under her arm.

"What happened?" Kelly asked as they walked out of the house.

Everything looked so normal outside. The sky was a bright blue, the birds were chirping. Peaceful was the word that came to mind. It was hard to believe in just a week's time she could be burning in eternal hellfire.

She didn't want to tell Kelly she had been threatened by the Powers That Be, or whatever they had called themselves. She'd been so damned scared she had forgotten who they said they were.

Brianna looked around for Kelly's car. "Where did you park? Down the road?"

"I walked. Nice way to avoid the question, though."

Brianna slipped Kelly a look. "You walked five miles in the dark?"

"Jogged is more like it."

Brianna hit the unlock button for her car. "Why were you fighting with Raum? Are you suicidal?"

They slid into the car and buckled. Brianna put the dagger in her glove box, then started the car and put it in reverse. *Just go through the motions.* If she thought too hard about what had transpired she'd lose what was left of her mind.

When she turned to look over her shoulder the black gate began to open.

Kelly growled.

Brianna thought about getting a rabies shot.

Kelly smacked her in the arm. "Do you know what he said to me?"

She resisted the urge to rub the sting out of her arm. "No idea."

"He told me they were the good guys, they were just misunderstood. Can you believe that?"

Brianna turned down the main road, her mind trying to focus on what she was going to say to Asmodeus when she arrived back on his doorstep. "Nope. Can't believe it."

She let Kelly ramble on about Raum as she tried to come up with something to tell Asmodeus. He wasn't a dense man, nor was he a pushover. Her reason for coming back had to be plausible. It had to make sense.

She could tell him her house had been ransacked. That angels had been sitting on her doorstep waiting for her, armed with fiery swords.

She'd been attacked by a burning bush on her front lawn.

"Brianna, you missed my street."

Brianna looked in her rearview mirror. "Shit."

"What's wrong with you? We're out. Safe. If you were going to stress out, you should have done it back at the mansion."

She gripped the steering wheel and tried to get her nerves under control. "Oh, it's just the whole thing." *Future burning, torture, dismemberment.* "I'll be better in a few hours."

"Well, you pulled off a damned good spell. Too bad it turned out the way it did. Normally to summon a being you have to have something of theirs in your possession. That just goes to show you possess more power than you believe."

Brianna almost rear-ended the car in front of her as she pulled up to a red light. She looked at Kelly. "What did you say?"

Kelly stifled a yawn. "You have more powers than you realize. I've been trying to tell you that for years."

Brianna made a U-turn when the arrow turned green. What she'd heard hadn't anything to do with powers. It was about a possession. She had something in her house, near her bedroom, that had once belonged to Asmodeus. Summoning him certainly hadn't happened because of any powers she contained.

Now she was getting somewhere.

All she had to do was find out what this object was and find a reason Asmodeus would need it.

Then she would need a plausible reason she had cared enough to bring it back to him, especially after he had threatened her and kept her hostage in his friend's house.

Not only that, she would have to figure out how to stay with him, making that reason plausible as well.

Oh, then she had to come up with a way to kill him, which she was absolutely certain wouldn't be easy.

And last, but certainly not least, she would have to actually kill him, figure out a way around his friends, and find a safe place to hide out. Naberius and Raum seemed like the vengeful kind for sure. They would mutilate her in a heartbeat if she killed their friend.

This was all based on if she succeeded in killing him. If she didn't...well, she didn't want to think about that.

She peeled into Kelly's driveway, hitting the curb and nearly taking out her mailbox. She could practically hear her car's shocks moan in pain. Before she came to a full stop she slammed the car into reverse. "'Kay, talk to you later."

"Are you sure you're all right? You seem tense all of a sudden."

Brianna plastered a smile on her face a car salesman would be proud of. "I just want to get the shop opened up, grab a shower and move on. I'll call you later."

Kelly nodded, opening the door. Her friend gave her a look of disbelief, but she didn't press for more information. "Call if you need anything."

Ha. What she needed was a permanent vacation on a deserted island that boasted of demonic protection. "Will do. Thanks, Kelly. For everything."

Kelly smiled. "See you soon."

"Sure thing." She waited for Kelly to shut the door.

One week. One week from now demons would be the least of her worries.

Chapter Seven

You have no purpose in this realm...

Asmodeus threw back another shot of vodka, the liquid burning a path down his throat. As Raum and Naberius sat at the kitchen table playing cards he sat fighting his own conscience.

He was losing.

For the first time in his life he had to think of consequences.

He had led two hundred angels in a rebellion, a fall and a few years of fleeting happiness in this realm. What had come of that had been horrendous for his brethren. Imprisonment, suffering and death.

He had not considered what a fall would entail when he had been in the midst of planning it. Lucifer's followers had endured their share of setbacks and anguish. He'd witnessed their fall, and at the time couldn't fathom their reasoning behind it. He couldn't understand their push for power. There was one Supreme Being with no room for another. Power had never been one of his goals.

What he had wanted had been simple. He had witnessed what the humans were offered by the Powers. Free will. Freedom to do what they chose, freedom to act independently, and most importantly, freedom to love. It was the connection humans shared with one another. The weeping he had witnessed when a loved one passed on. The joy they experienced when they brought a child into the world.

The sorrow, the guilt, the pleasures, all of which were foreign to him. He had wanted to experience those emotions with such intensity that he'd made a rash decision. In doing so he had convinced many angels to fall with him, with no thought to the penalty of his actions. Not one of them had thought of the repercussions.

Seeing Brianna in a state of panic over his insistence she summon Michael had sent him over the edge. He wouldn't drag another down with him. It wasn't right.

He had accomplished nothing in his life. His boys had meant everything to him and he had eventually destroyed them as well.

"What time are we heading out tonight?" Raum asked Naberius. Both had passed on the vodka. Asmodeus's hand actually shook as he poured another shot.

"A little after dark. Figured we would take Asmoday to Tony's," Naberius said as he laid out his cards.

Raum grinned and flung a card at him. "Have you ever had a deep-dish pizza?" When he shook his head Raum rolled his eyes and sighed. "Holy crap they're good. After dinner we'll head out for the Nephilim."

Redemption. Was that even possible? Is that what Naberius and Raum were pushing for? Did they think they would attain salvation? Or were they only staying out of the Abyss by keeping the Nephilim under control? The archangels had given one command to the rebels after they had served their sentence in the Abyss—control the Nephilim or go back.

He threw back his shot as his thoughts wandered to Brianna. She was such a good person, wholesome. She dealt in witchcraft though he had a feeling she did so with good in mind. He wondered what she was doing now.

£

"Fucking hell. What could it be?"

She opened her closet and started tossing shoeboxes behind her. She had collected so much ancient trash from Kelly's shop and her own, she didn't know where to begin her search.

She stopped throwing boxes and put her hands on her hips. Whatever it was she had of Asmodeus's had to be old. Really, really old. Dating back before the Flood.

Damn, she couldn't think of anything she owned that was *that* old.

She walked back out of the closet, kicking shoeboxes out of her way. *Sonofabitch.*

Okay, it had to be something in this room. Something close to where she had summoned him. She'd been on her bed, flipping through the spell book. Drinking a Pepsi—

Her gaze floated to the wall opposite her. In a glass case she had arrowheads mounted against a black velvet background. Ancient arrowheads, some Indian, some Viking—and some Neolithic.

I'll be damned.

She ran over to the glass case and hefted it from the wall. This might be a stretch, believing the arrowheads could have belonged to him, but it was all she had at the moment. She flipped the case over on her bed and took off the bindings. Her hands shook as she spread the black velvet across her bed. Finally her collection of ancient crap would pay off.

There were two Neolithic arrowheads. She took them off the Velcro.

She held them in her hand, studying them. She hoped this was what she was looking for.

Now, why would she take these to him? Why would he care, if indeed they had been his in the first place? She could see it now, her standing on Naberius's doorstep...

"Hi, I just thought Asmodeus, with all he has on his mind, would love to have this rusty arrowhead back. I know it must mean so much to him. I've no idea how they belonged to him by the way..."

Yeah, right. That would go over real well. He wouldn't be able to smell bullshit with the pile right under his nose.

There had to be another way. She pocketed the arrowheads. Why else would she appear on his doorstep?

It amazed her how quickly her boring, routine life had taken a turn into the unbelievable. On any give day she would open her bookstore, read, come home, get ready for the next day. The weekly call to her parents, the trips to the grocery store, the laundry...all routine. Her biggest issue two weeks ago had been a ChapStick left in the pocket of her jeans. Upon opening the dryer she had found all of her clothes spotted with a clear stain.

All relative when compared to what she now faced. She had always known demons existed. If you believed in Christian mythology you had to take the good with the bad. She'd even studied the ancient texts on angels and demons, and now she was wrapped up in a plot to kill one of them.

Crap, how was she going to intercept him?

He did say he was going out to hunt Nephilim tonight with Naberius and Raum. They had been talking about it at the kitchen table. Had Kelly heard anything when Brianna had left the room?

There was only one way to find out. She went to her dresser and picked up her phone.

Kelly answered on the fourth ring. "Miss me already?" she asked in a sleepy voice.

"I'm sorry for waking you up, but do you know where Naberius and Asmodeus are going tonight? Did you overhear anything?"

"Why would you want to know that?"

"Kelly, I can't explain right now. Do you know?"

Kelly sighed. "I know they're going to the woods in Hickory right after sunset, but I don't know what part. Naberius had called Raum while we were sitting at the kitchen table. That's when Raum popped in. Why?"

"Thanks. I'll explain later. Go back to sleep." Brianna hung up. She threw her phone on her bed and looked at the time. It was just after noon. She had plenty of time to get in the shower, run to her store and come up with something to tell Asmodeus when she accidentally ran into him tonight in the middle of the woods. Hickory Park was nestled on the edge of a wooded area, and they were most likely to park in the parking lot right in front of the play area.

Jogging. She'd go jogging.

Damn, she hated jogging. But this was a great start. She'd go jogging, get accosted by a Nephilim, and Asmodeus would save the day. She'd have to play up how heroic he was, flirt a bit, and *voila*! Instant infatuation from adoring female.

She jumped in the shower, adrenaline pumping. This had to work. What other option did she have?

None.

After showering and putting on her gray sweats, she decided she had more than enough time to open up her bookstore for a while. She couldn't go to the park until after dark, which would be around nine o'clock. She'd call her cousin, Tracy, and ask her to watch the store for the next week or so.

Or indefinitely, if such was the case.

On the drive to her bookstore, Charmed Books, she hit the drive-through at Arby's. She'd had nothing but coffee since yesterday at lunch. After she had come home with the new spell book she had forgotten to eat dinner, too excited about the strange language she had found.

What a nightmare. Witchcraft had always seemed like a tool that could aid in so many things. It could also destroy, and until last night she thought she had stayed away from the bad.

She parked her car and took a deep breath. Charmed Books was located in a strip mall. She'd taken a chance at renting the space because it had been expensive, but the store had taken off. It took her about a year to catch up on the bills with her revenue, but now she had regular costumers who enjoyed the personal touch she'd given the place.

There was a Krispy Kreme to the left of her store, and a Clair's Styling Salon to her right. Subway, Little Caesar's Pizza and Bill's Furniture Gallery capped off their little strip mall. She picked up her Arby's bag and locked her car.

Phillip, who worked at Little Caesar's Pizza, stood outside smoking a cigarette. He sported a barbed wire tattoo around his neck, tattooed sleeves on both his arms and a lip ring. A lot of people would take one look at him and walk the other way, thinking he was trouble. That just wasn't the case. He was the nicest person working at the strip mall. Always willing to lend her a hand.

"Hey, Brianna, you're a little late."

She smiled in greeting, though she didn't feel like making chitchat. "Life sometimes gets in the way." *Understatement of the year.* She rummaged through her purse, found the key to her shop and unlocked the door.

Before she could duck inside he called out, "A few boxes are waiting for you out back. Donations."

She nodded at Phillip. "Thanks."

"Do you want me to bring them in for you?"

Damn, she really didn't feel like yakking, but she felt bad for brushing him off. "No, that's all right. I'll get them."

He put his cigarette out in the can. "Call me if you need me."

"I will. Thanks, Phillip."

She opened the door and flipped her sign to open. As she switched on the lights some of her tension drained away. She knew what to do here, knew the layout and the things that needed to get done. Perhaps the repetitive tasks would calm her nerves.

She dropped her keys behind the counter with her purse and paper bag. The familiar scent of books and potpourri filled the air as she walked to the back door. She opened the back door and placed the door wedge under it, securing it so it wouldn't shut on her as she brought in the boxes.

The boxes weren't too large. She opened one to check the

contents. A few romance novels peeked out at her. Woodwiss, Holt and Kenyon.

The second box contained mostly recipe books. She hefted the two in, one by one, setting them just inside the back door. Thankfully the books that had been donated were normal, non-threatening books. Getting a donation of spell books or incantations would have sent her over the edge. Then again, most of those donations came from Kelly.

She brushed the thoughts aside only to dig up more unwanted memories. She looked forward to seeing Asmodeus again, which was perplexing to say the least. He was an enigma. Certainly not like any other man she'd been involved with, which held a dark appeal. What would it be like to call someone such as Asmodeus her lover?

She closed the back door on that disturbing thought. *I so don't need to go there.*

Brianna sat behind the desk and began to eat her ham and cheddar melt, letting the book jackets and quiet surroundings take away her anxiety. She had a lot to do before she took off for the day. She'd have to call Tracy, tell her some bullshit about going on a vacation, and ask her to watch the bookstore.

The Abyss. What a vacation.

She put her sandwich down and powered up her laptop. She was already getting antsy for tonight's mission, and it was only after two in the afternoon.

She browsed through her messages, skipping the ones from her mother. Her mom always forwarded jokes, nothing of great importance. One was labeled "must read" so she opened that one.

Why is a man so much smarter when he's having sex with a woman?

"Jeez, I don't know, Mom. Why?"

Because he's plugged into a genius.

Brianna laughed and shook her head. Her mom had such a warped mind.

Feeling a little warped herself she put the cursor on the

Google toolbar and typed in ASMODEUS, figuring she might learn a little about him to pass the time.

What came up shocked her.

£

The pizza Asmodeus had eaten settled in his stomach like a rock. It had been good as hell, but now he felt heavy and uncomfortable.

"You look like you need a Tums."

Asmodeus cocked a brow at Raum.

"It's a medicine for indigestion."

He only shook his head and kept walking down the wooded trail. Naberius had dropped them off and told them he would meet up with them around nine, which would give them about an hour to roam this park before they headed to Hickory.

Part of his stomach issue could be due to the fact he hadn't faced a Nephilim in centuries. Not since the night he had gone to the Abyss. The last time he had ever seen his sons.

He pushed the memories aside in an attempt to enjoy his surroundings. Last night he had been too busy, too full of anxiety to take in the stars and the moon, the cool night air. Tonight, as he hunted Neph with Raum, he could almost pretend all was right in his life.

The city lights weren't so bright he couldn't enjoy the stars. Focusing on the little joys that had been denied him might take his mind from what he would soon face.

The quiet sanctuary of trees and brush brought back cherished memories of the time he spent with his sons. He would never have a family of his own again. Even in this realm his brothers weren't awarded the same freedoms as the humans.

What would Brianna think of him if she found out about his dark past? The utter soulless act he had been forced to do to his own children. She would think him a monster, and she would be right.

Why did he care? He would never set eyes on the human again.

She deserved better than a man—a demon—such as himself. He focused on the surroundings again, hoping to get lost in the simplicity of nature.

Just as he started to become relaxed, the tingling began. A slight magnetism in the air, a quiet humming in his ears. The animalistic side of his nature alerted him to a predator in his surroundings. A Neph.

"You feel it?"

Asmodeus slowed his pace, materializing his sword in his palm. The familiar weight made him feel in control of the situation, though he was anything but. Sweat broke out on his forehead as though he were back in the fires.

Before he could control the tremors in his hands, a movement thirty yards ahead of them sent him into action.

The Neph sensed their power, catapulting the creature into a flight response.

He and Raum, both seasoned warriors, melded into an understanding. Asmodeus ran to intercept the creature from the front, jogging to the left, and Raum stalked it from the back.

Coming face to face with the creature was much more difficult than he had first imagined. It was as though he'd been thrust back into the past, his actions those many years before causing bile to rise into his throat.

The Neph bared its teeth, rushing him, knowing it had to eliminate the threat because there would be no running from it.

Killing an unarmed Neph posed no problem concerning strength. It was the emotional sting of the memories that halted his death blow.

The vision of his sons.

The Neph attacked him as his sword hung limp in his hand. His mind screamed attack, but in his heart he saw his sons.

He dropped the sword to the ground, both hands going around the Neph's neck, keeping its sharp teeth from tearing his flesh.

He stared into the Neph's crazed eyes, and that alone told him the creature was more animal than human. The pupils were like his own, horizontal, and the eyes were a sickly yellow. It was a monster, the only thing on its mind blood and survival.

But God, this was once someone's beloved child. Their pride and joy. Their life. This was why he had ended Bael's life. His youngest son had been spared the indignity of turning into one of these vile creatures.

Duty first.

As he struggled with the Neph, Michael's order tormented him.

The fallen watchers have created a new race of creatures whose only purpose is to feed from humans to live. The responsibility now lies with the fallen to eliminate these abominations.

All of the deaths and the sorrow concerning these creatures rested on his decision to fall. He deserved to go back to the Abyss. He deserved punishment. He had created this evil.

Choking the Neph with his left hand, he tried reaching for his sword with his right, his fingers digging into the dirt seeking leverage he couldn't attain. As he did, the Neph's grip on his throat went limp as it screeched. It fell off him and he was able to wrap his palm around the hilt of his sword.

Raum stood over the Neph, delivering the death blow.

Glancing to his left he saw the disembodied arm of the Neph where Raum had severed it with his sword.

He barely managed to get to his feet, feeling shaken to the core.

"Damn, Asmoday, I wasn't thinking. I forgot you haven't killed a Neph since..."

Asmodeus turned away, taking in much-needed air. The scene before him brought clarity back to a night in which he tried so hard to forget. Love had been torn from him, ripped away by his own goddamned hand. How fucking ironic. And heartbreaking. To know you were the one forced to end the life of your own flesh and blood was a pain that never went away.

How had Raum and Naberius let go of that night? Had they?

He de-materialized his sword, turning to face Raum. "That will not happen again." He could have endangered Raum with his inadequacy.

Raum looked stricken. "It happened to all of us in the beginning. It was hard to see... It was difficult not to see our own children."

Asmodeus waved his hand in the direction of the Neph's body without looking at it, and it disappeared. He did the same to the arm. So dismissive. This had been someone's child, and yet there would be no body with which to mourn. No questions answered. Where did the souls of his children go? Would he ever know? Were his sons suffering the sins of their father?

Naberius walked into the clearing. Asmodeus collected himself as best he could. Remnants of memories filtered through his mind, and he damned them all.

"You find it?"

Raum nodded. "We should call it a night."

"Let's finish our round at Hickory Park. Asmodeus is going to have to get used to this shit."

Asmodeus rolled his shoulders. He couldn't agree with Naberius more, and the fact that Naberius wasn't feeling sorry for him right now made the situation easier to bear. "I'm ready, but for one thing. Is there a way we can locate the parents of the Neph?"

At their looks of disbelief he held his hands out. "I know the demon who sired the child is likely serving his sentence in the Abyss, but surely one of you can talk to the Powers and gain the mother's location."

Naberius's eyebrows came together. "We've never done that before."

Well, he would ensure they do it from now on. The mother

of the fallen child deserved more than nights filled with questions, of birthdays gone by with no answers. "It's just a small courtesy I would have wanted, were that my child."

Raum nodded in understanding. "I'll take care of it."

As they walked back to Naberius's vehicle he finally felt as though he had done something right. Something good.

It was something he wanted to feel more of.

Standing in the middle of the woods at ten o'clock at night was not the smartest thing Brianna had ever done. Arriving just after sunset, she'd jogged around the trails, her mind coming up with terrible images of what a Nephilim might actually look like. She kept close to the parking lot, waiting to see a car full of demons pull in.

Yep, really smart.

To top it off there was no sign of life around the park at all. She hadn't even heard a bird chirping. Eerie silence and shadows cast by the trees and shrubs were all that surrounded her.

Where were they? Darkness had set in hours ago. They were supposed to be here by now, weren't they?

Learning what she had about Asmodeus thanks to Google—you really *could* find anything on the internet—probably caused some of her anxiety. She found out he had fallen out of lust for human females, which wasn't a surprise, but the fact he had instigated it all was more than a little daunting. According to Wikipedia, Asmodeus was a demon characterized by carnal desire, considered by some to be the Demon of Lust.

Holy crap.

Looking back, it wasn't so surprising he had asked her to join him in the shower so quickly after she had summoned him.

Now that she thought about it, he hadn't made a play on her since then. Plain old Brianna. No wonder. She couldn't even make the Demon of Lust desire her.

Just as she contemplated getting back in her car she saw

headlights moving down the road to the parking lot. She hid behind a tree, trying to get a better look at the car.

It was Naberius's black Saab.

Great. Time to rock and roll.

She turned around and jogged down one of the smaller trails. The only thing she could hear was the beating of her heart and the loud crunch her tennis shoes were making on the dirt trail.

Her plan, as sketchy as it happened to be, was to attract the Nephilim's attention when Asmodeus was close enough to help. It was a terrible plan, but it beat imprisonment in the Abyss.

She hadn't brought a flashlight, which was a terrible oversight on her part. Who jogged trails at night? How could she convince Asmodeus she hadn't been up to any ulterior motive?

Possibly because no one in their right mind would have attempted such a stupid stunt.

Then again, she wasn't in her right mind.

She rounded another turn in the trail. The moon shone through some of the tree branches, and she was able to see more clearly.

Her heart raced faster and faster as she jogged, though part of the breathlessness had to do with seeing Asmodeus again. He had barely left her thoughts all day. What the hell was wrong with her? He'd practically kidnapped her, held her against her will, and then he'd...he'd let her go.

Change of heart or wishful thinking on her part? Why had he let her go after his insistence she summon Michael? Was it possible he knew she had been summoned by the angels and given a mission?

Not likely.

A coyote came tearing across the path only a few feet in front of her. She yelped, skidding to a stop as she watched it run away. Guess she'd scared it more than it had scared her.

She listened as it tore down another path. The coyote ran

as though the devil were on its ass, not as though it were pursuing prey.

She turned to look in the direction it had come from.

Darkness. All around her.

Quiet.

Then she found it. A pair of iridescent eyes illuminated just beyond the trail behind a tree. The pupils, which were slit sideways, dilated ominously in her direction. For a moment she stood paralyzed. She couldn't see its body, but from the height of its eyes she could tell it was well over six feet tall.

Nephilim.

Excitement rippled through her as she turned and hauled ass back toward the parking lot. She heard twigs break behind her and knew the thing had bolted out after her.

This was a stupid plan! Stupid, stupid, stupid! She told herself not to look back, but like a dumbass she did. The thing was all legs and arms, elongated teeth, not a stitch of clothing on, and it was *fast*. Too fast. She'd never anticipated its speed.

She looked forward again and picked up as much momentum as she could. It didn't come as a great shock to her when she was suddenly tackled from behind.

She tried to scream out for Asmodeus, but couldn't. The creature had flipped her on her back and wrapped its long fingers around her neck, cutting off her airway.

This was not going according to plan. A long line of drool came from the creature's mouth and fell to her neck. Struggling was out of the question if she wanted to keep the Nephilim from crushing her esophagus altogether.

The creature growled, and she started to see stars just as it latched onto her neck with its razor-sharp teeth.

A tingling sensation spread through her as her body went limp. Her limbs were rendered useless, and though she was conscious, she couldn't fight to save her life.

She'd served herself up on a platter to this Nephilim, and it took no time in sampling what she'd offered.

Chapter Eight

She could feel the Nephilim taking her blood, consuming her life force, as she lay inept. Her entire body was numb, her limbs heavy and useless. The Nephilim wrapped around her like a breathing, drooling vise.

The creature growled, jerked and clamped down on her neck harder, as if in a frenzy as it straddled her. Death was coming quickly. The tingling in her limbs became hot. The blood in her veins felt like it was boiling.

The numbness faded away, and she was able to move her fingers. Strangely, she felt stronger.

Her limbs became light, and the stars in her eyes were replaced by a clarity she had never before experienced.

She desperately tried to recall a death spell, which was the hardest spell to conjure. She had never tried one before, as she had never needed one. Studying spells had always been one of her favorite pastimes, and now it seemed that was going to pay off.

She wasn't sure she could effectively pull the spell off, because she was certain the power she contained wasn't enough to make the spell work.

Only she could swear power seemed to flow through her. Raw power that traveled from her core being to the very tips of her fingers.

With renewed strength she wrapped her hands around the wrist of the Nephilim and pried the hand from her neck. Her throat seemed to heal itself as words poured from her mouth.

"Powers of the moon, stars that line the sky, this creature has trespassed and therefore must die."

For once she could feel the command surge through her body, collecting the energy the earth provided. She felt every pebble beneath her, every star above her. She was one with the earth. Never before had she felt such undiluted power. It made the hair on her body stand up, electricity seeming to move through the outlet of her body.

The Nephilim fell back, its eyes bulging from the sockets. It convulsed soundlessly, blood pouring from its eyes, ears and mouth.

Her blood.

The convulsing stopped and the Nephilim lay still. Her surroundings once again became silent, except for the humming she felt within herself. The raw power reverberated throughout her body, causing her senses to become heightened, her awareness absolute.

She placed her palm against her neck to staunch the flow of blood, only to draw away when a sticky substance covered her hand. It held only traces of blood sheltered in a mess of clear, thick liquid.

Saliva.

God, *gross*. The blood in her hand was interacting with the saliva. It sizzled, sparked and churned just as Asmodeus's skin had been doing the night he faced the three angels.

She became perfectly still as the implication of the anomaly hit her. It could mean only one thing—her blood had reacted with the saliva of the Nephilim. It had given her powers, or amplified whatever powers she may have had. She felt for the gash the Nephilim had made when it bit her neck.

It was healed. Gone.

She gagged. The stench was unbelievable. She wiped her hand on her jogging suit when she picked up on the sound of footsteps. It was as though she had stepped out of her body, traveled hundreds of feet, and heard the crunch of twigs and rocks. There was more than one person making that noise.

Shit. Asmodeus and his demons.

She panicked, glancing at the body of the dead Nephilim laying next to her. How could she explain that? She had to seem like a lady in distress for her plan to work. She couldn't tell Asmodeus about the powers she'd gained from the Nephilim's saliva. That could be of help when she killed him.

The footsteps began picking up speed. They were running now.

Without thinking she put her hands on the Nephilim, sparks shooting off her fingertips. She needed the creature alive, and though she couldn't do that, she sent some of the energy she was tapping from the earth into its muscles to stimulate movement. It was a survival move, and she instinctively knew what to do, her actions taking over. The Nephilim moved and she dragged the body over her and began feigning a struggle.

It was by far the most disgusting thing she had ever done.

When she heard the men draw close she screamed as loud and shrill as she could.

Seconds later rocks and dirt went flying over her face, and suddenly the Nephilim was pulled off her. A flash of steel and the head of the Nephilim went rolling.

This time she didn't have to act. She turned on her side and started gagging.

"Brianna!"

Strong hands turned her on her back. Asmodeus ran his hands over her neck, chest and abdomen, checking for injuries.

Damn. She didn't have any injuries.

Okay, time to play this up.

"Asmodeus!" she wailed, clutching his arms and summoning up enough panic to yield some tears.

He pulled her to him, running a hand through her hair. "You are fine. The creature did not bite you."

The hell it didn't. She raised her voice up a few notches, false terror lining every word. "I was so scared!"

"Everything will be all right," he said, holding her tight.

She'd never realized she could be so dramatic. It was kind of fun, actually.

She feigned a shiver. "I didn't know what to do. Thank goodness you came in time." *Oh puke.* She had to tone it down and make sure she didn't overdo it. Her life depended on this theatrical event.

"What were you doing out here?" He pulled back some and she held on to his shoulders, attempting to keep the connection between them.

"I was going for my nightly jog." She sniffed. Now that had to be *the* biggest lie of the night. "I don't want to go home. I don't want to be alone." She leaned into him again with a few shakes of her shoulders, as if she couldn't hold back sobs. This had to work. It *had* to.

His arms tightened around her. "You can come with us."

Bingo. Thankfully something in her life was going as planned. She sighed, leaning into him. A small part of her really did like being in his arms, feeling the strength and security that surrounded her. She had no time to contemplate where the feeling came from, and that was probably for the best, since she was planning his death at the moment.

She clutched his arm. He wore a leather jacket and jeans, looking as good as she had ever seen him. Damn. *Keep your mind in the game.* "Are you sure?"

"Of course. Can you stand?"

She sniffed again. "I think so." Hell, the way she was feeling she was sure she could fly.

Asmodeus swept a hand toward the body of the Nephilim and it disappeared. He put a hand on her elbow and another on her waist as he helped her up. She stood a little stooped, as if she hurt everywhere.

She placed a hand on her back. "I think I pulled a muscle."

Asmodeus tried controlling the rapid beating of his heart as he wiped dirt off Brianna's clothes, ignoring Raum, who had been gesturing to him while Brianna had been sitting on the ground. Naberius scanned the surrounding woods, but Asmodeus could sense no other Nephilim in the area.

He ran his hands up and down Brianna's arms, trying to keep her warm. She looked up at him, her eyes large and round. Protectiveness welled inside of him, and he was thankful they had been there in time to save her. "Let's get you to Naberius's. You will stay there the night."

Tears welled in her eyes. "Thank you."

They walked back to the car slowly, allowing Brianna to regain her footing. When he had spied her car in the parking lot fear had consumed him. If they had arrived even seconds later she would have been dead. She was lucky the Nephilim hadn't bitten her. A human became paralyzed from the poison in the Nephilim's saliva, which made it easier for the Nephilim to feed.

He helped her into the backseat of Naberius's car. Naberius tapped him on the shoulder as he said to Brianna, "Wait here."

Asmodeus shut the car door and turned to Naberius. Raum came up, and Asmodeus could tell there was a confrontation coming by the cold glint in his eyes.

Naberius kept his voice lowered. "Something's off about this. She would have been dead in seconds, or at the very least paralyzed."

Raum spoke before Asmodeus had the chance. "Can't you feel the power that surrounds Brianna? I did not feel that earlier today."

He did feel something wasn't right, but Brianna was too shaken up and he didn't feel they should interrogate her here and now. "Her fear has heightened her powers. Just as we show more power when we are emotionally charged."

"Bullshit. Why was she here? I find it highly strange she was here at this time of the night to jog. She can't see five feet ahead of her," Naberius argued.

"What motive could she possible have in coming near us again? There is none," Asmodeus said.

"She is hiding something." Naberius stepped toward him,

lowering his voice again. "She was too eager to come back to my house with us. Too trusting. She should, on all accounts, never want to go back there."

Asmodeus glanced at Brianna, who sat in the car with her head in her hands. The sight affected him in ways it shouldn't. "She was never harmed by us."

"She was held against her will," Raum snapped.

He turned his attention to Raum. "She was attacked by a Nephilim, and she realizes the only people who can keep her safe from such a creature are ourselves."

"She lies." Naberius turned away from them, his agitation on the subject apparent.

The scene was unfortunate, as it always would be when involving a Neph. He felt a connection with Brianna, more than likely because she had pulled him from his torment. He did not like seeing her like this, and he wanted to fix it. "Raum, will you drive her car back to the house?"

Naberius turned on him with a growl. "So you will leave it at that? You will do nothing?"

Asmodeus's anger rose as he stepped toward Naberius. Brother or not, the demon needed to back off. He said not a word as he opened the door to the car. "May I have your keys, Brianna?"

She took them out of her pocket and handed them to him, tears in her eyes.

He held the keys out to Raum.

"You are making a mistake," Raum said.

"It is my mistake to make."

He climbed in the car, taking a place beside her. She was shaking. He put his arm around her and drew her close, trying not to breathe. Nephilim had a terrible odor. It clung to Brianna. Still, he felt she needed the touch, the connection.

The circumstances between them couldn't have taken a sharper turn. Just that morning she had been a prisoner in Naberius's house, now she felt safe enough to go there of her own free will.

Naberius slid into the driver's seat. "What happened, Brianna?"

She swallowed visibly, looking as though she could barely keep it together. "I was jogging one minute, and then something just jumped me from behind."

"I'm surprised you're still breathing," Naberius said, backing the car up. "What the hell were you doing in the park at night? How could you see where you were jogging?"

Brianna merely looked down, bringing her shoulders up in a shrug.

Did Naberius not feel for what Brianna had been subject to? Asmodeus would demand an explanation from him, but he didn't want to upset Brianna more than she already was.

They drove in silence to Naberius's, though he could sense Naberius wanted to go much further with the conversation. The bastard was lucky he kept his damn mouth shut. Smart man.

As they pulled into Naberius's driveway, Brianna put her head in her hands. He ran a hand up and down her arm. She was shaking, clearly upset. How could Naberius not see she was genuine?

Brianna had to stifle a laugh. Whether it was from inappropriate giddiness or just a plain psychotic breakdown, she wasn't sure. She was covered in dirt, and the stench from the Nephilim made her lightheaded.

Having heard the conversation between the three demons, she was a little on edge. Her hearing had been amplified from the powers she had gained. It was an exhilarating feeling.

She would have to take this slow, gain their trust. Naberius and Raum had made perfect sense, and yet Asmodeus had defended her.

Why?

Asmodeus helped her out of the car, putting a hand under her elbow and one on the small of her back. She let him lead her into the house and up the stairs, as if she needed his strength to make it.

He opened a bedroom door and held out his hand. "I'll run a shower for you."

She nodded and walked into a large bedroom. It had a flat-screen television, a six-drawer chest of drawers with an antique mirror anchored on top, and a large bed covered in a gold and hunter green comforter. Two overhead lamps were secured to the wall next to the bed. The room reminded her of high-priced hotel accommodations.

Asmodeus walked past her into the bathroom. She glanced around the room, wanting nothing more than to test out her new powers. This was awesome. She had to calm herself down. In the car she'd nearly drowned in a fit of giggles. For years she had wanted to know what it was like to be a true witch, a natural, and now she knew. It was better than she had imagined.

She heard the shower turn on, and seconds later Asmodeus emerged from the bathroom.

"I'll get you a robe from Valencia. You left your bag of clothes here. Did you pack something to sleep in?"

She nodded.

"Are you okay?"

Was that concern in his eyes? "I'm better."

He put a hand on her forehead and quickly pulled away as if his action surprised him. "I'll be right back."

He walked out and close the door behind him. Why did he act as if he cared about her wellbeing? He was a demon. He cared about no one but himself.

Not to mention his friends were going to talk to him again, trying to convince him there was more to this situation, which there was.

How could Asmodeus not see the obvious?

To him there wouldn't be a motive, because he knew nothing of the angels or the mission they had given her.

She'd make damned sure he never knew.

She dismissed his show of concern. She had a job to do.

Now that she had these awesome powers that job was going to come much easier.

Taking her cell out of her jogging pants, she placed it on the dresser. She left the arrowheads in her pocket. She would have to keep this from becoming personal. She had never killed a person before, but then again, she'd never been threatened with the Abyss either. Killing him wasn't a choice. It was a necessity.

She turned to go into the bathroom and caught sight of Asmodeus's sword on the bed. She walked over to it, running her hand along the unadorned hilt. The steel was engraved with vines, and it shone from the light of the lamp, reflecting its light on the wall above the bed.

What weapon would she use to kill him when the time came? His own sword? That thought seemed dark, dishonest somehow. Heartless.

The door to the room opened and she stepped away from his weapon, dropping her hand. A robe lay across Asmodeus's arm. He handed her the robe and her bag. Out of the corner of her eye she saw his sword disappear, which made it quite apparent he didn't like her near it.

She took the bundle and thanked him, making her way into the bathroom. She had to regroup and think things through.

Her plan had been to get accosted by a Nephilim—check. Gain access to Asmodeus—check. Now she had to play up her feminine wiles, flirt a little, and earn his trust in the process. It was obvious Naberius and Raum were having their doubts about her attack, and soon Asmodeus would be questioning her as well.

Seducing him seemed like the easiest part of the plan. Hell, he was supposedly the Demon of Lust. It was perfect. Seducing him shouldn't be hard at all. Getting attacked had been harsh, getting access to Naberius's house had been precarious at best. But seducing the demon of carnal desire? Piece of cake.

She crawled out of her soiled jogging suit, took the arrowheads out of the pocket and placed the clothes in the laundry basket. As quietly as she could, she opened the medicine cabinet and set the arrowheads on the very top shelf, underneath a small package of tissues. She would need those later.

After pushing the teal shower curtain aside, she stepped into the warm shower.

Yes, she was on second base, and soon she would be rounding third. Easy enough.

She'd go out into that bedroom, show a little leg, flip her hair a bit, and thank him for being her hero for the day.

Why was she so nervous? All she had to do was seduce an ancient demon, gain his trust and kill him. Problem? Perhaps just a little.

She finished scrubbing off the stench, having to lather her hair twice, and shut off the shower. She leaned out of the tub and snatched the white towel off the towel rack.

First thing first. Pajama pants wouldn't help her cause. She was going commando under that robe.

She dried her hair with the towel and ran a brush through it, trying to give herself time to quit shaking. She needed to be fierce. It was him or the Abyss.

With a renewed sense of urgency, she slipped the robe on, brushed her teeth—bad breath was an instant turn-off—and pinched her cheeks.

There. She looked fresh—fresh for a ravaging.

She winked at her image in the mirror and left the bathroom. As she walked into the bedroom she saw Asmodeus reclined on the bed fully engrossed in a rerun of *The Golden Girls*.

She watched him as he watched the show. He seemed mesmerized by it.

What kind of demon watched *The Golden Girls*?

She winced when the little old lady made a smart-ass comment to Blanche and Asmodeus smiled. It was a tiny smile, but it made him seem less demonic somehow.

She walked farther into the room and he looked up. She'd left the top of the robe open a bit. Well, a lot. It was the first place his gaze wandered to.

He rolled off the other side of the bed, seeming to put as much distance between them as he could. "You should get some sleep. You've been through a lot and it's late."

"You're not sleeping in here?" Her gaze caressed the bed as she fiddled with the opening of her robe. Her heart threatened to beat right through her skin. She had to do this. It was her only option. *Get it together.*

He followed the direction of her hand, his eyes turning from light green to a green and yellow mix. She could sense his confusion. Maybe she allowed her nerves to push this part of the plan too fast. Fast wasn't good, but slow was worse given she had only a week to complete her mission.

He settled his wandering eyes, which were now changing to a yellow-black mix, to her face. "Actually, I'm heading out with Raum. Naberius will be here should you run into any problems, which I cannot foresee."

"Oh. I just thought we could watch some TV or, you know, whatever." Jeez, could she be any more obvious? She glanced down at her boobs. They looked perky enough.

"I'll see you in the morning." He turned, and without another word he left the room and shut the door behind him.

Oh, now that was something else. She'd have to step up her game. Stub her toe while she was in the shower and screech for help. Accidentally lose her towel while bending over.

Where was he going, anyway?

She sat on the bed and fell back against the pillows. The easiest way to kill Asmodeus would be to do it while in the throes of passion.

He *would* sleep with her, she'd make damned sure of it.

He probably didn't trust her, especially after Naberius and Raum's little speech. It surprised her the way he had defended her. In the car she had been reveling in the odd feel of her new powers, but now that she had a moment to herself, his actions seemed confusing. From what she had witnessed, he was the kind of man who missed nothing.

She shouldn't have pushed the seduction so fast. *Damn.* She wasn't thinking clearly. What with the new powers, the attack and the impending imprisonment, she was a serious basket-case.

As she reached for the remote she heard a knock on the door. She jumped up, threw her hair around for added volume, sat back down and relaxed against the pillows. If she wasn't so desperate her actions would seem comical, but her ass was on the line. She closed the robe a bit, not knowing who was at the door. "Come in."

Asmodeus walked in. "May I have your phone?"

She pointed at the dresser. Was he going to take it away again? "I put it on the dresser."

He picked it up and started pushing buttons.

"What are you doing?"

"Naberius showed me how to program numbers into these phones. I'm programming my number into yours. Valencia let me borrow her cell for the time being. I don't want you to think I've abandoned you." He finished up and handed it to her. "If you need me for anything do not hesitate to call. I can be here in seconds. I won't allow anything to happen to you."

She opened her mouth but nothing came out.

He winked at her. "I will see you in the morning," he said as he left the room.

She sank back against the pillows. Why was he being so pleasant? Where was the jerk who had bossed her around and kept her captive?

She reached back, grabbed one of the pillows and threw it across the room. *Damn.* What was she supposed to do now? Kill someone who was trying to protect her?

She slid out of bed and stomped to the window. What choice did she have? She had seven—no, six—days to kill him or she was going to the Abyss.

To hell with that. Perhaps he was going out to do

something bad tonight, and that was why he'd turned down her perky breasts. Demons did bad things, right?

She was going to find out.

She scrambled to the bathroom and threw on her blue silk pajamas.

As she went back to the window she tried to remember a locating spell. She would simply wait an hour then perform the spell. Then she would know where Asmodeus was, and she was sure he'd be involved in something illegal or amoral. One or the other. It would help her conscience for when she killed him.

Perfect plan.

Chapter Nine

Brianna snuck out of the two story window and butt-crawled to the edge of the shingled roof. Heights weren't exactly her thing, but she had no choice—current story of her life. She didn't want to perform any spells within the confines of the house in case Naberius could sense the energy she drew upon.

The power from the Nephilim was still going strong. She might have succeeded with her spell without the dirt, but it was better to do it the way she had always done it.

The night sky was clear and the air held a chill. The Santa Ana winds had kicked in. According to the news it had brought gusts of wind up to twenty-five miles per hour. Late summer in Los Angeles. You had to love it.

She dug her fingers into the shingles, eyeing the ground below. With her new powers she could probably jump to the ground without hurting herself. She felt invincible as the powers surged through her muscles. Nephilim had incredible agility, proven from her earlier attack. Would she also have that ability? The other option being to crawl down the side of the house—not something she wanted to experience.

A black iron gate surrounded the perimeter of the backyard, and beyond it she could see the other houses on the block. It would be just her luck to get spotted by a neighbor.

Hanging her feet over the side of the roof, she pushed off with her hands, swinging her feet away from the house.

She landed lightly, falling into a crouch, just as she had instinctively known she would. The drop hadn't so much as stung her heels.

Without hesitation she dug her fingers into the lawn and began her location spell.

"Dirt of the Earth, connection between, let the whereabouts of Asmodeus be seen."

She closed her eyes as a vision of a woman, crying and holding a young child, flashed through her mind. The young girl had a mop of blonde curls and bright pink cheeks. The woman sat on a blue and yellow striped couch. Asmodeus and Raum sat opposite her on a matching love seat.

For all intents and purposes, it looked like a domesticated scene. Raum even held a small teacup in his hands. Asmodeus merely sat on the couch, leaning toward the woman in a non-threatening manner.

Asmodeus spoke. "Mary, I know this is hard. I lost my sons from this condition, so I know what you are experiencing. At the same time, having been through this before, I cannot stress enough that we had no choice. Greg was no longer the son you raised."

Mary clutched the child on her lap tighter. "He's gone. He's really gone?"

"When was the last time you saw him?" Asmodeus asked.

Mary started sobbing. "A few weeks ago. He was normal. He's not a monster!"

Asmodeus got up from the love seat and kneeled in front of her. "Don't allow this to ruin your life. You raised Greg and you gave him a wonderful life. You could never have prevented the change. Nephilim are known to attack their parents. My oldest son tried to kill his mother. We are trying to protect you."

Mary quit sobbing long enough to ask, "He attacked his own mother? Why? What happened to him?"

Raum spoke. "We were ordered to kill our own offspring."

Mary shook her head. "Not all turn. Andras told me not all turn. Jordan is his child too. What will happen to her? What will happen to my baby?" She cradled her little girl, rocking her back and forth as tears ran down her face.

The vision faded away.

Brianna sat in the grass, collecting herself as the vision's remnants filtered away. Never had a vision come to her with such clarity before. It was as if she'd been in the room with them.

Asmodeus had killed his own children? What had that done to him? Had Michael been the one to command Asmodeus to kill his own flesh and blood? It made sense. That had to be the reason he had been so hell-bent on her summoning the archangel.

Asmodeus's children had turned into Nephilim and Michael had ordered their death.

God, she couldn't imagine seeing her own child turn into such a monster. How old had they been?

On top of that, he had been thrust into the Abyss for being the leader of the Second Angelic Revolt. In all that time in the Abyss what had he been able to think about? What had been his driving force? His focus?

His children.

His revenge on the man who had forced him to do the unthinkable. Michael.

Yet here he was, helping to keep the Nephilim under control all these years later. It must bring back all those memories he'd carried throughout the years. Memories of killing his own flesh and blood.

She ran her palms over the blades of grass, contemplating what her next move would be. She had seen enough in her vision to tell her what kind of man Asmodeus was. Certainly not the demon she had thought him to be.

What the hell could she do now?

Her phone vibrated in her pocket. She took it out and flipped it open. It was Kelly.

She glanced back at the house, hoping she wouldn't give herself away. "Hello?" She backed up next to a bush by the patio. If Naberius caught her in the backyard he would want to know what she was doing out there, and she had no explanation at the moment. Naberius was already suspicious, and rightly so.

"That bastard didn't remove the necklace."

Crap. The grounding necklace. "I'm sure he'll take it off you."

"That means I have to go back to that house again, and after being held there against my will it's not exactly a place I want to go back to."

Brianna placed a hand on the pot of the bush and leaned forward, looking at the windows of the house. Everything seemed quiet. "I'm already at Naberius's house. Just show up in the morning and I'll have Asmodeus take the necklace off."

"You're *what*?"

Brianna heard a noise. She looked back up at the house. No lights had come on. Everything was as it should be. "Long story. Let's just say I'm here to take out an insurance policy." That explanation sounded good. *Not.*

"Brianna—"

Brianna snapped the phone shut as a light from an upstairs window cast illumination all over the patio. She'd hung up on Kelly for the second time that day. Kelly was going to turn her into a ferret or something worse if she kept hanging up on her. Thank God she had that grounding necklace on.

Brianna stayed where she was, well hidden by the potted plant. She would have laughed at the absurd situation if the distinct sound of a window being opened hadn't reached her ears.

Naberius had heard her.

"Brianna?"

He didn't sound too happy, either.

"Brianna!"

Shit. She left her safe haven and crawled on her hands and knees to the side of the house. Their garbage can stood against the fence. She moved it to the side of the house and climbed up it, trying not to make too much racket. Once she gained her footing, denting their garbage can in the process, she hoisted herself up on the roof.

She kept flush against the wall of the house. Naberius couldn't poke his head out of the window because of the screen.

His loss, her gain.

She tiptoed ever-so-slowly to her window. Once she got there she slipped a leg inside. The screen sat next to the roof to the right side of the window.

She heard Naberius say, "I'll be right back."

He was coming to check on her. His room was right down the hall, so she had only seconds to get back in the room and pretend she was in bed or watching TV. There was no time to replace the screen. Thank God she'd left the TV on to hide any noise she might make.

She launched herself the rest of the way through the window and turned to yank the curtains shut. She jumped in bed and pulled the covers to her chin just as the door opened.

When he flipped the light switch on she squinted, sitting up in bed, the remote in hand. "What's going on?" she asked, attempting to sound tired.

He stopped just inside the door and looked around the room, his gaze unerringly drawn to the window. The Santa Ana winds threatened to showcase the missing screen. "I heard someone in the backyard. I thought I heard your voice."

He walked straight to the window and she froze, knowing he'd see the screen off.

Not knowing what else to do, she was about to scream when Asmodeus came walking out of the bathroom, toothbrush in hand.

"It was me."

Her heart did a stop, drop and roll. She slid under the blankets once more. This was *so* not good. Trepidation crawled into her gut as she held the blankets up.

He knew.

Naberius let the curtain fall from his hand. "Well, hell. Why didn't you just come in the front door?"

Asmodeus shrugged.

"Where's Raum?"

Asmodeus raked her with a glare before he answered Naberius. "He's back at his house. He said he will call you in the morning."

Naberius nodded. "All right. See you in the morning." He looked at her sheepishly. "Sorry about that, Brianna."

She was sure she mumbled something, but she was too busy eyeing Asmodeus to pay much attention to what came out of her mouth.

She was so screwed, and not in a good way.

When Naberius shut the door Asmodeus calmly walked back into the bathroom. She heard the faucet turn on.

Maybe she should just hightail it the hell out of there. Save her own ass.

Then again, that's why she was here in the first place.

Her surroundings grew dim as her psychic abilities sprang to life. Unable to control when they came to her, she could only sit back and watch the vision unfold in her mind.

A tall silhouette of a man spoke of the Abyss. She caught words here and there, her vision slurred and broken. "The decision is up to...goes willingly to...imprisonment....millennia in the Abyss."

Another voice came from far away. She couldn't place it. "I accept."

Then the silhouette dipped his head in acquiesce. "It is done."

A terrible pain slammed inside her chest as someone screamed "*No!*" over and over again. The pain in the voice made her blood run cold. She had the distinct impression it was Asmodeus.

Had she accepted her fate so willingly? Was the Abyss her destiny? That couldn't be Asmodeus screaming on her behalf. For one, he wasn't the type. And two, he didn't give a rat's ass about her.

Before she could be certain of anything, the vision was gone.

She tensed when Asmodeus turned off the bathroom light, emerged from the bathroom and leaned against the doorframe. He wore black silk pajama bottoms and nothing else. She'd forgotten how perfect he was. His chest was as impressive as the glare he was now giving her. Now wasn't exactly the right time to be noticing how delicious he looked with his shirt off. Especially after such a dark vision.

Was she the person the man in her vision had been speaking of? What was done?

Asmodeus ran his tongue across his teeth. "They have made great advances in toothpaste since I was here last."

She was sure she should say something witty and explanatory, but nothing came to mind. "I like mint myself."

"Hmm."

She felt like bringing the sheets up to her nose and disappearing. He was obviously waiting for her to say something. What could she say? "Did you want me to turn *The Golden Girls* back on? I'm sure they'll be playing reruns all—"

"What were you doing?"

There it was. There was no way out of this predicament. Her entire plan was ruined. Of course her vision would soon become reality. They always did, with or without her new special powers. It was the sole reason she had wanted to explore whatever powers she had. Could she change her fate with a spell, or, like most times, would she only create disaster? "What do you mean?"

He didn't look amused.

"Oh, you mean what was I doing outside?" Playing dumb was only going to get her so far. From the look on his face it would get her as far as six feet under.

"Brianna."

She held out a hand. "Okay. So I wanted to know where you went." Which was absolutely true.

He didn't look convinced. "Why not ask me?"

She sat up a little, adjusting the pillows. He had yet to throw her out of the house. That was a good sign. She tried changing the subject. "So, where did you go with Raum?"

"What were you doing?"

Apparently he wasn't ready to let her little excursion go. She bit her lower lip. She might as well tell him the truth. She'd just have to spin it a little. "I was doing a locating spell in the backyard."

"Why?"

"I didn't want to be alone."

"Naberius was right next door. I left you my number and you had your cell phone."

She took heart in the fact that he wasn't yelling at her—yet. "I was scared." This was the perfect time to initiate a little dependence on him and his strength. Men loved that. "I wanted you."

His expression softened a bit. *Score!*

"What did you mean when you said you were here for an insurance policy?"

Flag on the play. Jesus, he had heard her conversation with Kelly. Her mouth went dry as she looked at him. She swallowed. "Kelly wanted to know why I was back here. I told her about the attack, and how you saved my life." *And it's good!*

He raised an eyebrow. "Funny. I didn't hear that part of the conversation."

Ball intercepted by the opposing team. "I called her before I went in the backyard. I needed a spell. She called me back to tell me she still had the necklace on. Will you take it off her?" *Save!*

"Next time stay put." He snatched the remote from her hand.

Man that was close. He had doubts about her, but the hope she could turn this situation around kept her from running from the house. Not to mention the thought of the Abyss kept her where she was.

The bed depressed when he slid in next to her. "By the way, you can't lie worth a damn."

"What?" Her brain froze as he climbed under the blankets, his thigh brushing against hers, silk against silk. The muscles on his chest flexed, causing her to lose her train of thought. His biceps were a legend in the making, his shoulders rounded with muscles that spoke of brute strength.

"Have you heard the expression keep your friends close and your enemies closer?"

She scooted away from him, suddenly feeling fragile. *This is your chance. Make a move.* "I've heard something like that."

He leaned toward her, his eyes glowing. "Looks like we are going to be getting damned close then, doesn't it? There is something different about you. I can see it in the way you act towards me, the fact you were willing to come back to this house with me. I can feel a surge in the power you contain."

She was screwed. She didn't respond to his statement about her surge in powers. If he thought them enemies, she had no chance whatsoever of overcoming him. He would be anticipating any move she might make, always on the defensive. That didn't bode well for her mission. She was supposed to gain his trust, not garner his suspicion. "What do you mean? We're not enemies." She flinched when her voice broke.

And damned if he didn't catch it.

She had to think of a way to take his mind off her little excursion.

And fast.

Asmodeus no longer saw humor in the situation. The witch was lying. He could sense it, and he could see it in her eyes and the way her hands shook.

Brianna found it necessary to lie to him, and he found it necessary to label her an enemy. This was turning out to be a great working relationship.

Asmodeus leaned closer to her, until he could see the small

freckles scattered across the bridge of her nose. "The hell we aren't. I guess you can call us friendly enemies at the moment. I may not know what you are about, but I do know—"

Brianna stopped him with a kiss. It took him so by surprise he returned her kiss without thought of consequences. The soft feel of her lips on his threatened to disarm his resolve. She was up to something, and he'd best remember that.

Her hand traveled up his chest, the soft caress enticing him until he stopped it with one of his own. Having regained his senses, he searched for her other hand, securing it by his side.

He couldn't recall the feeling of his last contact with his wife. The warmth she had provided had been lost, seared from his mind by the fires.

Brianna had an ulterior motive, of that he was sure. He'd seen the lies written on her face, in the innocent blinking of her eyes. She was a terrible liar.

But she was a damn good kisser, using her body as well as her mouth to seduce from him his acceptance.

He gave it without thought. The intimacy created between them was to him what food was to a starving man. He'd lived so long without passion, he couldn't let it go, no matter what strings came with it. His blood heated, his cock grew hard. He fought the mindless need his body craved. He wanted to give in and get lost in the pleasure she would provide.

She tried tugging her hands away from his, but he wouldn't give her that freedom.

"I'm not going to hurt you," she whispered against his lips.

Her voice brought him out of his desperate need. The woman contained powers, powers that seemed to intensify, and through her actions tonight should not be trusted. "I'm not going to give you the chance."

She was human, and natural law did not permit this intimacy.

He rolled her onto her back, pinning her hands above her head. For a second he could read the surge of fear that traveled across her face. She quickly replaced it with half-lowered lids, lips parted for his pleasure.

"When you performed the spell, what did you see?"

Forced innocence once again flooded her eyes, and he could tell his question took her by surprise. "I saw you in someone's living room."

He'd been afraid of that. So much for her insistence of not being a witch. It seemed her spells were second nature to her. "And?"

"That was it," she said breathlessly.

She was lying again. Her black hair fanned about her, creating the perfect image of sweet innocence. But her eyes told a different story. She was not, and would not, be forthcoming with the truths she held. "What did you hear?"

She took too long in answering.

"I didn't hear anything. You don't with a locating spell. You just see the surroundings."

Unable to stop himself, he leaned down and gently bit the side of her neck, savoring the warm taste of her. The feel of her body beneath his. "Is that so?"

She squirmed beneath him, definitely liking what he was doing. He had to stop himself, but couldn't find the strength to wrench his mouth from her sweet, warm flesh. She was soft…forbidden.

He put her wrists in one hand and she sucked in her breath when he found the tender juncture of her thighs with his free hand. "I didn't hear anything."

His lips traveled from her throat to the sensitive spot just below her ear. "Right. This coming from a witch who denies being a witch."

She brought her right leg up over his hip, opening up for him, arching her back to give him better access. "I'm an aspiring witch."

He ran his hand over the soft silk covering her thigh, teasing her. "And your display earlier? You were trying to seduce me, as you are doing now. The question is, why?"

She turned her head to kiss him again and though it was nigh impossible, he pulled back before their lips met. If he didn't put distance between himself and Brianna he would lose control of the situation. "Trying to avoid the question?"

Her look of seduction melted away, replaced by pure annoyance. "I guess I'm trying to figure out why I should be answering your questions when you think I'm your enemy anyway. You aren't going to believe anything I say."

"I will start believing you when you begin speaking the truth. Until then we have reached a hiatus." He summoned the handcuffs he had seen in Naberius's basement, slipping them over her wrists. Before she had time to digest that action, he put a grounding necklace around her neck.

She tried bucking him off, thrusting her hips against his. "What are you doing?"

His cock hardened painfully. "Taking out an insurance policy."

"Take these *off*."

He watched her struggle against her constraints. "Like hell I will." He slid off her and grabbed the remote from where it had fallen from his hands. He turned on *The Golden Girls*.

So much for passion.

"Asmodeus. You can't expect to leave me like this throughout the night."

"It is the only way I will get some sleep. Now quiet down. I like this television."

He barely managed not to laugh as she tugged, pulled and jerked the cuffs until he thought she would break her wrists.

"How can I sleep like this? It's painful."

Asmodeus lost his temper, the humor in the situation gone. "You want pain? Keep fucking with me. Those cuffs are more for your benefit than you realize."

Brianna yanked a few more times before giving up. She'd bet the skin on her wrists was red and chafed by now. *Damn.*

She should have known she couldn't lie to a demon and get away with it.

She tried to relax. Fighting with the restraints wasn't getting her anywhere. "Okay. What if I told you the truth? Would you take them off then?"

"No."

Oh, you have got to be kidding. "Why the hell not?"

He turned off the television and the bedside lamp. "Because I need to get some sleep."

"I'll lose circulation. I can't sleep like this."

"You will live."

She yanked one last time, flinching when pain shot up her arms. She was so mad she was close to tears. "I should have figured I wouldn't get any compassion from a man who had none to start with."

"You know nothing about me, so you base your assumptions on nothing." In the darkness his voice was like a physical caress. It sent shivers over her skin.

"I know more than you're aware of," she snapped. She immediately wished she hadn't said that as he turned the light back on. Asmodeus leaned over her. His eyes were changing from light green to yellow singed with black, a sure sign he was pissed.

His face was only inches from her own. "What do you think you know?"

She didn't answer him. She wasn't that stupid.

"Well, you just answered my previous question. Before you start judging me, which you have already done, think of one thing. Had you been in my place, what would you have done? They couldn't have been saved. If there had been something I could have done to save my boys I would have done it, consequences be damned. If you would have handled the situation differently please do tell. I've been playing that night over and over in my head throughout the years and I've never come up with something that would have brought my boys back to me. You complain about pain? You know nothing of pain."

Again, she didn't speak. His eyes were illuminated, his body tense as he leaned over her. She figured the best course of action would be to keep her mouth shut.

He turned over and shut off the lamp. She lay there beside the ancient demon staring at a ceiling she couldn't see.

She'd hurt him. Saying she was sorry wouldn't take the pain away, for either of them. Soon, unbeknownst to him, she *would* know pain. The Abyss would take care of that innocence.

Her plan had been that of an amateur, juvenile and foolish. What could she do now? She couldn't just give up. Yet how could she kill Asmodeus when he had already been through so much? Especially now that he had protected her, even after she had lied to him over and over again. Why couldn't Michael just give him a break? The others who fell with him were free, why not him?

If only she could obtain an audience with Michael and pose the question to him. If she tried to summon him she'd have to do it far away from Asmodeus or she'd be screwed. Asmodeus would try to kill Michael and she would be in worse trouble than she already was. The question was, how could she get away from him now? She'd put herself right back where she started—a prisoner.

There were so many questions she wanted to ask him. When she had searched his name online she had come across something that called him a Watcher. He had been a Holy Watcher, then noticing what the humans had, fell from grace and became a Rebel Watcher. Had he really fallen out of lust and, as the article stated, "cohabited with the daughters of men" wherein the Nephilim had been born?

She grew tense as she lay next to him.

She'd have to sort everything out in the morning.

She just wished she could shake the feeling she had betrayed Asmodeus.

Chapter Ten

"What kind of kinky shit went down in here last night?"

Brianna squinted at the light her eyes met when she tried to open them. She attempted moving but came up short, unable to pull away from the bed. It was then she recalled the handcuffs. Her shoulders burned and her back was stiff and sore.

"Y'all don't waste any time, do you?"

Who the hell was talking? Brianna brought her head off the pillow, ignored the stab of pain that shot through her shoulder blades and looked in the direction the voice had come from. When she saw it was Raum she let her head fall back onto the pillow. He had on red boxer briefs and nothing else.

"Get out," Asmodeus growled from beside her, turning on his side and taking the blankets with him. Jackass. As long as *he* was warm and comfortable—not exactly what she had experienced last night.

"Well, hate to break up your den of sin, but her little friend Kelly is here demanding you take something off her. I was more than obliging, but she punched me in the stomach, the little witch."

"That's right. Now, out of my way. I need to talk to—" Kelly stopped short when she saw Brianna. Kelly's face was a mask of shock. Mortification crept up Brianna's spine when she realized what they must look like. "What in the hell is going on?"

Brianna closed her eyes, silently cursing Asmodeus. This was humiliating.

“He put one of those damned necklaces on you too. What’s with the handcuffs, though?”

Brianna opened her eyes in time to witness Raum give Kelly a wink. “I’m betting they were playing a little game of cop and wench myself.”

Kelly’s eyes widened as she looked down at her. Brianna refused to say anything to either of them. She just wished they would go away. Quickly.

As the effects of sleep wore off, Brianna felt the weight and pull of the grounding necklace, making those awesome powers she had gained useless. Just one more obstacle to overcome if she stuck with her mission.

The blankets once again stirred and cold air hit her leg. Asmodeus sat up and began to stretch. Must be nice.

“Can you take these damn things off me?” Her voice was hoarse. She stomped down the traitorous thoughts about how gorgeous he looked when he first awoke. He looked down at her, sleep tugging the corner of his eyes, his features relaxed as she glared back at him.

He slid out of bed. “Sure thing.”

The handcuffs disappeared. She tried bringing her arms down by her side but she couldn’t. They were too stiff and heavy, and she couldn’t feel her hands. She bit back a moan.

Kelly stomped over to her side, casting a glare at Asmodeus. “You’re such a jerk!”

Kelly rubbed her arms, sending unwelcome feeling back into them.

Asmodeus looked unfazed by Kelly’s outburst. “I’m not taking the grounding necklaces off either of you. Not until I figure out what the two of you are up to.”

“I have a job to do,” Kelly sputtered. “I can’t even read people’s palms with this contraption around my neck. It gives me headaches.”

“Sorry,” Asmodeus mumbled, disappearing into the bathroom.

Brianna counted to ten. She had a new plan rolling around

in her head. She'd get her and Kelly out of this mess soon enough. Well, Kelly anyway. Her own future wasn't looking too great, not after that telling vision last night. If she effectively summoned Michael he might be able to help her with her dilemma.

"Come on, Brianna. Let's get the hell out of here. I'll find a way out of these necklaces."

Raum slowly shook his head. "If Asmodeus put the necklace on you, he has to be the one to take it off."

Kelly squared off in front of Raum. "You obviously don't know me very well. I do whatever it takes to get things done."

Brianna rolled her eyes. If Kelly kept talking like that they'd never get out of here alive. She tried rubbing her wrists, but it hurt too much. Her skin was raw.

Asmodeus came out of the bathroom and saw her tending her wrists. She let go of her wrists, not wanting him to see he had hurt her. She had to remain strong or she was going to lose it in front of everybody.

Before she realized what he was doing, he kneeled in front of her and took her hands in his. The pain disappeared.

In that moment she didn't know if she was frightened of him or drawn to him. His show of concern for her wounds disconcerted her. She didn't know how to respond.

"There's something I want to show you. Meet me in the library."

Before she could say a word Kelly barked at Asmodeus, "In case you didn't know, we're leaving. Now."

Asmodeus, still kneeling, glanced over her shoulder. "*You're* leaving. Now. Raum, take her out of my presence."

"Sure thing."

"What? Let go of me." Kelly smacked Raum's hands away, but she wasn't fast enough. He hauled her out of the room with ease.

Now alone with Asmodeus, Brianna felt awkward. Nothing was as it seemed between them. He was on the defensive, and she was stuck in her forced offensive struggle against time.

For a moment she considered telling him everything. The angels who summoned her, the mission they gave her, and the fiasco with the Nephilim. Could he help her? Would he help her?

He didn't give her the chance. He stood and walked to the door, his black silk pajama bottoms clinging to the muscles in his legs.

"I'll be waiting for you in the library."

She only nodded, knowing the moment had passed. It would be so easy to slip into hopelessness. Despair tugged at her spirit. She felt like calling her mom in Indiana, asking her advice, though there would be none to give.

Jesus, she might never see her mom again.

"Brianna?"

She wiped her eyes and faced Valencia who stood in the doorway. "Yes?"

"Would you like something to eat?" Valencia asked.

"No, thank you."

"Are you all right? Is there anything else you need?"

Valencia had the ethereal appearance of an angel, her long, dark auburn hair cascading down her back, her cheeks flush and bright. Brianna's preconceived notions on demons were shattering all around her. "No."

"I'll be downstairs if you need anything."

Brianna choked down a sob. She left Valencia standing in the doorway as she made her way into the bathroom. She couldn't do this anymore. She wasn't a liar or a schemer, which was why everything was falling apart around her. She wasn't a killer, even if that decision meant death and torture for herself.

She shut the bathroom door and broke down, sliding down the door, hoping none of the demons could hear her, but knowing full well they could.

Everything seemed hopeless, and she couldn't do anything about it. Nothing could be done about her situation. The angels had set her up for failure, and fail she would.

She would accept her fate.

There was no other choice available.

£

Brianna's head pounded something fierce. She had taken Valencia up on her offer and had gone downstairs asking for aspirin. She now stood with her hand on the doorknob to the library. She couldn't imagine what Asmodeus wanted to show her. Everything had gone wrong last night, leaving him suspicious of her motives, with good reason.

There was no chance he would believe anything she said now, and she couldn't blame him for that. She blamed herself for lying and her attempts to manipulate him.

She slowly turned the knob and opened the door. Not knowing what to expect made her headache worse.

She closed the door behind her. Asmodeus sat behind the large oak desk. He must have showered and dressed in another room. He wore a white collared shirt left completely unbuttoned, teasing her with his masculine form, and his hair was wet. He looked up as she made her way to the desk.

It would be easy to see herself liking this man if they had met under different circumstances. He was intelligent, gorgeous, and he carried himself well. He had an analytical way of thinking that she admired, a trait she had always wished to possess. She was finally seeing the man, not the demonic façade he tried so hard to convey at times.

He stood and motioned for her to sit in his vacated chair.

As she took the seat he pushed an opened book toward her.

Damn, not another book.

"What's this?" he asked.

She had no idea. The pounding in her head crushed any interest in reading. "You tell me."

Placing a hand on the page, she leaned forward and

studied the script. She couldn't read the writing. It contained symbols she had never seen before. It didn't compare to the demonic language, which closely resembled Hebrew. It looked more like Egyptian symbols.

Out of the corner of her eye she became aware of Asmodeus leaning over her right shoulder. He smelled of soap and musky cologne. She recalled the feel of his body on top of hers, the soft touch of his lips.

She took a deep breath. "I've never seen it before. The writing reminds me of ancient hieroglyphics."

"Yes it does. I tried to decipher it using the ancient language and it did not coincide."

Why would he assume she contained knowledge of this writing? Because of the demonic spell book she had summoned him with?

She placed her thumb and forefinger to her temples. Her headache was becoming a migraine. Stars floated behind her eyelids. "Do you think this book is important? Does it carry any significance for you?"

She put a hand on the page to save her spot and flipped the book closed. On the cover was a star in the middle of a circle, both in flames.

Jerking her hand from the book, she stood and bumped into Asmodeus. She had heard of this book before. There had been many copies that claimed to be the *Demonic Book of Spells*, though none had turned out to be legitimate. The flames on the cover were dancing and casting light, which made her believe she was looking at the original.

"What is it?" he asked, picking it up.

"You shouldn't have touched that." If the rumors were true, the book contained spells of possession, manifestations and incantations. You could make someone schizophrenic from the spells held within those pages. You could make people do terrible things. Dark power radiated from the cover.

"I found it in your house last night."

Stunned, she could only gape at him as the seconds passed

by. "You did *not* find that in my house. And wait, why did you go to my house?"

He slapped the book back down on the desk. The eerie glow of the flames on the cover drew her gaze. *Christ, the spells contained within...*

"It was under your bed. Raum and I went to your house before we went to Mary's."

That was impossible. She had never laid eyes on it before. "I don't perform spells such as those contained in that book. I never have."

"You summoned me. You read the summoning spell written in the demonic language you claim you don't understand. Do not stand before me and tell me you do not delve in dark magic." He put a finger under her chin, commanding her gaze from the dancing flames on the cover. "Did you obtain more powers from this book? Have you been working the spells therein?"

She shook her head, slapping his hand away. "Asmodeus, I have never laid eyes on that book. Never." She held his gaze, willing him to see the truth in her eyes.

He stood before her, his eyes lighting to a vivid yellow. "I believe you."

Her gaze was drawn back to the moving flames on the cover. "Why didn't you ask me about this last night?"

"I wanted to look it over first." He sat on the chair and opened the book.

"Why isn't the *Demonic Book of Spells* written in the demonic tongue?"

"Because the demon who made it did not want others sharing in his knowledge."

"I thought demons couldn't command the energy of the earth. Where did that book come from? What powers do the spells draw from if not the energy of the earth?"

"No one knows where it came from, and the powers are rumored to come from both the energy of the earth and from one's life force." He idly flipped through the pages. "Who could have placed this in your house?"

"No one. The only other witch I know is Kelly, and she doesn't mess with that stuff either. She's the one who taught me to stay away from it. The spells from dark magic can consume you, turn you into something you're not."

"Have you noticed a change in her as of late?"

"No. She would *never* touch that book." Kelly hadn't been acting different, and she'd be the last person to get into something like that. It would destroy everything Kelly had worked so hard to obtain. "Why were you searching my house last night?"

Asmodeus's eyes began to glow. "Naberius and Raum were positive you were acting last night at the park. They argued you used a spell of some sort, and you were never in any danger from the Nephilim. Of course I stood up for you, saying you hadn't been dishonest with me. He convinced me to go to your house and search for a motive for your reappearance."

Damn.

"Brianna, I can smell a lie. I had put my guard down where you were concerned, but I can assure you, I will never again make that mistake. You've been lying to me since we met again at the park. I want to know why."

She stepped back when he got to his feet, the action making her slightly dizzy. Things were quickly going from bad to worse.

"Kelly knew where we were going last night. She was in the kitchen when Naberius made the call to Raum to discuss where we would be meeting. She also has access to your house." He glanced down, running a finger over the ancient spells written on the page. "What is it you are not telling me?"

If she told him about the angels they would undoubtedly arrive en masse to apprehend him, and her. She couldn't risk it. She couldn't lie to him anymore either. Pretending she didn't know what he was talking about wouldn't work. "I can't tell you."

His face grew dark. Sparks of energy split the air around

them. "What does Kelly have to do with it?"

"Nothing. She knows nothing."

His eyes grew darker. "I find that hard to believe."

She fumbled for footing. "I—"

"Somehow you became more powerful after the Nephilim attack last night. I could feel it, as could the others. Is that something you were going to try and use against me? Is your motive behind all your lies to send me back to the Abyss?"

Her chest tightened with fear. The emotion in his eyes nearly brought her to her knees. She couldn't lie to him any longer. Somewhere along the way she had gone from fearing him to respecting him.

"Brianna. Explain yourself."

"I..." She put a hand on the desk to steady herself as a wave of nausea hit her. Her vision became hazy. "I'm just coming down with something." Her head felt like it was going to implode.

The stars in her vision multiplied, and she couldn't support herself any longer. She would have slid to the ground if Asmodeus hadn't helped her into the chair. She was having trouble breathing.

This wasn't a cold. It was coming on too strong.

Asmodeus kneeled in front of her, taking her face in his hands. From her haze she briefly wondered if that was concern she saw on his face. "Brianna, did the Nephilim bite you last night?"

She couldn't answer him. Her body went limp, just as it had when the Nephilim had bitten her.

"Brianna?"

Asmodeus lifted her up as she closed her eyes, unable to expend the energy to keep them open.

"Naberius!" Asmodeus ran to his room as Brianna went completely flaccid in his arms. Her head fell against his chest. The powers and energy that surrounded her were fading—

powers she could only have attained had she dealt with the *Demonic Book of Spells*, as he had once thought, or from the bite of a Nephilim. If she had been bitten it would only be a matter of time before the powers left her and the toxins in the Nephilim's saliva killed her.

He kicked the door to the bedroom open, splitting the wood, and laid her on the bed.

Naberius came up behind him. "What happened?"

"I think Brianna was bitten by the Nephilim last night." He placed his hands on her face, which was losing all its color. She was covered in a fine sheen of cold sweat.

Naberius bent over her, examining her neck. "The powers could have come from the toxins mixing with her blood. That's only if she contained any of the powers she claims she doesn't possess."

"What can we do?" She was growing cold to the touch. He had healing powers, but nothing that would touch the toxins from a Nephilim. Not if they were already imbedded in her blood.

"Raum," Naberius yelled. He turned back to look at Brianna. "We can try and combine our powers to heal her, but I don't know if it will work."

Raum ran into the room. "What? Jesus, what happened?"

Kelly barged into the room after Raum. "What are you doing to her?" She tried pushing past Raum, but he held her back.

"She's dying!" Kelly screamed, fighting against Raum's hold.

Asmodeus stood and faced her. He grabbed her from Raum, bringing her face only inches from his own. "She was bit by a Nephilim last night. Do you have a healing spell?"

She glanced down at Brianna. "I-I don't delve in dark magic. That kind of spell would contain dark magic. It's the only form of incantation that would bring back people from certain death."

She was lying. He could feel it. He let go of her and stepped back. He didn't trust himself not to kill her. "Then Brianna will die."

Indecision clouded Kelly's features. She knew about the *Demonic Book of Spells*. It was obvious. If she was any friend to Brianna, she would perform a spell to heal her.

Brianna began convulsing on the bed.

Kelly looked back to him, terror lining her words. "I don't have my book with me."

"I think I know where it is." He concentrated on the book in the library. Because of a protective spell, or power of some sort, the book could not be materialized. He flashed himself to the library, took it from the desk and flashed himself back to the room. "Will this work?"

Kelly snatched it from his hands in a greedy lunge. "Take off the necklace."

As she held the book a glint in her eyes spoke of hunger. Just how long had Kelly possessed this evil that it affected her in such a way? He didn't hesitate to take the necklace off her. Brianna's life depended on it.

"Everyone needs to leave."

"No." He couldn't leave Brianna in the hands of this woman. Something deadly emanated from her aura. Now that she held the book he could sense her darkness.

She cradled it against her chest and slowly shook her head.

He wanted to kill her with his bare hands...watch the color drain from *her* face. How could he trust her with Brianna? He looked down at Brianna lying on the bed. She'd gone completely still. She was going to die if something wasn't done.

"Let's go." He motioned for Naberius and Raum to leave the room. He took a step toward Kelly and willed himself to keep his hands off her. "If she dies, you die. Are we clear?"

Kelly nodded. The last thing he wanted to do in that moment was leave Brianna's side. She was helpless, and in the hands of a dark witch.

Before he changed his mind he turned and left the room, closing the door behind him.

“What the hell is going on?” Raum asked as they gathered in the hallway.

Asmodeus folded his arms across his chest and stared at the ceiling. Raw violence traveled through his body. “Last night I felt more power coming from Brianna than she originally possessed. We all did, which was why you figured she was lying. I confronted her with the book just now and she began to shake, and she fell limp. She didn’t get her powers from the book. She was bit by the Nephilim.”

“But that would have killed her, not made her more powerful,” Raum argued.

Asmodeus faced his Rebels. “It would have killed her were she an ordinary human, which apparently she is not.”

Chapter Eleven

"You with me, Brianna?"

A warm hand rested on Brianna's forehead. She opened her eyes to find Kelly sitting beside her. Her entire body ached. Every muscle, bone and joint. She tried to sit up but was unable to do so.

"Relax your body. You'll be weak for a few moments. Just rest for the time being."

"What happened? Where am I?" The last thing she remembered was being in Asmodeus's arms as he carried her. Where was he now? She wanted to be cradled against his chest, feel the security and warmth he provided.

"You're still at Naberius's, in Asmodeus's room."

Her body tingled as her strength started trickling back, though the powers she had possessed from the bite of the Nephilim were gone, leaving her strangely empty. "Did he heal me?"

Kelly shifted on the bed and Brianna saw the *Demonic Book of Spells* lying in her lap. The flames on the cover reflected their light in Kelly's eyes. "No."

Kelly wouldn't meet her gaze, and her short answer to Brianna's question hadn't made the situation any clearer. "What are you doing with that?" Brianna asked, gesturing to the book.

"Why didn't you tell me you were bit by a Nephilim last night?"

A coldness rolled off Kelly, and the question caught Brianna off guard. She didn't answer to Kelly, and she wasn't going to start now. The fact that Kelly sat before her holding the spell book told her much about her friend. "What did you do?"

"The saliva from the Nephilim interacted with your powers, heightening them, and in the end it counteracted them. Basically there was a fight transpiring in your body, and your powers lost. We both know your powers are lacking. You should have informed me what had happened."

Brianna caught an underlying threat in Kelly's words. Yesterday the thought of Kelly threatening her would have seemed absurd. After this revelation Brianna couldn't put it past her. "What are you doing with that book?"

Kelly got up from the bed, cradling the book to her chest as if she were afraid Brianna had intentions of taking it from her. Her actions bordered on feral possessiveness. "We're different, Brianna. You wouldn't understand. I used this book to heal you. There *is* good in this book, and you have proven it."

The flame on the cover cast shadows on Kelly's neck. The grounding necklace was gone. Had Asmodeus taken it off her? "Where is your grounding necklace?"

"Asmodeus removed it so I could perform the spell on you."

"He knows you have the book?"

Kelly didn't answer.

The book *had* come from Kelly. Kelly was the only human who had access to her house. Kelly was also the only witch Brianna knew, and one had to be a witch to use the *Demonic Book of Spells*. What made Brianna feel worse was that she had just stood up for her friend and Kelly had made a liar out of her.

Heat crept into her face when she thought of what she had done to Asmodeus the night before. He had defended her to Raum and Naberius and she had made a liar of him. Karma was a bitch. "Kelly, you know you can't play with a book like that. There's nothing good in that book. You taught me that."

Kelly sneered. "One of the spells in this book just healed

you, bringing you back from certain death."

"Kelly—"

"I have a business to run. This isn't a hobby to me like it is you. You play with witchcraft, yet I live by it."

Brianna had never seen Kelly so defensive before. "You're dealing with dark magic. It's dangerous."

"It's only dangerous when you don't know what you're doing. In your hands this book could be potentially harmful. You are ignorant of our ways, and you have never had a good grasp on spells or incantations. I do."

Kelly's words hurt. She was laying bare all of Brianna's weaknesses, pounding them into her, letting her know just who was the more powerful of the two. The challenge she detected in Kelly's words and actions raised alarm bells in Brianna's mind. "How long have you been dealing with dark magic that you know what you're doing? Where did you get that book? Who taught you to read it?"

"Don't worry about where I got it or how I came to understand it," Kelly snapped. "The fact remains I know how to use it, which tilts the favor in my direction."

"What favor?" Not that Brianna expected to get any sane answers from Kelly. It was useless. Her words were making less and less sense. "Kelly, you're a good person. If you practice dark magic it could turn you. It will corrupt you."

Kelly laughed and the sound chilled Brianna. "Who's to say I'm not already corrupted? You're so young. Sometimes I forget that."

Brianna felt as though she were speaking to a stranger. "You're not much older than I am."

"You've no idea, do you?"

Brianna lay very still. Was Kelly into the dark arts further than she had originally thought? To what extent had the darkness corrupted her friend? "What are you talking about?"

Someone pounded on the door. A volley of sounds erupted in the hallway, as if her hearing had just cleared.

"Brianna!"

It was Asmodeus. Before she could call out to him Kelly started mumbling a spell. As she did, her eyes changed from blue to white. There were no pupils.

Just as the door opened Kelly disappeared.

Asmodeus barged in, scanning the room. "Where is Kelly?"

Brianna's gaze was fixed on the spot where Kelly had disappeared. Humans couldn't do what Kelly had just done. Brianna had never heard of such a thing.

"She's gone. She just disappeared. Her eyes turned white as she used a spell. Asmodeus, how could she do that?"

Asmodeus practically ran to her, a worried expression straining his face as he sat next to her on the bed. "She put some sort of ward up over the room. We've been trying to get in." He placed a hand on her cheek.

"Kelly—"

"Don't worry about her right now." Asmodeus got up and went back to the door. "Raum, did you hear what Brianna just said about Kelly?"

"Yes."

"Find her," Asmodeus said.

"Will do."

Asmodeus shut the door and walked over to Brianna. "How are you feeling?" He ran his hand over her forehead, a gesture he had done more than once. In that moment her dishonesty about the angels bubbled up within her, and the way she had lied to him left her disgusted. Her one goal in life had been to hone a craft she had no business with, and it had landed her in this mess. Now she didn't know what to do, who to trust. Her best friend had just turned into someone else before her eyes.

"The book belonged to Kelly," she said, stating the obvious. For some reason she felt guilty by association.

"Kelly will be dealt with, and I don't want you to worry about her. Leave that situation to me. I want you to know you can trust me."

She didn't comment. The silence that hung between them

was awkward.

He took a deep breath. "I know that sounds odd, coming from a demon, as that label intones a sense of evil, and in many ways it should. My goal throughout many centuries has been to take my revenge on Michael, though I've come to realize that will not bring back my family, nor alleviate the sense of being alone in this world. It will only bring on more pain."

It took her a few seconds to digest that bit of information. He had obviously put a lot of thought into his decision. It was surprising he let go of such venomous hatred so easily. It also told her he wasn't exactly the monster she had first thought him to be. God, that she'd been willing to kill in cold blood to save her own ass. Her eyes began to burn, her vision blurring as she tried to sit up. She was forced to lie back down, her strength slowly coming back.

He helped her recline against the pillows. "If you tell me what is going on I may be in a position to help. If it involves Kelly we can figure out what to do together. You are the only person, other than Naberius and Raum, that I know who are in close vicinity. I feel an obligation to you, but I can't help you if you don't apprise me of the situation. Answer me honestly—what transpired last night at the park?"

She tried blinking away the gathering tears, only to cause them to fall down her cheeks. That he said they could work through this together, after her sneaky resolve to kill him, made her feel awful.

He put his hand under her chin, using his free hand to wipe away her tears. "Brianna, what is it? Were you aware of what Kelly was doing?"

She shook her head. "It's not something I can share with you. I wish I could." If she told him what had happened, she was afraid the angels would come.

He didn't say anything as he studied her face.

His examination left her uncomfortable. She couldn't hold up to his scrutiny, so she completely changed the topic. "Can I have something to eat?"

The defeat in his eyes was evident. The isolation. Naberius had his own life, which he shared with his beautiful girlfriend. Asmodeus and Raum seemed to get along, but what was the companionship of one old acquaintance? He probably felt just as alone as she now did. How could she ever have considered killing him? What kind of person did that make her?

He stood. "I will return shortly."

She waited until he shut the door and then let the tears fall. She wanted to scream at the top of her lungs that this wasn't fair. She'd made a simple mistake. How could she be punished for a millennium for one simple mistake? And her best friend wasn't the person Brianna had come to know and love. Kelly carried something dark within her. Brianna didn't even know if Kelly could be saved.

She wiped at her eyes, not wanting Asmodeus to walk in and see her bawling. She'd felt his disappointment that she wouldn't share with him what she knew about the angels, but how could she? There wasn't anything either of them could do anyway. They were going to the Abyss, and that was that.

She controlled her emotions as best she could before he came back. Fate was having a ball with her, but she was still in control of some things, such as her reaction to the problems she faced.

When Asmodeus opened the door she was able to sit up a bit more, and she had quit blubbering. He carried a plate of spaghetti and had a can of Coke under his arm.

"Valencia said you might like this. It's leftovers from last night."

The tomato and garlic aroma did nothing for her, but she'd asked for the food so she would attempt to eat some of it. He set the plate on her lap and handed her a fork. "If you don't like it she said she'll make you something else."

"This is more than fine. Thank you."

She took a few bites as he settled himself on the edge of the bed, facing her. He seemed content to watch her eat.

She pushed thoughts of Kelly aside to concentrate on her

own immediate future. What would the next few days bring? If she didn't kill Asmodeus the angels were going to deliver their punishment. What would it be like to be subject to the horrors of the Abyss?

She opened the Coke. "What's the Abyss like?"

Outwardly he displayed no change in emotion, but she was beginning to notice the small things about him. A slight variation in his breathing pattern let her know her question had taken him off guard.

"It depends on which level you are on."

She put the Coke back on the nightstand. "Levels?" They hadn't mentioned anything about levels.

From the look on his face she could tell he didn't care much for the subject, but he answered her.

"There are three levels. The first level is reserved for angels who have been disobedient within their own realm or those who would benefit from philosophical teachings. The second is for angels who have fallen, and the third level is for those who have incited falls and started rebellions. I guess you could call it rehabilitation, with the overall purpose being to reinstate the angels back into the ranks."

"What happens in the levels? Why are they separated?"

"The first tier isn't very bad at all. It's more like a learning experience, where one is taught the principles in which we exist. The second is much the same way, and the third is more punishment than anything."

Mulling over the information, she twirled spaghetti onto her fork. She wasn't an angel. Every level of the Abyss was meant to teach angels, not humans. "Has a human ever been exiled there?"

He laughed, though the sound contained no humor. "Absolutely not. Humans wouldn't be able to withstand it."

She abruptly lost her appetite. "Oh."

She began thinking about all the things she'd miss. Her freedom. Her family.

Cold weather.

She leaned away from the pillows without her whole body going into pain mode, and put the plate on the nightstand.

"You don't like it?"

"It's fine, I'm just not hungry." Not when she was going to Hell and her best friend was dealing in dark magic.

"Would you like to go out for dinner later?"

His question came out of nowhere, and it rendered her speechless. Was he asking her out on a *date*? He still wore that white shirt, buttons undone, leaving his incredible chest open to her view. She swallowed, not knowing what to say.

"I've been to a diner named Tony's. It was pretty good." He leaned back and waited for her to answer.

She caught something more in his gaze, as if he were still assessing her. Then it hit her. This would be no ordinary date. He was searching for answers. "You're going to try and figure out what I'm hiding."

Asmodeus locked eyes with her. "Absolutely."

Her psychic gift unexpectedly flared to life. This night would pose a major change for her. Something was going down tonight, though she was unable to grasp if it would be for better or for worse.

If she were taking into account the past few days, she'd bet her life on worse.

Chapter Twelve

Kelly leaned against the back of the chaise lounge on her back porch, giving her body time to adjust so she could regain her strength. She had put up a ward over her house a few days ago, and even she couldn't transfer herself through the border.

Using the powers the *Demonic Book of Spells* required tapped every ounce of energy she possessed. The dark spells were taking more and more out of her, but as she'd been promised, she would gain a resistance against their need.

The chaise sat on her covered patio, but she'd swear she could still feel the sun's rays drawing the moisture from her skin. She moved around to the front of the chaise to sit down.

Thank God she had found a way to get that grounding necklace off her. She clutched the book in her right hand. Now that she had it back in her possession she could get back to studying its contents.

"Kelly?"

Kelly watched in amazement as Lev walked out of her house. At six foot eight he barely fit through her sliding glass door.

"Lev? What are you doing here?" How had he gotten in her house with the ward in place? Though she would never tell him, she'd put the ward up to keep him out specifically.

"I made coffee." He ignored her question and sat opposite her, his signature sunglasses in place. Certainly he no longer felt the need to hide his identity from her. She knew what he was. Had known from the beginning.

"What are you doing here?" she asked again. She ran an appreciative eye over his body, which he'd dripped into a pair of jeans and a black T-shirt. Though his physique was nothing to dismiss, it was his aura that had drawn her to him. Because of the powers that ran through her body, she was able to see other's auras. Human auras were sometimes difficult to perceive. Angels, from what she had heard, had warm, light auras.

Lev's aura was dark. Powerful.

She compared his aura to Raum's, surprised to find herself doing so. Raum had a powerful aura, and though he was also a demon, he didn't contain the darkness that Lev possessed.

He lit a cigarette, settling back in his chair. "I see you brought the book back. Why?"

A week ago he'd wanted her to get the book out of her house. He'd informed her that using the spells had the potential of enhancing her powers, but addiction to those spells might pose a problem. He had convinced her taking a break would clear her heart and mind. The night she had performed her locating spell on Brianna, using her hairbrush, Kelly felt it necessary to place the *Demonic Book of Spells* under Brianna's bed beside her sweater box.

"I had to. Brianna had taken it to Asmodeus." The pressure dropped in the air surrounding her. Leviathan hadn't physically moved, and yet Kelly had experienced the surge in his powers.

"Is Asmodeus aware of the book's location?"

She hadn't had time to think that through. Of course he would know where the book was. Asmodeus would come to her house, or send one of his Rebels in his place. The bastard would want it back. She'd healed Brianna like he'd asked, but she'd had to get out of Naberius's house before Asmodeus could put the grounding necklace back on her. She had high-end clientele to think of.

She shifted in the chaise. "I disappeared. It's going to be quite obvious where the book went."

"That wasn't very smart of you."

She hated when he talked down to her. In the beginning of their relationship he had brought her gifts, made her feel like she was the only woman in the world. Now he belittled her every time he came over. He scolded her when she performed spells, and they had quit having sex. It was like he wasn't interested in being intimate with her anymore.

"Don't you think he'll be over here to retrieve it?"

She shrugged. "Probably."

He didn't like her answer. The air around her snapped to life, more violently than a few moments before. Other than that he hadn't moved. He never moved. He was merely there. The man was so much more than his outward appearance. He contained powers she could only dream of.

"I told you the book would overwhelm you. You've proven it in your inadequacy to keep it to yourself. It should have never ended up in Asmodeus's hands. You are careless."

Her temper snapped. "You told me to get it out of the house, to let it go for a while. I took it to Brianna's house because you asked me to. This is your fault, not mine. I would have kept it here—"

"Silence!" He leaned forward and flicked his cigarette onto her lawn. "Do not raise your voice to me. If it were not for me you wouldn't have the damned book in the first place."

When his voice took on that tone it was time to back off. Lev scared her when he got like this.

"That book can give you everything you've ever wanted in life. Power. Success. Love. But you aren't using it as I instructed you. You only perform petty spells, which only serve to drain you."

Lev had informed her she could siphon another's life force, to counteract the drain of her powers. It was something she refused to do. She didn't need to siphon. She wasn't in this to become powerful, though the power was indeed addicting. She kept the book to help her at her craft. "I am feeling drained, but I can't siphon from another witch."

He didn't say anything. This was as cold as she'd ever seen

him. The façade he had made for her benefit was diminishing.

"What is it you want with me?" she asked quietly.

He smiled. "Have we come to this turn in our relationship already?"

His words confirmed her fear. He had never been interested in her. She was a means to an end. She should have known.

"What do you want?" she repeated.

"Siphon the power from Asmodeus and his demons and bring it back to me. Siphon from the witch as well. If you do not do this I will take the book back and you will die."

She gasped. "Are you threatening me? What can you do with anyone's life force? You're immortal."

"From your first spell you have started to die. That's why the spells are taking so much of you. They feed from the power of your life force, not the energy of the earth, as your pathetic spells do. That is what enables you to wield dark power. To keep your life force flowing you must siphon from another being with powers. Or you can siphon from a normal human, though they usually die in the process. I want the immortals' life force because with it come their powers."

What more powers could he possibly want? She tossed the book to the ground in front of him, though it took every ounce of her willpower to do so. "Then I quit. I didn't become addicted as you had once warned me."

He smiled. "Nothing in life is what it seems. It's no longer about addiction. It's about survival. Whether or not you ever perform another dark spell you still need to siphon. You've let your life source seep out, and that's not something you can merely close up. That's why you've been so tired. Why the spells are taking so much out of you. You need to siphon from another source to stay alive."

The day Asmodeus had released her and Brianna, she had come home and slept the day away, which was why she had forgotten about the necklace until late that night. The truth of his words cut deep.

No. This was bullshit. She was human. She couldn't siphon

off another living thing. "It is physically impossible for me to siphon from another."

He laughed, rising from the chair to tower over her. "You contain the power to do so now. It will come naturally to humans in your position. It's called bonding."

"Bonding?"

"It's in the book," he said, picking it up off the ground and tossing it into her lap. "And if you choose not to take from another it's your death. Choose not to bring these powers to me, it's your soul."

She felt cold as he walked away. She had never imagined her involvement with the book or with the demon would go this far. Things were getting out of hand, and Lev had no intention of helping her. "What do I do about Asmodeus?"

"I don't really give a damn," he called out, just before he disappeared.

£

Wednesday night at Tony's was karaoke night. Brianna wasn't in the mood for karaoke, but it added a nice distraction from the terrible thoughts running through her mind. Asmodeus had taken her back to her house so she could get dressed in her own clothes. She hadn't packed anything for a night on the town.

She decided on a little black dress, because she wasn't quite sure what she and Asmodeus were going on. A date or an interrogation. She figured the little black dress could help in both.

Asmodeus wore black slacks with his white collared shirt. His hair was pulled back. He looked like an Armani model. Apparently half the women in Tony's thought so too, as she'd caught more than one staring in his direction.

The hostess, another one with wandering eyes, sat them in

a booth with a view of the lovely street. The street lamp shone in their window, casting a glare. Cars honked and people passed by, staring in at them. The hostess placed the menus on the table, which was covered with a white and red checkered tablecloth. Brianna settled down and pushed the menu to the edge of the table.

"You know what you would like to order?" he asked.

The waitress walked up to ask them what they wanted to drink.

"I've been here before. You only come to Tony's for the deep-dish pizza. At least the locals do."

He smiled, placing his menu on top of hers. "I am ordering that as well."

The waitress pulled a small notepad out of her black apron. "Two deep-dish pizzas. And what would you like to drink?"

"I'll have a Coke," Brianna said.

"I'll have the same."

The waitress nodded and took the menus, and with one last appreciative glance at Asmodeus she left.

"When have you been here?" she asked, trying to act nonchalant and attempting to keep the conversation light.

"The night you came back."

"Oh." Not the night of the attack. Not the night he'd caught her lying. The night she'd come back. Why those words affected her so much she had no idea. It wasn't as though this was going to turn into a long-term relationship. Well, in the Abyss maybe, though she highly doubted lustful thoughts would come into play there.

Still trying to keep the conversation light-hearted, she raised an eyebrow and nodded toward the stage. "So, are you going to get up and sing tonight?"

Asmodeus glanced at the microphone sitting on the small stage. "Is that what they are setting up to do? A band played the last time I was here."

"Well, anyone can go up there and sing, so if you feel the

need." She watched as he gave the stage another look.

"No thanks. You?"

She picked up her fork. "I'd rather stick this fork in my eye."

"I'd be forced to heal you, then I would be hauled away to a laboratory. Perfect night."

"Which reminds me. Why do your eyes look normal right now?" He wasn't sporting the freaky horizontal pupils. His eyes looked as normal as hers, only the light green of his eyes were rare. She'd never quite seen that color on another person.

"I can change them if I wish."

She leaned back in the booth, feeling at ease with his company. She hadn't thought this date would be so relaxing. "What's it like to have all of those powers?"

He shrugged. "I can't answer that. It would be the same as my asking you what it's like to walk."

Point taken. The thought of having such power was overwhelming.

Looking outside, she watched a couple walk by, hand in hand. The scene made her realize she had taken her freedoms for granted. She'd worked so much at her bookstore she hadn't found enjoyment in a simple afternoon walk. A sunset.

"You are concerned about the repercussions of your summoning me."

Ha. There was no need to worry about it. The consequences had already been laid out. She was screwed. Slowly coming to terms with the fact that she was going to burn in hell wasn't pleasant. "Not really."

A waiter stepped up to the microphone and tapped it a few times. Hearing the resounding thunks throughout the dining area, he smiled. "Okay, folks, this is karaoke night at Tony's. We'll have someone at the DJ booth, so go on up and tell him what song you want to sing, and if we have it we'll set it up for you. Just fill out the slip of paper with your song choice if it gets busy and we'll call you up."

An older man immediately went up to the booth and soon

he was singing "Jailhouse Rock" by Elvis. He wasn't bad, actually.

The waitress delivered their drinks.

Brianna took the paper off the top of the straw and watched Asmodeus. He was turned in his seat, seeming to enjoy the old man singing, the same as he had enjoyed viewing *The Golden Girls.* Whether it was TV or karaoke, he became mesmerized by the distraction, taking pleasure where he could.

A few other brave souls sang—one butchering the song they chose—and Asmodeus finally turned back to her as the waitress arrived with their food.

He promptly peppered his pizza to death.

What freedoms were most important to him? If he had the choice to do whatever he wished, what would he do first? "If you had one week to live, what would you do with it?"

He didn't hesitate with his answer. "First I would spend it in good company. I'd enjoy great food," he said, raising his fork, which dripped with cheese and ham, "and I would have as much sex as I could."

Some of the Coke she had been drinking dribbled down her chin when she laughed. She quickly dabbed her face with her napkin. One minute he seemed dark and mysterious, and the next he was an open book.

He smiled. "You?"

She put her napkin back on the table, enjoying the simple innocence of his smile. He looked like he hadn't a care in the world. A drastic change in the way he usually carried himself. She liked this side of him. "I guess I'd do the same." They had less than six days left to them, and when she failed in her mission they would take him as well, in whatever manner they could.

Guilt washed over her because she had yet to tell him about her assigned mission. He was aware she was hiding something, but there was no way she could enlighten him, which was why they were here in the first place.

"What are you thinking about?"

She pushed the bad thoughts aside and said the first thing that came to mind, hoping to keep him in his playful mood. "I'm thinking there's a beach close by. Ever been to the beach?"

A distant look replaced his smile. "A long time ago."

He suddenly seemed tense, and she wanted his playfulness back. "Why don't we go there after dinner?"

Out of the corner of her eye she saw the waitress lead a familiar face to a booth a few rows from theirs. It was one of the angels who had summoned her from the library. He was dressed casually in a blue T-shirt, and he was seriously smaller than he had been in his own realm. He looked like a normal human, not at all like the Warrior Angel he truly was.

"Sounds good."

She turned her attention back to Asmodeus. She should have told him what had happened in the library. The appearance of the angel made it feel as though it were she and Asmodeus against the angels. They were in this together.

"Asmodeus..."

She caught the angel at the booth slowly shaking his head. He motioned for her to look outside. When she did, she noticed another angel standing under the street lamp, illuminated by the soft yellow light.

"Uh, Asmodeus..."

"I am aware." Asmodeus leaned forward. "The question is, how did *you* recognize them?"

She brought her gaze back to his. Asmodeus looked calm. Resigned. She had no desire to answer his question, so she completely ignored it. Truce gone. "What should we do?"

He studied her for a moment. The assessment in his gaze made her feel like an errant toddler. "They won't do anything in front of the humans."

"So what do we do?"

"We finish dinner and go to the beach, as was your wish. I say we behave as though we have only one week to live."

Could he make that innuendo any more obvious?

Unbeknownst to him, the scenario was true. Scanning the muscles his shirt couldn't hide, she figured there were worse ways to go.

She glanced behind him to the angel. He eyed her over the rim of his coffee cup. His unwavering stare was starting to creep her out. She tried ignoring him, looking back at Asmodeus. "I think we can work something out."

"You know, I like this new side of you. Laughing in the face of danger. Thumbing your noise at the powers that be."

Is that what the angels would think she was doing? *Shit.* Anxiety filtered through her body. "Do you think they are going to do something? Why is it they just don't take you?"

His smile was anything but pleasant. "Because they know that unless they come with an army they will go home in pieces."

She glanced at the angel in the booth. He didn't look incompetent to her at all. "How can you be so sure of your abilities?"

"How can I put this to you so you will understand it?" He folded his napkin and placed it on the table. "Dogs are friendly, looking only for companionship. Unless, of course, you breed that dog differently. Or torture it. When a dog is tortured it has a heightened sense of survival. Survival becomes ingrained in their defenses. It's not that the dog is bad. It's aggressive. It's a learned trait, and the dog believes to stay alive it must fight anything that seems to pose a threat. I guess it's safe to assume the angels view me as a tortured dog. They realize what I am capable of if provoked or attacked. They are not sure what I will do, or who I can summon to fight with me. I view them as a threat to my survival."

The waitress chose that moment to come up to their table and slide the bill toward Asmodeus. "Do you need any boxes?"

"No, I think we're good. Thank you." Brianna put her napkin on the table, feeling sick to her stomach. Sometimes Asmodeus seemed so normal, at other times his intensity knew no bounds.

Brianna cleared her throat. "So, do we go to the beach or do we head back?"

"Why wouldn't we go to the beach?" he asked, placing cash in the leather pouch for the bill.

Duh. "Because we're being blatantly followed by angels that have been sent to apprehend us…you, I mean."

Asmodeus didn't miss her slip up, though he quickly masked his surprise. He waved a dismissive hand. "I'm not going to let them interfere with the first date I've ever been on. What kind of man would I be if I let them ruin our night?"

Was he serious? "Yeah, but—"

"Do you want to go to the beach or not?"

His apparent ease with the situation unsettled her. "Well, I'd like to live through the night, for one."

"You're with me. Don't worry about them."

She wished she had as much confidence as he did, considering the precarious situation they faced. It was as though he dared them to try something. "I guess we can go to the beach if you think it's safe."

He stood and held his hand out. "Don't let them worry you any longer. Leave the worrying up to me."

"You're showing no signs of worry at all," she said, taking his hand and scooting out of the booth.

"I'll let you know if we need to worry. Right now there is no need." As if to prove his point, he turned to the angel sitting in the booth and waved. The angel didn't look pleased. In fact, he had a decidedly agitated look on his face.

Asmodeus laughed.

They walked out of Tony's, her hand in his, and she had the distinct feeling the angels would not follow them.

When she slid into the passenger seat of Naberius's Saab she turned around to look in the window of the restaurant.

The angel was gone.

She scanned the street for the other. He was gone as well.

"Where did they go?"

His arm brushed hers when he leaned back to check for other cars as he backed up. “Couldn’t care less.”

Either he was crazy or he was absolutely confident in his abilities against the angels. She was betting crazy.

When he came to the edge of the parking lot he turned to her with a smile. “Which way to the sand, sweetheart?”

Yep, he was most definitely crazy.

Chapter Thirteen

"I never learn my lessons with humans."

Leviathan surveyed the living room in Kelly's house one last time. He had gone back to check on her to make certain she was studying the aspect of bonding. Either she had vacated of her own free will, or Asmodeus had taken her and the *Demonic Book of Spells*. Whatever the case, the bitch was currently using a spell to keep him from locating her whereabouts, of that he was certain.

Dumb move on her part. When he eventually found her—and he would—he'd make her beg for mercy. Begging for compassion from someone who contained none would not get her very far.

"Let's go, Dog."

His black lab came trotting out of Kelly's bedroom. She stopped in the middle of Kelly's living room and pissed on the floor.

He knew he liked that dog for a reason.

"Good girl." He turned to leave the room, unsatisfied with his findings. Dog finished her business and thumped over to his side. He bent down and scratched her head.

As he walked out of Kelly's house he felt a tingling sensation from the ward she had put up. Silly girl. He was a demon from the first fall with Lucifer. Not remotely a part of the lustful idiots who had fallen with Asmodeus. Those dumbasses had been apprehended within years of their fall. Not so with Lucifer's demons.

Lucifer. The prick. That man was psychotic. Being on Luc's shitlist wasn't somewhere you wanted to be. Unfortunately he was currently at the top of that list, and if he didn't do something that pleased the schizo soon he was going to get killed.

Unless, of course, he attained the powers from the witch.

He opened the door to his Ford F-350. Dog jumped up and sat in the passenger seat.

"You piss in here and I'll make a seat cover out of your ass."

Dog whimpered and let her tongue fall out of her mouth.

"No slobbering either."

As he put his sunglasses on, he recalled the time Kelly had asked him why he had named the lab Dog. He had told her to spell Dog backwards.

She'd seemed adequately appalled.

His other dogs had been appropriately named Michael, Raphael, Uriel and Gabriel, after the four Holy Watchers. At Christmas he took pictures of the dogs with antlers on and sent them to the angels. Strange, he'd never received a card in return.

He started the truck, becoming more pissed off by the second. He'd given the *Demonic Book of Spells* to Kelly for her benefit as well as his own. Now the ungrateful bitch had taken off on him. Or worse, she could have been apprehended by another demon.

She didn't contain the power to hide from him for long. She was a fake. Fucking tarot card reader. Brianna was the one with the power, which was why he needed Kelly to bond with her. Kelly was easily manipulated, whereas her friend was too strong-willed. His attempt to get the book out of Kelly's hands for a while had failed. He had wanted her to become weak, and she had been getting weaker by the hour. She would have turned on her friend in days.

Then Asmodeus had burst into the picture, ruining everything. He suddenly felt like the captured villains in the

Scooby Doo cartoons. *If it wasn't for you meddling demons...*

He was going to name his next dog Asmodeus. He'd buy a poodle and put a pink ribbon around its neck.

He had no more time to waste. He had to find Brianna and force her to summon Kelly. Kelly was more than likely in a bad condition by now. He doubted he'd have trouble getting her to bond with Brianna.

Killing the two would bring an improvement to his current mood. He put the truck in reverse and smiled at Dog. "Time to find the wicked witch, ToTo."

£

Asmodeus leaned out of the car to take his shoes off and roll up his slacks. The breeze coming off the water was a welcome change to what he had become accustomed to for the last few centuries.

Brianna had tried to hide the fact she had been watching for the angels during the ride to the beach. Three different times he'd had to turn around because she'd forgotten to tell him what turn to take.

He stood and put his shoes and socks on the driver's seat and shut the door. Brianna stood in front of the car waiting for him. She had worn a little black dress that clung to her every curve.

He walked up to her and took her hand as though he had done it a million times before. It felt natural to walk hand in hand with her. He absently ran his thumb over her silky skin as he thought over the past few days. She'd been less than forthcoming with him, and though it should anger him, it didn't. The sight of her lying prone on the bed, drained of color, left a terrible ache in his being. The last time he had experienced fear like that had been when he had seen her car in the parking lot at Hickory Park.

It was damned confusing. He was falling for her. He could tell by the way he became concerned every time her safety was at stake. Damned if he knew when it had happened. But the truth was there would never be a relationship between them. It was against the laws of nature.

As they reached the edge of the sand he couldn't help but think he didn't deserve this small reprieve. For more than half of his life he'd been punished. He was waiting for something terrible to happen. Something that would take all of this away.

As they silently made their way toward the crashing waves he felt a connection with her. An understanding. Brianna took his company for what it was worth, not for what he could give her. She'd accepted his trust, and in turn gave him her trust as well. It was a liberating feeling to be with someone and not try to hide who and what you were. Quite unlike what he had shared with his wife.

He had to stop contemplating what a wonderful woman Brianna was, and start concentrating on why he had worked to get her alone in the first place. She was still hiding something. He figured what she hid from him had more to do with her safety than it had to do with his. Perhaps that's why she had come back. She was frightened. He wouldn't be surprised if she had had a confrontation with an angel about her summoning him.

She squeezed his hand, taking him from his thoughts. "Wow. The breeze sure does get colder the closer you get to the water."

He let go of her hand and shrugged out of his shirt.

"No, I wasn't hinting for anything. Keep your shirt."

He helped her slip into it, his hands brushing against the softness of her skin. Memories of their intimacy clouded his vision. She was a passionate woman, and also cunning. If he hadn't stopped them the night before, she would have accepted him into her body. The grounding necklace caught the light of the moon, and the sight of it around her neck made him angry. He'd take it from her without her knowing.

Removing the necklace might be a mistake, but it was a mistake he was willing to make at the moment. He dematerialized the necklace without another thought.

"Nonsense." He took her hand again, a feeling of possessiveness overcoming him. A part of him wanted to tell her to run, to get as far away from him as possible. The other part wasn't willing to let her go.

There could never be anything significant between them. He'd learned his lesson. Demons and humans couldn't coexist. Not to mention she would grow old, he wouldn't. His wife had aged with the passing of time and he had remained youthful. It wasn't something he wanted to revisit.

"Okay, what are you thinking about?" she asked as they came to the water's edge. "You look like you're thinking too hard."

The moon and the stars were bright tonight, and under them, with her dark hair tangling about her face, she looked like a vision.

"I was just thinking I hadn't told you how beautiful you look tonight."

She smiled and turned to look at the water. Something was bothering her, and it wasn't the appearance of the angels. How had she recognized the angels? He had read the recognition in her eyes the instant she saw them. What was she hiding? He wished she would trust him with whatever it was she was withholding.

Apparently her trust didn't extend that far.

Hell, if his wife had never trusted him how could he expect a woman whom he'd just met to trust him?

"I'm to the point I don't know what to believe anymore."

He found her response confusing. Was she lost in thought, or was she answering his earlier comment? "You do not think yourself beautiful?"

She laughed, the sound carrying in the wind. "I'm referring to Kelly. To the situation." She turned, her gaze catching his under the moonlight. She looked vulnerable and innocent. "My feelings for you."

At her words something inside him broke free of the constraints he had placed for his own protection. He had loved once, and those people had been ripped from him. Ironically by his own hand. If he allowed Brianna in what was left of his heart, what would happen to her? What injustices would she suffer from loving him?

Instead of replying to her, he turned to face the blackened water of the ocean. Everything changed with time. Especially one's feelings for another person. How would she feel about him when everything around them fell to pieces? And it would. It was only a matter of time.

Brianna felt like an ass. Somehow she had forgotten the reason for his presence. He was currently with her because he was trying to find out what she was hiding, nothing more. He wanted to know her motive for coming back to Naberius's house. They were friendly enemies. He had made that perfectly clear the night before. Enemies did not share their feelings on a moonlit beach.

The silence was broken by Asmodeus's cell ringing.

He fished it out of his pocket and flipped it open. "Hello?"

She dragged her foot through the sand, wishing she could bury herself in it.

"It is the *Demonic Book of Spells* that makes her ill. When the witch uses spells contained in that book she is not only using the energy of the earth, but the energy of her life force as well."

Brianna stilled, knowing he spoke of Kelly. Raum had found her.

"I will be there shortly."

He closed his cell and put it back in his pocket. "You will accompany me to Raum's."

He turned on his heel and headed back to the car.

So it was back to the old Asmodeus? Withdrawn and calculating? She moved quickly to catch up with him. Why was he acting so indifferent to her? "Where does he live?"

"He lives a few miles from here, in a house overlooking the beach."

"Kelly is ill?"

"Do not ask me any questions."

She put her hand on his arm and pulled him to a stop. He slowly turned to face her. Again, he reminded her of a cold, terrifying man. If she didn't know any better, if she hadn't felt the warmth beneath the façade, she would have believed him capable of anything.

"What are you afraid of?" she asked, confused as to why he had gone from a laughing gentleman to total indifference.

"I am afraid of nothing."

"You are," she argued. Was it her? Did he find her lacking? He was holding himself back from her, but why?

He locked eyes with her. "If I am afraid of anything, it is hurting you. If you knew what was best for you, you would leave the conversation at that. The only reason you are with me is for your safety."

Her safety? "Are you deliberately trying to hurt my feelings?"

Without answering her he turned and began walking back to the car. With no choice left to her she followed. When they reached the car she took his shirt off and handed it back to him. He slipped it on without another look in her direction.

During the short ride to Raum's the silence seemed to gnaw at her. When had she gone from planning to kill Asmodeus to having feelings for him? That's what was happening, wasn't it?

She searched his profile. The hard line of his jaw, set in anger, made him look dangerous. Would he hurt her? Never. She could feel the truth of that deep inside her soul.

Was she falling for him? Yes. It was likely from all of the times he had saved her life. Always there when she needed him. He seemed unbreakable. Her feelings toward him could be nothing more than that of indebtedness, because she didn't really know him.

No. That wasn't exactly the truth. She'd witnessed his pain when she had performed the locating spell. Plus he'd fought Nephilim when they undoubtedly reminded him of his own terrible past. He'd also shown concern over her when she had nearly died from the Nephilim bite.

Asmodeus pulled into a U-shaped driveway and she made the effort to quit thinking about him. He made it obvious there could be nothing between them, and in truth she had no idea why she even considered her feelings toward him. What was the point?

She shoved her thoughts aside and focused on her surroundings. Raum's beach house was a two-story dwelling with white paneling and blue shutters. Not exactly what she had envisioned him living in. It seemed too...quaint.

Asmodeus put the car in park and left it running. "I will not be long. Stay in the car."

"Why?"

He stared at her as though she wasn't very smart. "I don't want you to interfere, so I'm asking you to stay in the car."

"You didn't ask me to do anything. You told me to stay in the car."

He shrugged. "Same thing."

He opened his door and slid out. She forced herself to look out of the windshield and forget what a Neanderthal he was. What kind of relationship could she ever have with him? He needed to realize he couldn't order people around.

A relationship? Where were these thoughts coming from?

As she sat in the car waiting, three women in tight jeans, short skirts and enough makeup to put Tyra Banks and all of America's Next Top Models to shame walked by. They glanced at the car as they made their way to Raum's front door.

Who the hell were they?

They didn't bother knocking, they just opened the door and walked in.

Brianna sat in the car for a few moments. How long was Asmodeus going to be? What were they doing with Kelly?

More importantly, who were those sluts?

With a huff of impatience she opened her car door and climbed out. She straightened her dress as she walked up the stairs to Raum's front door. The wind had picked up, causing her hair to whip around her face. She ran a hand through her hair and raised her hand to knock, then dropped it when she heard a female voice croon, "Asmoday, you were supposed to come back last night. What was more important than us?"

She didn't hear him answer the slut, so she leaned her ear against the door.

"Why are you leaving so soon?" she heard through the door.

Leaving? Who was leaving?

The door began to open and her brain caught up with the words she heard. She straightened and glared at Asmodeus, who stood before her wearing a frown.

"I'm almost finished. Go back to the car." Though he seemed calm she noticed the illumination in his eyes and the way the muscles in his jaw worked.

"Who the hell is she?" One of the girls whispered loudly. Brianna looked in their direction and gave them a once-over.

Sluts.

She looked back at Asmodeus. "Where is Kelly? What's going on?"

Before Asmodeus could answer her, she caught sight of Raum. He walked out of a hall into the living room.

When he saw her standing at the door a look of confusion crossed his features. "Brianna? What are you doing outside? Come in." He motioned for her to enter his house.

Brianna smiled at Asmodeus and took Raum's offered hand. She noticed the sluts were steaming in their hip-huggers.

"A mortal, Raum? Why?" one of the hookers asked.

Mortal? What the hell were they? Other than sluts, of course. Asmodeus walked out of the room, toward the back of the house.

"She's not mine. She's Asmodeus's."

Brianna shook her head, ready to deny that bit of garbage, when the tallest of the women leaned close to her and sniffed. Like a dog. The woman was sniffing her *like a dog.*

"Hmmm, O positive."

Unwilling to let that bit of rudeness go, Brianna leaned toward her, sniffed and crinkled her noise. "Hmmm, HIV positive."

"Okay," Raum said, pushing her toward the front door. "Waiting in the car might be the best idea."

"Of course. Kick *me* out, not the three hookers." She tried pulling away from him. "Where is Kelly?"

Raum said something to the sluts, but she didn't catch it. The three women seemed seriously pissed. The tallest one looked as though she'd do some severe damage, and Brianna did a double-take when the slut's eyes turned white. Pure white.

Raum opened the door. "I'll fill you in later. Kelly's not at her finest at the moment."

"Those girls are demons?" Didn't demons eyes turn red?

Raum looked puzzled, pausing with his hand on her arm. "No."

"That girl's eyes...they turned white."

Raum looked back at the women. The taller woman's eyes went back to normal. He sighed and tried nudging her in the direction of the door. "Here, why don't I walk you out to—"

"Raum, who are they? Are they here for Kelly?" She couldn't leave Kelly in here alone.

He shook his head. "No."

The tallest woman jutted her chin out and ran a tongue over her teeth. Her very pointy teeth. She seemed normal, except for the two fangs in her mouth.

Goose bumps spread over her skin. She could swear she felt those sharp fangs sink into her flesh. *O positive. Yikes.* How did the vampire know what her blood type was? "I think I'll go wait in the car." What next? Was Santa Claus going to come down the chimney bearing presents?

Raum quickly agreed. "I think it's a good idea. Asmodeus will be out short—"

"I'm not telling you a goddamned thing. My life and practices are none of your goddamned business."

Brianna turned back when she heard Kelly's strangled yell. Though Kelly had screamed those words, it didn't sound very much like her. She sounded as though she were in terrible pain. What were they doing to her? "What the hell is going on?" Brianna tugged her arm out of Raum's grasp and made her way down the hall.

Raum was behind her, but he didn't try to stop her. She listened to Kelly's voice and found the room they were holding her in. Just before she entered the room Asmodeus blocked her way.

"I told you to wait in the car."

"What are you doing to Kelly?"

He stood immobile inside the frame of the door. "The only pain she is experiencing is through her own actions."

What was that supposed to mean? She tried peeking around him, but he continued to block her view.

"Brianna, go back to the car. There is no more to be done here, and I will be finished momentarily."

Kelly laughed from somewhere in the room. The sound sent goose bumps over her skin. "It's you he wants, Brianna. I know that now. It's always been you."

Brianna put her hands on Asmodeus's chest, stood on her tiptoes and tried to look around him. It was futile. He was just too massive. "What are you talking about?" she asked Kelly.

"Do not talk to her," Asmodeus warned.

Kelly's voice changed to one with a desperate edge, a whisper of warning. "Brianna, your life is in danger, and Asmodeus is trying his best to keep that information away from you. I need your help. Why won't you help me?"

Before she could respond, Asmodeus picked her up and slung her over his shoulder. He stalked down the hallway and she made no attempt to get out of his hold. Fighting him would have only caused her more embarrassment. As if leaving the house with her ass up in the air, thrown over Asmodeus's shoulder wasn't embarrassing enough.

She couldn't see the reactions of the sluts because her hair obstructed her view. She was sure she didn't want to see their smug faces.

"What is she talking about? Why is my life in danger?" Brianna grunted when Asmodeus adjusted her weight. Kelly couldn't possibly know about the angels, so she must be referring to something else.

"If you listen to Kelly's ramblings you are a fool. I warned you to stay in the car."

He walked out of the house and down the stairs.

Not willing to let the matter drop she asked another question in hopes of an answer. "Do you know what she is referring to? Who wants me?"

When they reached the car he set her down and put his hands on her upper arms, forcing her to face him. "You will get in the car and you will wait for me."

Unwanted tears gathered in her eyes. Her emotions were confusing enough without his constant dismissals. "Why is my best friend saying those things? Why are you treating me like this?"

Instead of answering her he gently cupped her face and lowered his lips to hers. She was too surprised to argue, too surprised to care why he was kissing her. She had so many questions, so many emotions tearing through her mind, she felt like a spinning top in a child's hands.

The kiss started out slow and sweet, but it quickly became rough, a command to comply. His muscled form pressed her against the car, blocking the cold of the night. As his lips possessed hers she could feel the desperation, the utter loneliness that threatened to consume them both.

She'd been jealous of the sluts in the house. Pure female jealousy made her want to mark him for her own, and she did so by bringing her arms around his neck and pulling him closer, opening herself up to him.

His hands fisted in her hair, and she welcomed the pain. She wanted his protection, but she didn't have the sense to ask him for it. She didn't trust his reaction toward her mission, even if she no longer had any intention of carrying it out.

When she felt his arousal, hard against her body, it ignited her own. Wanting to feel more of him, she parted her legs slightly, bringing an arm down and wrapping it around his back.

Asmodeus had lost himself in Brianna's innocence. When he had seen her tears amidst her confused question as to his treatment, he could not stop himself from claiming her. He wanted her. Had always wanted her.

Her body was pliant against his. When she wrapped an arm around his back, pulling their bodies closer, he nearly lifted her dress to take her. Somewhere in the recesses of his mind he realized now was not the time or place.

He broke the kiss and stepped back, putting much-needed distance between him and the one thing that was forbidden to beings such as himself. Brianna leaned against the car, her hair disheveled, her lips full and parted. The door to the house opened. Raum came forward and stood on his porch.

"What do you want me to do with Kelly?"

Asmodeus looked back at Brianna. His only thoughts revolved around finding a place they could continue their passion in private. With sheer determination he forced those thoughts away. Brianna was the one thing he could never have.

"Keep her for now. Guard her. We must find out who she keeps referring to. I'll be in touch."

Raum nodded and went back in his house.

Brianna put a hand on his chest. "Asmodeus, there's something I need to tell you."

A shadow crossed in front of the house. He stepped away from Brianna, scouring the surroundings. A dark presence had manifested itself, though he couldn't locate where it had gone.

"Asmodeus—"

"Quiet."

She did as he asked. He no longer sensed a shadow, nor saw anything that would give him suspicion. The shadow could have been anything.

"What is it?"

So much for her being quiet. "Nothing."

He moved to open the door for her. Without a word she slid in the car. He walked around the car, taking one last look around. Nothing but the sound of the ocean and the light from the moon surrounded them. He sat in the driver's seat, dismissing the shadow that was more than likely brought on by his contradictory emotions. He couldn't let Brianna become a disruption. There were things he needed to do, leads he must investigate.

"Where are we going?" she asked.

More than anything he wanted to say somewhere they wouldn't be interrupted, somewhere he could feel the heat of her body and taste the sweetness of her skin.

Now that he had regained his senses, he realized he needed to separate himself from her. She was growing on him. Her tears had affected him, as had her heartfelt question. She might need his protection, and he would provide it. But she also needed protection from him, and he would give it.

Chapter Fourteen

Asmodeus had a special talent for teasing her. Once again she had opened herself up to him, and once again he had denied her. At least there was an upside to his current dismissal; she wasn't in handcuffs this time around.

With the car window rolled down she relished the cool breeze as it ruffled her hair. Clouds were moving in, and the clean, damp smell in the air promised rain. Asmodeus handled the car with an expertise even she lacked. She chalked it up to men and their toys. An ancient such as him shouldn't look so at ease in the driver's seat of a Saab, but he looked as though he were born to take to the streets with such a sweet ride.

She needed to tell him about her mission and the time frame allotted to her. It now seemed like the right thing to do. She wasn't exactly sure how she would go about it, but it needed to be said. If the angels came, so be it. The angels were now checking up on her, which had her wondering what they would do next. What did they know? Could they read her thoughts? If they could, they knew she no longer considered carrying out their mission.

"Asmodeus, I need to tell you—"

"I understand, Brianna. I'm going to take you to Naberius's and leave you under his protection. I'm going back to Raum's."

"But—"

"Naberius will take good care of you."

What the hell was he talking about? "Why can't I stay with you?" She felt him pulling away, just as he did at the beach when she admitted she had feelings for him.

"This is the best way."

"For you," she said, unable to keep the hurt from her voice. As if she didn't have enough to think about. Why was she letting this bother her so much when she had much bigger problems to face?

"This has nothing to do with me." He stopped at a red light and ran a hand through his hair. "No, it has everything to do with me. You're safer at Naberius's house. He can protect you just as well as I can."

She was finished arguing with him. He obviously knew what was best in any given situation. To hell with this. She would get to Naberius's, wait until Asmodeus was gone, then she would leave. She'd go back to her shop in the morning and live the rest of her five days in quiet denial.

When Asmodeus was a few minutes away from Naberius's house he called Naberius on the cell, asking him to open the gates and apprising him of the situation. Arriving at the black gate, she felt like a prisoner all over again. She was determined to leave tonight. Naberius couldn't save her from her true destiny, a punishment no other human had ever been subject to before.

Whatever Kelly had been talking about couldn't be any worse than that fate.

What would happen to Kelly? Could she be saved? Not that she could do much for her friend, especially after Kelly had been so hateful to her.

What kind of friend did that make Brianna? When Asmodeus had taken her from her home Kelly had come to break her out. She had risked her life for her. Kelly had taught her so many things in the years they had known each other. She had taken her under her wing and provided her the learning tools to help with spells, tarot cards and palm reading.

And now, when her friend needed her the most, she was going to turn her back on her? She couldn't do that.

She wouldn't do that.

As they pulled to a stop Brianna's plans had changed. She had to figure out a way to get Kelly out of Raum's house. She would help Kelly let go of the *Demonic Book of Spells* and the pull it had on her, because it was obvious the book was having a negative effect on Kelly's life.

Asmodeus started climbing out of the car.

"Thanks, but I can find my way in. Have fun with your fanged sluts."

She opened the door and found the restraint not to slam the damn thing shut. She walked around the front of the car, through the headlights, and kept her head held high. This rollercoaster was going to end tonight, and once again her life would get back to some sense of normalcy.

For a few days, anyway.

Asmodeus waited until Brianna walked in the house. He put the car in reverse and backed out of the driveway.

This was for the best. What could he give her? Nothing. He had nothing to give. Hell, he was living off money he had borrowed from Naberius. He was driving a car loaned to him from Naberius, and he had no home to speak of.

He had no purpose.

Once again on the street he slammed the car into drive. Brianna could take care of herself. She contained the power to do so, if only she would believe in it. Tangling herself in his life would be the mistake of a lifetime. He couldn't fathom why she couldn't see that simple truth.

He glanced at the empty passenger seat. His shirt carried a small trace of her perfume. He tried blocking it out, but it proved to be too difficult. It was as if her presence lingered, taunting him with the possibilities of what could be.

He focused his thoughts on the road, and what he would do when he arrived back at Raum's house. What Kelly had said earlier had been nagging him. Was there someone after Brianna, or had Kelly lost touch with reality? The latter was a definite possibility. Kelly had gone from being a vibrant blonde, full of life and fire, to being a gaunt shadow of her former self. The book had taken its fair share out of her, and she had allowed it.

He'd heard of the book's existence. The demon rumored to have written the *Demonic Book of Spells* had incorporated spells that required power from both the energy of the earth and the energy of the spell caster's life force. A spell ensured the book could not be materialized, even by that of its maker. Why the book had been created remained a mystery.

Where had Kelly acquired the book? How had she come to understand the language? She could study the script for years, but without a proper teacher, one who was familiar with the book, she couldn't possibly have mastered a grasp on the language. Even he hadn't been able to understand the book. The language had been demonic, but it had a dialect all its own.

There was a demon helping her—there had to be.

Asmodeus came to a red light. He pressed down on the brake and let his head fall back against the headrest. This didn't feel right, but leaving Brianna was his only option. She deserved so much more than he was able to give her. She deserved all this world had to offer. He wasn't of this world. He would never be a part of this world.

A thought kept nagging him. Naberius was happy. He had a wonderful life with Valencia, and they had made their relationship work. He lived in a nice home, led a respectable life. Didn't he deserve happiness, such as what his friend had found? Was it possible?

Visions of Brianna haunted him. He recalled the first time he had seen her, terrified at his presence, yet gathering her wits about her and commanding the situation, aiding him when he needed it. Brianna having a fit, handcuffed to the bed, her hair fanning out around her face. Brianna standing in front of the ocean, trusting him with her private thoughts.

Brianna. His thoughts had centered on her since she had summoned him. She was an enigma, something of which he could not define. Someone who had angered him, cheered him and drove him crazy.

Someone he wanted in his life, whatever that life may be.

The light turned green and he pressed the accelerator to the floor, turning the wheel all the way to the left until it would go no farther. He heard a terrible grinding as he saw smoke in the rearview mirror, likely coming from the tires as they spun in place. Within seconds he was headed back in the direction of Naberius's.

This could go down in history as the biggest mistake he ever made, but he was willing to take that chance at finding the elusive happiness that had been denied him for so long.

£

Brianna stalked up to the room she had so recently vacated, excusing herself from the forced pleasantries she'd encountered downstairs with Naberius and Valencia. She didn't have much time left, and she blamed her soon-to-be near-death experience for her new don't-mess-with-me attitude. What the hell could these demons do to her? Nothing compared to what she would soon be facing.

She didn't bother to go over her plan in her head. She didn't have time to think things through. Kelly had been her friend for years, and if the book had a negative impact on her, Brianna was going to be there to pick her friend up and help her.

She opened the door to the bedroom and slammed it shut behind her. She stomped over to the dresser, picked up her cell and used the clip to attach it to her dress. Walking straight to the window, she dismissed the memories the room held for her. Not all of them were pleasant anyway. Hell, most of them *weren't* pleasant.

She opened the blinds and pushed the window up. She was met with black bars.

What the hell? Those hadn't been there the day before.

She yanked the screen out, tossing it to the hardwood floor. Did those sons of bitches think for one minute a few black iron bars would keep her prisoner in a room? As long as she used nature as a backdrop, she could make her own damned spells.

The grounding necklace.

She reached up, and to her surprise she didn't feel it. When had Asmodeus taken it from her? She couldn't recall when he'd done so. But whatever the time, or whatever the reason it worked to her advantage now.

She wrapped her arms around the offending bars and muttered, "Trees of green, sky of stars, rid me of these prisoner's bars." The bars disappeared, leaving her holding nothing but the cold night air.

"Amateurs."

She climbed out of the window, aware she no longer had the powers she had the last time she was on the roof. She would have to find a safer way down than jumping.

She crawled carefully to where the garbage can lay next to the fence. Unfortunately it was no longer by the house. Figured. They must have moved it.

Had they known she would be performing the same kind of stunt?

She sat, inching her way over to the edge of the roof and the fence below. Something had come over her since her rejection from Asmodeus, and it felt good. She felt liberated. No one was going to hold her down, and the personal doubts she used to carry were long gone.

She had less than six days to live her life. She didn't have the time to live her life half-assed, and she no longer had the patience.

£

Asmodeus punched the intercom when he arrived at the

black iron gates. He waited impatiently, wanting to ram Naberius's damn gates down with the car. Ironically with Naberius's car.

"Hello?"

"Let me in."

"Sure thing," Naberius said, and the gates began to open.

He took his foot off the brake and accelerated up the drive to the house. Admitting he was wrong wouldn't be an issue. It would be gaining her forgiveness, which he wasn't so sure would be forthcoming. He'd noted a change in Brianna tonight. Not defensiveness, but a transformation from wallflower to hellfire. The light in her eyes and the strength in her gait as she had walked in front of the car had been that of a woman with purpose and determination.

He hoped her determination wasn't that of hating him.

He parked the car and headed toward the house. He hadn't felt such dread before a confrontation.

Naberius met him at the door. "What happened? Brianna seemed pissed."

"I'll fill you in later."

Naberius shrugged, allowing him to head up the stairs without further delay. He took the stairs three at a time, anxious to tell Brianna his change of heart.

When he came to the bedroom door he stopped and gathered his composure. Brianna was going to be irate. For once he had to think of something to say, something that would let her know what she meant to him. They hadn't known each other long, but through their harsh and dangerous experiences he had come to rely on her company. He almost expected it, took it for granted.

He cleared his throat and knocked twice.

He didn't hear her moving around, so he knocked again. Leaning in, he couldn't hear the shower running. There was no way she could have gone to sleep already. She would have been too keyed up.

He opened the door and a cold breeze hit him.

Across the room the window was open and the screen was lying on the floor.

Brianna was gone.

Chapter Fifteen

Brianna had taken her heels off in the taxi, unwilling to subject her feet to any more torture. Of course it was a silly gesture considering her future place of rest, but she figured she'd make herself as comfortable as she could before then.

She had a general idea of the direction she was headed in, but didn't know Raum's address. She told the cabbie the neighborhood she wanted to go to, and when the cabbie pulled onto the street she eyed the houses in search of Raum's.

When she finally found Raum's house she had the cabbie drop her off farther down the street. The cab driver turned around, expecting payment. She didn't have her purse with her. She accidentally left it at home. All she had was her cell she'd picked up before leaving Naberius's.

Feeling like a terrible thief, she leaned forward and looked into his eyes, whispering, "Oceans apart, rivers divine, never have we met, your face or mine." She glanced at his I.D. on the dashboard of the cab and took note of his name. Before she got sent to the Abyss she'd mail him the cab fare.

She opened the door and climbed out, surprised at her growing confidence in her powers and abilities. The cab driver drove away without another thought to a woman he had never met.

Feeling stronger, she set her shoes on the concrete and slipped back into them. Between Kelly and herself they would overcome the darkness that had taken over Kelly's actions. They had to. She wasn't sure she wanted to know what would happen to her friend if they didn't succeed.

Sighing, she crossed the street and started making her way to Raum's. The sound of the ocean reminded her of the feelings that had taken over at the water's edge with Asmodeus. For a short time she had witnessed his sense of humor, his carefree side. She could see herself falling in love with him. She could imagine waking in his arms, feeling the security he would provide.

She shook the feelings away as she came to Raum's house. Asmodeus did not want a relationship with her. He had made that perfectly clear, which was just as well. Neither of them had a future.

Looking behind the house she noted there was a back door with a staircase leading in from the beach. That would be her only chance to gain entry without being seen, especially if the vampires were still there. Hopefully that staircase didn't lead to Raum's room.

She wasn't sure if the fanged sluts were still here. They, along with the demons, would undoubtedly feel her presence. Wouldn't they? She wasn't sure, and she had no time to contemplate it further.

As she walked over to the door she could swear someone was watching her. She stopped by the side of the house and looked around. She started to shiver from the wind coming off the water. Her teeth began chattering.

Someone *was* watching her. She could feel it.

She turned full circle, seeing no one. She didn't feel like the person watching her was Asmodeus or Raum. She felt suffocated.

It could be one of the fanged sluts, but even they wouldn't raise the hair on the back of her neck. Not like this.

With no other option left to her, she walked to the side of the house in an attempt to find anything out of place before she broke in. Just as she came to the driveway a voice rose above the sound of the ocean.

"You led me right to her. Thank you."

She spun around to where she had been standing, and there above, on the roof, was a man. He sat on the edge, his booted feet dangling, watching her with glowing red eyes.

A demon.

He didn't move. He only crooked a finger in her direction, and before she realized what he was doing, pressure built inside her chest, levitating her. There was nothing to grab a hold of as she floated through the air. She tried thinking of a spell, but terror had a way of keeping any rational thoughts from taking hold.

When he wrapped his hands around her, sliding her onto his lap, a light hit the driveway. A car had pulled in.

The man put a hand over her mouth, and her throat constricted. She couldn't make a sound.

It was Asmodeus. She was certain. There was no way she beat him here, unless he had gone somewhere after dropping her off, but she knew without seeing him that he was the one getting out of the car.

She tried to move, to alert Asmodeus to where she was, but the man held her tight, cutting off her air supply in the process. When she tried to take in a breath the suction of the demon's palm wouldn't allow it.

She heard Asmodeus run up the stairs to the front door as stars danced in her line of vision. When the man finally let her breathe dizziness washed over her from the air she took in.

"Say goodbye to your sweetheart."

Her surroundings dimmed, and before she could blink she was at her house, her familiar couch and love seat staring back at her. The man dropped her on the floor. She didn't know how long she sat there as waves of dizziness overtook her, leaving her nauseous.

"I don't have time to waste, so summon your bitchy friend and let's get on with this."

Brianna sat on her floor, dazed from what had just transpired. Her head was still spinning from their travel. She'd never experienced anything like that. It was unnatural, and the effects hadn't left her yet. Her thoughts were scattered, but she was cognitive of the fact this man spoke of Kelly. He could be referring to no other.

He let out an exaggerated sigh. "I had forgotten. You humans don't like our style of transportation."

As she tried to recover, she was fervently aware of the man's proximity. He stood only a few feet from her, but she swore she could feel him breathing down her neck. The power emanating from him was dark, and it seemed to envelope her, as if he were deliberately trying to intimidate her.

He was doing a terrific job.

"I brought you something to help with your summoning spell. Not that you need it, but what the hell?"

He tossed a box of tarot cards on the carpet in front of her. They were Kelly's Goddess Tarot cards.

"What do you want with her?" she asked, finding her voice.

"She's deteriorating from her constant use of the *Demonic Book of Spells*. I warned her of the book, but she wouldn't listen."

He was not here to help Kelly, of that she was certain. The man's aura was dark and terrifying. He was out to help no one but himself. "I will not summon her."

He crouched in front of her, grabbing her chin and forcing her to look at him. "You will."

His eyes were scorching red. The air around the demon crackled to life, and the coldness of his aura seeped under her skin, causing her to shiver. "Why don't you summon her yourself?" she said, knowing full well he couldn't control the energy of the earth.

He released her and stood in one fluid motion. "Dog."

It was a soft spoken command, and out of the hallway came a huge black lab. It had a pink spiked collar around its neck, and its tongue hung out of its mouth. It came to sit by them, looking as though it were ready to play fetch on a warm sunny day.

"I don't feel like getting my hands bloody, so I hope you'll excuse my laziness." The demon pointed at Brianna. "Enemy."

The dog went from a drooling, content-looking pooch, to a snarling hound from hell. It growled, took a breath, and growled more while staring directly into her eyes. The dog's eyes turned to slits as it bared its teeth and snarled.

"One more command and that pretty face of yours is going to resemble ground beef."

She didn't reply, only kept her eyes locked on the dog and prayed for a miracle.

"Summon Kelly." He folded his arms across his chest as if her compliance were a given.

She swallowed and slowly reached out for the tarot cards, hoping she wouldn't alarm the dog, sending it into vicious action. She wrapped her hand around the cards. There was no way in hell she was summoning Kelly, ferocious dog or not.

She didn't know if she should try and stall the demon, or fuck up a summoning spell so it would be ineffective. Then again, deceiving a demon, especially one as dark as this, wasn't going to work.

"What is your name?" She tore her eyes away from the demented hound from hell and looked up at the demon.

"None of your damned business. Commence with your task."

So much for that. She turned the cards over and over in her hand, trying to decide what to do next.

"Perform the goddamned spell!"

She laid the cards on the floor, her hands shaking, figuring if she didn't touch them while she said her summoning spell, the spell wouldn't work. She hadn't been holding the arrowhead that had belonged to Asmodeus when she had effectively summoned him, but that success might have been from the strength of the spell she had used, one that was directly linked to Asmodeus.

She pretended to touch the cards, skimming her fingers just above them, knowing—praying—the spell wouldn't work. She didn't have the power within her to make a summoning spell work without touching a personal item from the individual she was calling on. "Light of the sun, reflecting on the moon at night, locate Kelly, bringing her within sight."

Kelly appeared just behind the demon, her hands in cuffs and her visage a haggard nightmare.

Her cheeks were sunken in, her skin a dull yellow. She looked as though she were fighting for every breath she took. When Kelly's gaze landed on the demon she promptly started laughing.

Brianna stared at Kelly in astonishment, no idea how the spell had worked. It shouldn't have. She didn't have the power to pull off a summoning spell.

She'd sold her friend up the river.

"You fucking bastard," Kelly said with a smile.

"You're looking good, sweetheart." He cocked his head to the side. "The stench and look of death suits you."

Kelly's gaze fell to Brianna. Kelly was slumped on the carpet, leaning her back against the wall as if she needed support. Her arms were lying lifelessly on her lap in the handcuffs. She seemed to sober instantly. "I take back what I said. There is nothing good in the *Demonic Book of Spells.*"

Brianna glanced at the dog, which was back to a slobbering, content pooch, and started crawling slowly toward Kelly.

Kelly shook her head. "Stay away from me," she warned.

Brianna didn't stop.

"You are doing exactly what he wants, Brianna. He wants me to bond with you, and the closer you come to me the less I am able to control myself."

Brianna stopped. What did Kelly mean, bond with her?

The demon walked to Kelly and stood over her. "Did you do your homework on bonding?"

Kelly's lip curled. "I browsed the book, yes."

"Then what are you waiting for?"

"I will not do as you asked. I won't give you that power."

The demon looked less than pleased. "You would sacrifice yourself for her? The only way you will recover is by bonding with a witch such as Brianna. I suggest you smash the remaining do-gooder in yourself and get on with it."

Brianna watched as Kelly eyed her with hunger. Brianna shrank away. Bonding didn't sound too good.

"I won't." Determination settled into Kelly's features.

The demon made a tsking sound, shoving his hands in the pockets of his jeans and taking a deep breath. It was as though he forced himself to look put out by Kelly's response. "Kelly, Kelly, Kelly, what am I going to do with you? You never listen to me."

Kelly's lip lifted in distaste. "Asmodeus is out looking for you. He'll probably be here in minutes."

Hope bloomed in her chest. "How do you know?"

"He called Raum looking for you. Raum is out looking too."

The demon looked as though he'd like to kill them both with his bare hands, then he quickly masked the look of hate with one of nonchalance. "Like I give a shit about those two second-rate demons. Even combined, their powers are not as potent as mine."

Brianna remembered Asmodeus's explanation of his powers in Tony's. Now would be the perfect time to put a little fear into this demon. "I summoned him from the Abyss. He still contains all of his Angelic power. They had to return his powers so he could withstand the Abyss. I'm thinking he might be more powerful than you think he is."

He seemed to be contemplating what she had just said. She slid a glance at Kelly. Even if Asmodeus came in and saved the day she wasn't sure Kelly would make it.

There was a chance Asmodeus might be able to heal Kelly, as he had done with her before.

"Where is the *Demonic Book of Spells*?" the demon asked Kelly.

"Raum has it."

"You dumb bitch."

Brianna flinched as a light filled the room. Before she opened her eyes she sensed that it was Asmodeus. She wasn't sure if her psychic abilities chose that time to spring to life, or if it was the familiar feel of his presence.

"It would seem you have some explaining to do, Leviathan." Asmodeus stood in front of the demon, his back to her.

Leviathan's face was a mask of hatred. "Do you honestly believe you can stop me? A demon from the second fall up against a demon such as myself?"

Another light flashed through the room, quickly followed by another. Naberius and Raum stood next to Asmodeus. She breathed a sigh of relief. The cavalry had arrived.

Leviathan no longer had a smug expression on his face as he stared at the men standing before him. He backed up.

When Asmodeus advanced, Leviathan threw his hand out and she ducked, remembering what power Asmodeus had used on the angels. The stagnant air in the house turned turbulent. She could hear the crackle of static electricity, feel the hair on her arms raise.

Glancing up, she caught Raum approaching the demon from the side while Naberius hung back, waiting to make his move.

The demon materialized a sword, as did Asmodeus and Raum. Before Raum could lift his sword the demon turned to him, and an invisible source slammed Raum into the wall, sending him through the plaster. Naberius thrust out his hands as Raum slid to the floor.

The demon grunted from whatever power Naberius had used, and brought his sword up as Asmodeus attacked him.

She started crawling to Kelly, then thought better of it. Kelly had warned Brianna the closer she got, the less she was able to control herself. How in the hell could she help Kelly if she couldn't get close to—?

"Brianna!"

She flattened herself to the floor without looking up, and something skimmed the hair on her head. A half a heartbeat later a sword slammed into the wall to her right, clattering harmlessly to the ground.

"That was close," Kelly said in a deadpan voice. Brianna looked at Kelly, who seemed bored with the demons fighting in Brianna's living room. Kelly eyed the spectacle as if detached from the scene.

She'd lost her damned mind.

Brianna belly-crawled to the side of the couch just as the sword embedded itself into the brown fabric, barely missing her. She gasped, pulling back. Where could she hide that a damned possessed sword couldn't nail her in the ass? It was as if this Leviathan guy was merely playing with her.

"*Damn.*" Naberius came to her and hauled her to her feet, wrapping his hands around her arm painfully.

"Look out!" she screamed as the sword vibrated again, tearing the material of her couch. Naberius held onto her with one hand and waved his right in the direction of the sword. The power he was using filtered through his touch, and she shivered from the onslaught. The sword disappeared before it became airborne.

A searing pain hit her in the side as she and Naberius were thrown into the wall. His body took most of the impact, but the effect was bone-jarring enough for her. When she regained her breath, she rasped, "Are you okay?"

"Never better," he said as he spit blood.

Asmodeus charged the demon as her house violently shook. As they fell to the floor, the demon disappeared.

Raum began limping toward Kelly. "You had to have known that would happen."

Kelly shrank away from Raum, but he ignored her as he bent down, put a hand on her shoulder and both disappeared.

Knowing what that de-materializing shit was like, she felt sorry for Kelly.

Seeing Kelly in that condition had shaken her to the core. She doubted Kelly could be saved. She looked as though she were beyond help.

"If you need me, call." Naberius flashed out of her living room holding his side.

Brianna slowly got to her feet. The situation was over so quickly she could barely wrap her mind around what had just transpired in her living room. Was that it? Did no one think the demon would come back?

She stood before Asmodeus, questions swirling through her mind. He didn't look as though he just went toe to toe with a demon. "Don't you think he'll come back?"

"He's badly wounded. I doubt it." His sword disappeared, but before it did she saw the blood on it.

"Oh." He must have stabbed him with it as she battled the attacks of the air sword. She looked around her living room. It was a good thing she didn't rent. "Who was that?"

Asmodeus walked over to her wall and lifted his hand. The large hole Raum's body had made disappeared. "Leviathan. A demon from the first fall."

Why would a demon from the first fall want to help Kelly? She quickly came to the conclusion that he wouldn't. "Why does that demon want Kelly?"

Asmodeus's hair was loose, falling behind his collar. The residual effects of his power began to ebb away. The glow in his eyes was fading, turning back to normal. If eyes that had horizontal pupils could be considered normal. "He doesn't."

"He wanted her to bond with me so she could heal herself."

Asmodeus shook his head. "He can control Kelly. Her spirit is weaker than yours. If you bond with her, you won't just be healing her, your powers will be hers. He wants those powers, along with the book. With both the powers and the book he will be damn near unstoppable. Demons were not meant to control the energy of the earth. That was a power bestowed only on certain humans such as yourself. He could bond with you, but why not have the powers of two witches?"

She ignored the way her body responded to the sight of Asmodeus. Only hours before she had stood before him, admitting to feelings he had cruelly dismissed. Then he came to her rescue. Again. "Unstoppable to do what, exactly?"

"Control humans. Weather. Anything."

Well, that sounded great. "What will happen to Kelly?"

He didn't answer her. She could tell by the look on his face Kelly didn't have a chance. "Certainly there's something we can do."

"Kelly chose her own destiny."

His cold tone reminded her of her earlier resolve. The elation she had felt when she had chosen her own course of action. At the same time, if he hadn't popped in she would still be in serious trouble.

Why was she always conflicted when it came to this man?

Something rubbed up against her and she jumped away from it. Turning, she saw the dog the demon had left behind. "Oh shit."

Asmodeus bent down and put his hand out. The dog walked to him, head down as though it were afraid it would get hit. Before the dog made it to Asmodeus, it made itself flush with the floor, afraid to go any farther.

"The poor thing," she whispered.

"Get me something to feed it."

She went into her kitchen and snatched up some lunch meat. She walked around the dog slowly then handed the food to Asmodeus. He held it out to the dog and with one paw the dog crawled toward him. The dog brought another paw forward, and another, until it was directly in front of Asmodeus.

He held the shaved ham out. The dog carefully nipped the edge of the ham and slid it off Asmodeus's hand. Asmodeus waited until the dog had eaten the meat, then reached out to scratch it behind the ears. "Now go lay down."

The dog licked his chops and took off.

Asmodeus took a step toward her. "I wanted to apologize for my actions earlier this evening. I had no right to treat you the way I did. Can you forgive me?"

She closed her eyes, trying to keep the steely resolve that

threatened to dissolve at his words. They were too different.

A relationship wasn't something she should even consider. "I don't understand. You confuse me. One minute you act like a gentleman, and the next you act cold and indifferent." She took a deep breath and opened her eyes to look at him. "What do you want from me, Asmodeus?"

The sadness was back in his eyes. A longing. "I want you. Only you."

Unwilling to accept his words, she shook her head and walked to her room, intending to shut him out of her vision. Her life. She didn't have the time to try and figure out his mood swings, or why he couldn't make a decision on if he wanted her or not. Sure, he could say he wanted her now, but the second she accepted that, he would undoubtedly change his mind.

"Brianna."

She shut out the sound of his voice, slamming her bedroom door. The stress and realization of what she faced was becoming a reality. Even if she told him about the angels, and the fact she was facing imprisonment in the Abyss, there wasn't a damn thing he could do about it.

Her bedroom door opened and she pivoted to face him, ready to take on the ancient pain in the ass. Asmodeus stood just inside her bedroom. He was so...ethereal. He looked as though he could fix any and every problem, and she wished that were the case. More than anything she wanted to run into his arms. She ached for him to tell her things would turn out for the better, the Abyss would hold no terrors for her future.

But he couldn't do that. He didn't even know of her problems, and she wasn't about to tell him.

His expression was soft, yet stern. "Tell me what is bothering you."

She could never do that. She wasn't sure how he would react, or what the angels would do. Telling half-truths was the only option available to her at this point. "The future isn't clear to me. I don't know what I feel when I look at you. Every time we get close, you don't hesitate to push me away."

Asmodeus sat on the edge of her bed, turning away from her. "I should be doing that very thing now, though it's becoming more and more difficult as time goes by."

She pushed down the hope that statement brought. He was clearly telling her that though he wanted her, he didn't like the emotion. Was fighting it. She didn't know how to respond.

She had no future. She didn't have to stand there and sort through her feelings. In a few days none of this would matter. Sharing her body with him would be a faded, though cherished, memory.

Is that why she thought she cared for him? Was she rushing things because she could see the end of her life draw near? It couldn't be she had fallen for him for any other reason. Just one date wouldn't change things between them. She hadn't known him long enough. But why would he have feelings for *her*? He had no idea whatsoever of his impending imprisonment.

Tears threatened to fall.

Proving he possessed powers she couldn't even fathom, he responded to her without facing her, seeing her tears without physical proof. "Please do not cry, Brianna. I can take your anger, but I cannot stand strong against your tears."

She smiled weakly. "So I have a secret weapon I didn't even know I possessed? That's good to know."

"Come here, Brianna."

Her heart seized and her tears immediately stopped at the seductive sound of his voice as it curled around her, drawing her closer. Six—no five—days were left to her. What would she do with them? Leave the pleasures of this life, crouching into a corner, afraid to touch the fire? Or would she seize on every opportunity that presented itself?

Just as she focused in on the intense heat of his eyes as he turned to her, the light in the room dimmed. Candles suddenly appeared across her dresser, end tables and desk, casting an ancient yellow glow throughout the room.

She brought her gaze back to his. "Plan on lighting the

place on fire?"

The light in his eyes intensified. "Only you."

Wanton abandon threatened to take over her timid actions when he uttered that corny line. What would it be like to give in to every desire she secretly held? Having decided she was going to the Abyss, there would be no strings, no attachment. Just sex.

She recalled Asmodeus's words.

Good company, great food and lots of sex.

They'd covered the first two.

There would be nothing to hold her back. No promises of tomorrow. Plans and relationship snags wouldn't exist for the two of them.

She slowly walked toward him as he pushed from the bed and stood to face her. He was by far the sexiest man she had ever laid eyes on. Hands down. His long blond hair made him look medieval, the light stubble covering the lower half of his face made him look devilish.

And the air that surrounded them...it was alive with energy. She could actually feel it.

She paused mid-stride. Like him, she would take something with her to the fires. An aching. A longing, though not of vengeance.

The fires. That's all she could think about lately. Glancing around the room at the tiny flickers of flame dancing on the candles, she couldn't imagine the horrors she would soon be facing. Terror ripped away her arousal, piece by piece, threatening to consume her. Fear gnawed at her until her chest constricted.

Burning. Fires.

She felt as though she was falling into a deep, dark chasm, and no one would be there to hear her screams for mercy. For help.

Then Asmodeus was standing before her, wrenching her away from the darkness, as his hands cupped her face. Thoughts of his anguish and suffering, spanning centuries, nearly brought her to her knees. She needed to feel his arms around her, needed to feel the false security he would provide. But more than that, she wanted to erase his horrendous memories for the time being, much more than she wanted to carry his touch with her.

She wanted to show him love and acceptance. Foreign feelings for him—even if it would only be a fleeting escape from what they would soon face.

As he dipped his head, bringing his lips to hers, she stomped down the fear that lodged in her chest. He was not a mortal man. He was an ancient, immortal demon. When she focused on that truth, it was more than daunting. But as her tongue found his, and his warmth mixed with hers, he was only Asmodeus, a man she had come to respect. A man who was constantly in her thoughts.

No longer would she question the whys of her feelings. The why didn't matter. He was here. He was holding her.

And he wanted her.

Wrapping her arms around him, she drew him closer, melting into his body. He was solid muscle and harnessed power, and she clung to it. Desperately trying to push the terror threatening to sweep her away, she suppressed a shudder.

He pulled back. "Brianna, what is it? What are you not telling me?"

She looked into his eyes, dark and illuminated, and forced herself to keep his gaze. "Why do you ask that now?"

He ran the pad of his thumb across her face. "You are crying."

She brought a hand to her face and felt the tears she hadn't known were falling. "I'm sorry."

He tenderly brushed hair from her face. "Don't apologize. Why are you crying?"

She shook her head, not wanting to focus on the bad. She wanted to lose herself in his touch. "Can we forget? For a short while can we just forget?"

She could tell he was trying to read her again. His eyes

bore into hers, forcing her to look away. Was he worried about her? Or was he merely curious to know what she was keeping from him?

He let the subject go and took her hand, a smirk picking up the corner of his mouth.

"Where are you taking me?" she asked as he led her out of the bedroom.

"The first place I remember seeing you. Everything before the shower was fuzzy, but I recall you looking at me in the shower. You intrigued me."

Her cheeks grew warm at the memory.

He turned the water on. "Besides, I can smell that dumb bastard's scent on you. I want it off."

Pleased with the possessive streak, she suddenly realized the base of her desires. She wanted him. And she wanted him to want her. Period.

By the look he gave her when he faced her again, she had her answer. He forgot to keep a rein on his physical appearance. He looked feral...magical. His eyes had gone black, his aura had melted into light, mixing with the turbulent air around them.

She began undressing, feeling a heaviness in her breasts, an aching between her legs. She pulled her black dress over her head, and before she finished with that task, he had unfastened her bra. A rush of anticipation left her breathless.

He slipped his hands into the waistband of her black thong and pulled it down her legs, kissing her inner thigh, behind her knee, her calf. She stepped out of the clinging piece of fabric, her hands on his shoulders for balance. As he stood back up he let his gaze wander all over her naked body.

She felt no embarrassment, only a gradual heat that traveled from her face and down to her core.

As he unbuttoned his shirt, she moved to unbutton his pants, her hands fumbling with the zipper.

"Fuck it."

Apparently patience wasn't one of his fortes. His clothes

disappeared. She stood back and ran an appreciative eye over him. He was perfection personified. Muscles covered every damned spot on his body. His waist didn't dissolve into small hips. He was thick. Everywhere. Massive.

When she finally brought her eyes to his, she could see a faint smile tugging at his lips. He took her hand and stepped into the shower.

The water hit her back as she climbed in, and she recalled the first night he was here. What she had had to do to get him cooled down. He'd asked her to join...

She turned away from him, afraid he would read the fear in her eyes and mistake it for fear of him.

The tortures of the Abyss were taking hold again. She closed her eyes and tried desperately to will her fear away. She wanted to get lost in the feel of his hands, the strength of his body.

The water tickled her chest as she let go of her apprehension.

Asmodeus knew something was wrong when Brianna turned away from him. He couldn't shake the feeling that whatever she wasn't telling him had to do with her safety. After she had recognized the angels in Tony's, he knew she had been confronted by them. The question of what had transpired in that meeting remained.

Nothing would harm her as long as he remained by her side. He wouldn't allow it.

Dismissing any threat, he picked up the soap and lathered his hands. He had Brianna right where he had dreamed of having her, and thoughts of mayhem and alliances were not what he should be focusing on.

Not when she was naked and wet, her ass pressed against his erection, begging him to take her.

He brought his arms around her, running his soapy hands over her breasts, her throaty moan making his dick harder. Her long, wet hair cascaded down her back like a waterfall, the water dripping from the ends. She leaned into him, pressing her body closer to his as he ran the pad of his thumb over her nipples.

Her head fell back against his chest, her eyes hooded, a slight smile on her lips. He leaned down and kissed her neck, aware of the trust she was giving him. Her hands settled on his hips, her nails digging into his skin, pulling him closer.

This was such folly, becoming involved with a human again. He knew better, yet the sounds Brianna was making goaded him. Her strength in the face of all that transpired brought out a protective streak he hadn't known existed.

He lowered his right hand, his finger dipping into the hot core of her sex. She groaned, her knees giving a little. "That's it, Brianna. Forget everything and focus only on this moment."

She pushed against his fingers, her hand coming to rest on top of his, holding him there. He took the hand covering his and guided her own fingers into the soft folds between her legs. Their fingers entwined as he massaged her clit, and she moaned with pleasure. He bent his legs and kneeled, turning her to face him, wanting desperately to taste her. When he leaned into her heat, licking the tender flesh, she moved her hand. He grabbed her wrist and brought it back. "Don't stop. Keep touching yourself."

She dipped a finger deep inside as he flicked his tongue across her clit, once, twice, suckling it as she fisted her other hand in his hair. As she withdrew her finger, glistening not only with water but with her own heat, he took it in his mouth, sucking gently.

He knew she would be passionate from their other encounters, but he had no idea just how much her passion would ignite his own.

As he licked and teased her, she put her hands on his shoulders, leaning heavily on him. Her moans came faster, louder and more guttural. He quickened his tongue, probing her core with his fingers until she fell apart in his arms.

She slid down to her knees in front of him, found his

mouth, and angled her head to kiss him deeply. Emotions threatened to consume him as he held her close. She gave herself to him completely, her palms holding the sides of his face as his arms wrapped around her.

She broke their kiss, her lips traveling down his neck, over his chest. She traced the lines of his abs with her tongue, making his cock so hard it was painful.

Dipping her head and getting down on all fours, she flicked her tongue around his head, teasing him. Moving lower, she licked and sucked his balls, sliding her palm over his cock.

He took a steadying breath, willing himself not to throw her down and take her. The need to drive his cock deep inside her was nearly overwhelming.

She slowly licked the length of him, then took him into her mouth, running her tongue back and forth, eliciting a growl from him. Her head bobbing, she palmed his balls, her other hand at work on the base of his cock.

The sight of her fucking him with her mouth, her ass tilted up, glistening from the water, brought him close to coming. "Brianna—"

She sucked him harder, faster, tightening her hold on him. He tried pulling away, on the very edge of release, but she held firm, swirling her tongue around his head. When she took all of him into her mouth he lost control.

Every muscle in his body tensed as he came in her mouth. She sucked, swallowed, and took more. He held her head, reeling in pleasure as she licked him.

He turned off the shower with his powers, picked her up and brought her to her bed. He laid her out, relishing this moment and taking in her beauty. Her breasts were more than a handful, and he had the wicked image of sliding his cock between them as she opened her mouth to taste him once again.

Her waist was small, her hips perfection as they gave way to shapely legs which were slightly parted, allowing him to see her pink, swollen sex.

He fisted himself as he kneeled on the bed between her legs. He was already hard again, the sight of her on the bed pulling on every ounce of lust burrowed in his body. The connection he had with her was rare—he'd never felt this before.

"You're ready again?"

He grinned at the surprised look on her face. "We're just getting started, Bry."

Brianna's breath caught at the heated way he looked at her. The sweet way he had shortened her name. No one had ever called her Bry before. It was intimate. Endearing.

"Spread your legs wider. I want to look at you."

She could feel herself getting wet again. She was so sensitive down there from his earlier assault, she was sure only a touch would send her over the edge.

Life was so unfair. Five short days were all that remained to experience what Asmodeus had to offer. Only five days to see what was inside his heart. She'd had privileged glimpses of the softer side of him, the tender side, and she craved more.

With one finger, he slipped past her folds, edged his way inside, and withdrew. Taking his drenched finger, he teased her by gliding it around her clit, running his skilled hand everywhere between her legs. Everywhere but where she wanted him to touch the most.

She moaned, spreading her legs farther, begging him without words to bring his attention to where she throbbed.

"I love looking at you."

Her eyes half open, she looked at him, caught sight of the blackness that had spread in his eyes, the feral look that should terrify her. But in that moment she was his, would do anything he asked of her. He was becoming familiar. The sound of his voice, his touch, his face...everything.

With a flick of his finger he moved over her clit, causing her to jump and groan with pleasure. With both hands he spread her folds wide, staring into her core, causing her to become so aroused she whimpered. To be so exposed to him, to beg for his touch, broke down the barriers she had tried to build. Shattered them.

He slipped his finger inside, drawing out the wetness, spreading it all over her clit, massaging her. Teasing her. Her legs started shaking from his assault. "Asmodeus, please..."

He slid his body over hers, kissing her breasts, licking her nipples, nibbling on her neck. His weight on top of her was invigorating. Dominant. She nuzzled her face into his neck as he slid his length inside.

He stretched her as she dug her nails into his back. Jesus, he was big. Her muscles expanded, taking in his width and length.

"Are you okay?" he asked breathlessly.

He held back in fear of hurting her. In answer, she arched up to meet his hips, taking in more of him. He reined in his power, careful not to hurt her, and that made her want to cry. He was hers, she decided in that moment. He was hers for the short time left to her.

He groaned, driving himself inside of her. The pleasure was fierce, wicked and explosive. Moving his hips in a circular motion, he ground against her clit until she saw stars. She dug her nails into his back, teetering on the verge of orgasm. He thrust hard, his cock stretching her to the limit as spasm after spasm rippled through her. She cried out his name, her cheek next to his, her arms securely wrapped around him.

She was so tight now, all of her muscles contracted in blinding ecstasy. He growled, and she felt him grow and twitch inside of her as his body tensed. He thrust twice more, each lacking the intensity of the last. Finally, on a sigh, he grew still, his forehead against hers.

She held him as his body relaxed. There had to be a way to save him. She couldn't let them take him back to such torment. Not after she'd seen his heart, his soul. He didn't deserve what they intended to deal to him.

She held tight to him, making a silent promise.

They would not take him. She would go to the fires willingly, but they could not take him. She wouldn't allow it.

She had no choice but to summon Michael and make her plea.

Chapter Sixteen

Lev sat at his kitchen table, quiet and unmoving. Rarely had he tasted defeat such as he did now. His plan to get back on Luc's good side had failed miserably. Now the plan to acquire more powers than the bastard had failed, leaving him little choice but to face the oncoming battle, which would come any moment now. Luc would send an assassin. It was inevitable.

His wounds had healed already, though it still stung that the second-rate demon had overcome him. He'd tried to scare Asmodeus into thinking he would kill Brianna, but the bastard had realized it had only been a ruse. If he killed the witch then his plan would fall apart around him. Using his powers on his sword, fending off the other two demons and keeping Asmodeus from slicing him in two, he had been pulled in too many directions.

He should have just killed the bitch and been done with it.

Though if he had done that, he would still be left with his current problem. He had to find a way to obtain more powers.

He smelled an acidic stench in the air, indicating one of Luc's assassins would soon be materializing. His sword hung loosely as it sat underneath his sweaty palm. He eyed the blade, enjoying the deadly beauty of its razor-sharp edges. Failing in hand-to-hand combat was an anomaly for him, save for his last battle, and he wasn't about to repeat that failure. He had to control his rage. Anger would not help him in a fight, it would hinder him. And he could not lose focus when a battle with Luc's assassins was on the table.

Luc's assassins were made up of the elite of their kind. Luc sent them in to do a job, and the job was done, no questions asked. To fail as an assassin was to die.

A weight in the air around him told him the assassin had arrived. Lev slowly flexed his fingers around the hilt of his sword and stood to face the demon.

"I see you are ready for me."

The demon looked much like himself. Black hair. Light green eyes that were slowly becoming red. The air crackled, powers colliding and bending under the pressure of their proximity, both showing off their powers. The demon wore loose-fitting denim. A black T-shirt. He stood before Lev as though he already knew the outcome of the fight. He was that sure of himself.

If Lev knew anything, it was his strengths and weaknesses. Retreat had been his only option at Brianna's house. The second Asmodeus had plunged his sword in his gut he had dematerialized. He hadn't even had the strength to bring Dog back with him.

Though he was still tired from his earlier battle, fighting this demon was not an option. It was a necessity. This assassin would only keep coming after him, slowing him down in his pursuit for power.

The assassin had to be eliminated.

He didn't twirl his sword or try to intimidate with words or actions. Luc's assassins were beyond that. He merely waited for the attack, knowing it would come swiftly. He would not be kept from gaining powers from Kelly and retrieving the *Demonic Book of Spells*.

The assassin didn't hesitate to engage. Lev deflected the first swing of his opponent's blade, gritting his teeth when his arm shook from the force. Luc's assassins were gifted with more powers than the average demon, which aided them in their missions.

The chair he had been sitting on was knocked to the ground as he lunged at the assassin, backing him into a corner.

The demon disappeared, only to reappear behind him. Lev ducked the swipe of the assassin's blade, and counterattacked with a thrust of his powers, which sent the assassin flying into the wall on the far side of the living room.

Before the demon could recover, Lev whipped his arm back and threw his sword, which became embedded in the demon's chest, pinning him to the wall.

He thrust his hand out, and his sword flew back into his grip. The wound would take a few minutes to heal, and the assassin would be struggling against the pain. Liquid fire entered his body as the demon's eyes blazed bright red.

Lev fought the blinding, burning sensation, the realization he may lose this battle against the superior demon igniting desperation. He bounded over the couch as the demon regained his footing. Both hands on the hilt, he thrust his sword into the assassin's neck and twisted it. The sizzling pain in his body reaching a fevered pitch, his vision began fading. The demon fought back with powers Luc must have given him. The fire in his chest threatened to take him down.

He could not lose. He had to finish this before he became ineffective.

As the assassin struggled to get free, he wrenched his sword out of the demon's neck and brought it around for the final blow. The assassin's sword buried into his thigh just before his head fell from his body.

Lev collapsed on the ground as wave after wave of pain consumed him. Though the healing process had already begun, heat built around his wounds, both internally and externally. Fire consumed him, causing his stomach to lurch.

Through the pain he grasped the demon's sword and wrenched it out of his flesh.

Unable to support himself, he fell on top of the demon as a black void settled around him.

£

Asmodeus smoothed a long, black lock of Brianna's hair from her face. He lay on his side, Brianna curled into his chest. Her breathing was shallow, her mouth slightly open as she slept. The light from the morning sun filtered through her curtains and fell across the bed.

Knowing full well he should be out finding Leviathan, he couldn't find the willpower to leave her side. The awareness of the trust she gave him settled into his soul. After everything that had transpired between them in the last few days, he would have never imagined a bond being formed. For the thousandth time he didn't feel he deserved this reprieve.

There would be hell to pay for his actions—literally. He couldn't fathom why he had done the unthinkable, but he wouldn't change a second of it either. As Naberius would say, he'd done fucked up.

He'd also thought of asking her to summon Leviathan, but he didn't want her involved if he could help it. He wanted to keep her safe. No man, demon or not, would take her from him.

She snuggled closer to him, murmuring something intelligible, then stilled with a small sigh as her palm came to rest on his chest.

He put his hand over hers, watched as her eyes fluttered open. Her hair fanned out on the pillow and over his arm, her eyes heavy with sleep.

She was the most beautiful woman he had ever set eyes upon.

"Good morning." He leaned down and lightly kissed her lips. She responded by slipping her leg between his and wrapping an arm around his waist.

"What time is it?" Her voice was hoarse. Deep and erotic.

"After ten." He ran his hand down her back, cupped her ass and pulled her closer. His erection settled between her legs and she moved against him.

"Someone's up," she said, pushing at his shoulders to turn

him onto his back. She crawled on top of him and started kissing his neck.

He felt content just running his hands up and down her back, feeling the dip at her waist, rounding to full hips. He held onto her hips, his own rising to tease her as he rubbed himself against her.

"Mmmm, that feels good."

He lifted her hips just enough to slip inside, watching her face as he did so. Her brows came together as though she were in pain.

"Did I hurt you?" He started to withdraw.

"No. No, you didn't. It feels...so...good." She began to move against him, sliding up and down his erection.

They took their time, making love slowly, languishing in the feel of their bodies coming together. Sunlight streaked the room, the scent of the candles from the previous evening wafting in the air. How he had come from the Abyss, only to land in Heaven, he would never know.

As she rode him she made the most erotic sounds he had ever heard. His orgasm edged close, and he gritted his teeth, holding back until he made sure she was pleasured first.

She leaned back, her breasts thrusting out as she rocked back and forth. He brought both his hands to them, pinching her nipples between his fingers. She moaned, quickening her pace, leaning forward so her clit would brush against his pelvis. He let her control their pace, intoxicated with the erotic vision she created as she fucked him.

Her long, black hair cascaded down her back, her lips were parted, and her eyes were slightly closed. With her face flushed, her body perfect, he had trouble figuring out why she would want to be with him.

"Asmodeus..."

He let go of her breasts, grabbed her ass and plunged himself deep inside her as she came.

He waited until her body finished contracting around him, and rolled her onto her back in one fluid movement.

She whimpered, bringing her legs up and over his back, wrapping her arms around his neck.

The position allowed him to go deeper inside her warmth, and her heat enveloped him. He took her slow at first, wanting the sensations to last. When she came again he quickened his pace. When she whispered his name his orgasm came on strong and fast. He held onto her as his world came apart around him, all because of the trust given to him from the petite woman who held onto him just as tight.

He pushed himself up to his elbows to look down at her. The brilliant yet sleepy smile she gave him melted his heart. Just a week ago he didn't have a heart, and here he was, giving it away.

She brushed a strand of hair off his forehead, tucking it behind his ear. "Will you do me a favor?"

He was sure in that moment he would give her anything. "The favor?"

"Will you check on Kelly for me? I'm worried about her."

His breath caught as he saw the hope in her eyes. Kelly was beyond his help, but that was not something he would bring to Brianna's attention right now. Brianna was aware of the seriousness of the situation, and she held on to blind hope. "I will."

"Thank you."

"I'm going to jump in the shower first." He wanted the tension gone. Just the mention of Kelly had Brianna frowning. "That is if you can control yourself for five minutes."

She pretended to look shocked, smacking him on the rear. "You're the nympho."

"I'm a what?"

She laughed. "Nymphomaniac. A sex addict."

Truth was, though many would argue he was the demon of carnal desire, he hadn't felt this way until he had her. She had a way of pulling him in, making him crave her more with each and every touch. He leaned down and kissed the tip of her nose, and pulled her out of bed with him.

"What are you doing?"

"I'm living up to my name."

"Asmodeus!"

He flipped her over his shoulder as she giggled. Promising himself after the shower he would leave her be for a few hours, he made his way into the bathroom.

£

Brianna waited until Asmodeus flashed himself from her house. The dog was secured in the garage with food Asmodeus had materialized and a big bowl of water. They would decide what to do with the dog later. Asmodeus told her he would be back within the hour, so she had to move fast.

She grabbed the black leather spell book and settled on her bed, flipping through the pages. She hoped she would find something in the spell book pertaining to Michael, or at the very least, something about angels.

The writing was in the demonic tongue, and it was difficult to decipher names and meanings. She didn't want to say a spell and make a colossal mistake, but she had to do something to gain an audience with the archangel.

She picked up the dagger she had brought to her room, eyeing the strange writing on the blade. The angelic writing looked nothing like the demonic writing in the book. It was etched in beautiful lines, loops and slashes.

Sighing, she put the book down and studied the script on the dagger. She was well versed in Hebrew and Latin, though this looked nothing like either. She couldn't risk bringing another demon to this realm. She had to summon Michael.

She would have to create her own spell. Kelly had taught her how to do this, and she had effectively pulled off her own spell on the bars in Naberius's house.

Determined to obtain audience with Michael before

Asmodeus came back, she decided to go a little primitive. Gritting her teeth, she brought the blade across her palm, creating a long, shallow line of blood. She wrapped her injured hand around the blade, causing further pain.

"Heavenly host of love and wrath, messengers of darkness and light, I summon your strongest angel, Michael, to bear witness to my plight."

She sat on her bed, shaking and afraid of what she would see, who she would summon, if anyone. For a full minute she sat, still as a statue on her bed. Had she really thought she could effectively summon Michael, the greatest of all the angels? She pushed the pain of her throbbing hand aside. It didn't work. She should have known it wouldn't.

As she got up to wash the blood off her hand, a soft light illuminated her room, touching every corner. It wasn't a flash of light. It stayed and enveloped her with a feeling of hope and trepidation. Peace and fear.

Who the hell did she think she was, summoning a being such as Michael? All of a sudden she wanted to rescind her spell. She didn't want to face him.

Shaking off her fear, she held onto her resolve. If there was a way to save Asmodeus, she would endeavor to find it. He deserved that much. He deserved someone who loved him enough to do such a thing for him.

And she did love him. She couldn't deny the way he took her breath away, the way her insides burned as she looked at him. Waking in his arms had been pure bliss. He needed a champion, and she was ready to play the role.

Until she saw the form of a man emerge from the light, drawing the light into him as if he *were* the light. Her room darkened as he materialized from the radiance.

Did she say champion?

Before her stood a man of incredible size and an undeniably dark aura. Because he had come from the light, she couldn't make sense of the darkness that came off him in waves. Angels auras were supposed to be bright.

He had blond hair, much like Asmodeus, and he wore it down. His eyes were blue, not black as she had thought they would be.

Though his eyes weren't black, he did have a decidedly agitated look on his face. She figured he wasn't too pleased she had summoned him. "What is it you seek, Brianna?"

"You're Michael?"

"I believe that is obvious enough, even for a human such as yourself." He folded his arms across his massive chest. "You have two minutes."

She fought the urge to stutter and wet herself. The beauty and darkness coming from him confused her. Knowing she had to pull it together, she took a calming breath. Reaching somewhere deep inside of herself, she leveled her gaze on him. "I summoned you to talk about Asmodeus."

His eyes narrowed slightly. "What about him?"

She swallowed and stood her ground. A wave of uneasiness settled in the air between them. Or was that just her? "We're in a dilemma of sorts."

"I am aware."

Well, at least she didn't have to explain the circumstances in the two damned minutes he was giving her. "I don't think he deserves to go back to the Abyss. Is there something that can be done?"

"You are a twenty-four-year-old human. How is it you can arrive at an informed decision where Asmodeus is concerned? What do you know of him?"

She felt two inches tall. "I know he's kind. Protective."

Michael's eyes turned black, and his white robe fanned around him as if he were surrounded by wind. She quickly stepped away from him. Now *this* was what she had expected, but it wasn't something she wanted to face.

"Come here, Brianna."

Do I have to? She almost said the thought out loud, but in a moment of pure genius she kept her mouth shut. She walked over to him on wooden legs, each step closer, each step a bit more hesitant than the last.

Without preamble, he bent down and put his forehead to hers. Everything around her began to spin, twirl and coagulate until she was hit with a vision.

In picture-perfect clarity she saw Asmodeus.

He stood with numerous demons—or angels, she couldn't tell. They seemed to be huddled in a small passageway made of white clay...or some similar substance. Unnaturally bright light surrounded them. They wore little clothing, only a pair of white, silky pants. They held no weapons, and all resembled each other. Blond hair, tall, muscular.

She recognized Naberius and Raum instantly, because Naberius was the only angel present with dark hair. Raum stood next to him, silent and regal. They flanked Asmodeus as he held his hands up to indicate he wanted silence.

As the crowd fell silent she gazed at the faces that were present. Some seemed indifferent, and others seemed terrified. There was an energy in the air, and she had the distinct feeling the energy originated from the group huddled around Asmodeus. Their powers seemed to merge together, until they were one.

"My brothers, we stand before a precipice made of our own choosing. The decision you make here will affect you for the rest of your days. Lucifer's demons were thrown from the Host, exiled to Earth with no hope of redemption. Yet I must ask you, do you see their suffering?"

Murmurs from the crowd erupted, shouts of "no" and "nay" resounding through the halls. For whatever reason, she knew they spoke a different language, but what she heard was English.

Asmodeus spoke above the den of noise, his deep voice carrying to those in the far back. "Free will. They do as they please while we, those who remained faithful even as we were dealt so little, have nothing of which to call our own. The echelon chooses not to hear our desires. We are to follow orders blindly, until when? Will there ever be an end?"

Shouts rang out in the crowd, and the awe-inspiring light around them began to fade.

She felt the crowd's fear. As the light faded, more and more of the faces wore a mask of terror. A few fled, tearing at their clothes as they did so, anguish in their voices ringing out.

Most stayed, eyeing the fading light as if they did not want or need it. Though she only saw this through a vision, she could feel the love, the utter warmth, pulled out of her as the light faded.

"On this day we shall take a stand. We shall inherit the earth. Those who are with me, make your decision now." Asmodeus brought his arms up, and she had a distinct feeling he was speaking to the light. "Those who are against me, heed my warning. I shall not be denied what has been given unto the humans. Free will."

A chorus of cheers went up, and the resounding roar gave way to only two words—free will.

That vision faded, replaced with a small, comfortable-looking domestic scene. A cauldron hung on a hook in a stone fireplace, and an older woman sat by the fire, a wooden spoon in her hand. The door to the cottage opened, and Asmodeus walked in.

Michael's voice penetrated through Brianna's mind, a whisper invading her thoughts. "That is Asmodeus's wife. He failed to mention to her what he was, and she has grown old as he has remained youthful. The passage of time was harder on humans back then. They aged quickly. She no longer trusts him, yet still, he lies to her."

"Isabel." Asmodeus greeted her with a kiss to her forehead. Isabel pulled away, flinching visibly.

Brianna pushed away the sharp sting of jealousy. This was Asmodeus's wife. The mother of his children.

Asmodeus ignored her as two boys shuffled into the cottage. The oldest resembled his mother, but had his father's eyes. He held two rabbits in his hands. The light in his eyes spoke of strength and determination. He seemed ready to take on the world.

The youngest resembled Asmodeus. Though he was all arms and legs, no older than seven or eight years old, his face was the spitting image of his father. He flounced over to his mother and threw his arms around her.

She smiled and kissed the top of his head. "Jorian brought home supper, though I pointed to the rabbits, Mama. I saw them first."

The boy Jorian put his bow and arrows in the corner of the cottage and went back outside without a word.

Asmodeus came to kneel next to his wife, and Isabel positioned herself as far from him as she could. Asmodeus, the pain in his eyes evident, ruffled the young boy's hair and left the cottage.

Again the scene faded, and Michael's voice broke the silence. "Because of his actions, he created a race of demonic creatures. I believe you recall your own encounter with one of them."

The next vision slammed into her. Asmodeus was bloody and fighting for each breath he took. Isabel was screaming, holding onto a young man. He had been the young boy in her earlier vision, now a few years older, and he clung to his mother's skirts.

They stood beside the cottage that she instinctively knew was their home. Chaos ensued around them, men running, women screaming. Bodies of Nephilim and young men littered the ground. The cottage was engulfed in flames, the orange glow eerie against the black, star-covered sky. Isabel looked terrified, yet the young boy was remarkably calm in spite of the circumstances.

Asmodeus stood before them.

Tears coursed down Asmodeus's face, mixing with dirt and blood.

"Stay away from him. You are the devil. You are evil!" Isabel clutched the boy to her chest, bending down and wrapping her arms around him as Asmodeus slowly advanced.

"Go into the dwelling, Isabel. Now."

Isabel glanced beyond him as a man ran his sword through a young girl. The girl's scream was cut short. She crumbled to the ground. As if that wasn't disturbing enough, the man brought his sword down on the tiny body one last time.

The girl's head was severed from her body.

Asmodeus's wife became even more hysterical. "Leave him. Leave Bael to me!"

Asmodeus kept walking, finally reaching her and wrapping his hand around Bael's arm. The little boy didn't cower. He only looked at his mother with wide, tear-filled eyes.

Isabel went wild. She hit Asmodeus, and he allowed her to take Bael from his grip.

Bael smoothed his mother's thin, graying hair from her face. "It will be fine, Mother. I love you. It will be fine." He hugged his mother, then turned to his father.

Asmodeus shrank away from him.

Again, the little boy was the reassurance in the situation. "I understand, Father. I don't want to be like them." He held out his tiny hand. "Father, will it hurt?"

A gut-wrenching sob escaped Asmodeus's lips. He didn't answer his son as he led him away, the sword in his hands red from Jorian's blood. This she realized from some instinct. Somehow Michael was giving her details that seemed to be important.

She saw Michael standing to the side, his blond hair and white robe moving in the wind, his eyes darker than the blackest night. He held out a hand. "You will stay here and slay him."

Asmodeus growled at Michael. His lips pulling back, he bared his teeth. "I will take him away from this massacre. I will see it done, though not here." His voice broke as he kept walking. "Not here."

Michael let her go and the vision faded away. Her heart broke for Asmodeus as she crumpled to her knees. The pain he had experienced throughout his life. The horrors. Her chest felt hot, as though a flicker of flame had ignited in her bloodstream, and it traveled throughout her body. She vaguely had the notion she could kill in that moment.

"Is that the kind of man who deserves another chance?"

Forgetting her fear of Michael, she practically snarled at him. "You are a cruel being. Don't you think he has been through enough? Don't you think he's been hurt long enough? I'll do anything. Take anything from me. My firstborn, my soul, but just give him another chance."

Michael stood before her, completely unfazed by her verbal attack as though he were detached from the scene. "The decisions he makes in the next few days will not only affect him, but those around him. His situation is precarious at best. A man such as he knows nothing of unconditional love, the kind of love that can redeem past sins. You have had your audience with me. Call on my services no more. You will find no compassion from me."

Before she could tell Michael what a lousy bastard he was, he disappeared.

She lacked the energy to get off the floor. Their situation was hopeless. Michael had been her last hope, and he had crushed her with his coldness. He seemed to hate Asmodeus as much as Asmodeus hated him.

What next? Dare she even ask? There were no more options left to her. No more strategic steps to avoid the Abyss for either of them.

Knowing Asmodeus would be back any minute, she forced herself up. After she washed the blood from her hands she busied herself with making her bed and picking up her room. She tried to keep her thoughts from the impending fires, and the sad fact Asmodeus would soon be going back to his own torment.

The decision to keep the knowledge of the Abyss and her mission from Asmodeus might have been bad judgment on her part, but the time to tell him had passed. If she told him about the angels, the angels would arrive en masse, not allowing

Asmodeus to plan a strategy. The angels would take her and Asmodeus's last days together, and they would be left facing the fires sooner than anticipated.

As she took the laundry to the garage, Asmodeus flashed into her living room. She paused in the kitchen, holding her laundry basket. There was no hope for Kelly, so why was she holding her breath?

"She's getting worse, but that is to be expected. She will not get better."

Brianna nodded, hot tears pricking her eyes. She knew what he would say before he went to check on Kelly. She had needed an excuse to get him out of the house so she could summon Michael.

Why the hope? It seemed she carried hope in all things, and each hope was being unceremoniously crushed. She turned to put her hand on the doorknob leading into the garage, but his voice brought her up short.

"There's something else we need to discuss."

Dropping her hand from the doorknob, she turned to face him once again. What else could possibly have gone wrong?

Asmodeus indicated she should take a seat on the couch. Her anxiety was at an all-time high. Letting out a frustrated sigh, she put the basket by the door and sat on the couch. He sat next to her, and she could tell by the rigid set of his mouth this wasn't going to be a pleasant conversation.

"What we did was foolish, Brianna. There's a high probability that you're pregnant. You realize this, don't you?"

"Of course it's occurred to me." Especially when she had seen the flashback of that fateful day with his sons. But the one thing he didn't know was she wouldn't be carrying his child. Ever. She was going to the Abyss. A Nephilim they would not make.

With the vision of his sons fresh in her mind, she lifted her hand, placing her palm on his face. She imagined the pain he had endured when he had been forced to take the lives of his children.

"Brianna..."

The concern etched on his face nearly killed her. She wanted a better fate for him. A better life. And she had failed to assure that future for him. Was he destined to be imprisoned? Could no one fight for him and win?

Would anyone else ever try?

She leaned forward and kissed him lightly on the lips. "With everything that's going on, with Kelly and the book, I just want to take this one day at a time. Please. I can't handle much more."

He seemed to want to say more, but he let the matter drop. Her first concern wasn't saving a child she may or may not be carrying.

Her main concern was saving a man who, in some amazing, crazy circumstance, she had come to love.

A man who deserved happiness.

Chapter Seventeen

Asmodeus leaned against Raum's porch overlooking the ocean, his fingers digging into the seasoned wood. The sun cast its orange light over the shallow waves and the endless blue water beyond. Reflecting over his life and the decisions he had made had never been one of his traits, but it seemed that was all he was doing as of late.

He'd made a mistake where Brianna was concerned. The reality of what could transpire should she be pregnant ate at his soul. The possibility brought back the harsh pain of the past, making it seem like it had happened yesterday. The blood. The anguish. It was not something he could revisit while maintaining his sanity. The fight Jorian had given him had sickened him, but the calm acceptance of Bael, who had yet to turn, had destroyed him. He was no longer the same man he had been. He would never be the same.

He couldn't face that situation again. It would kill him.

And praying was not permissible from beings such as him.

What was foolish was Brianna didn't seem concerned about what they had done or that she may be carrying his child. She'd read the stories of what had transpired, but she hadn't been there to see the carnage firsthand. Still, she should be more concerned than she was, which made him think there was much more to the situation than met the eye.

When the sliding glass door opened he took a deep breath to control the rapid beating of his heart. Raum came to stand next to him.

Asmodeus slid his hands into the pockets of his jeans, his thumbs hooking on the seam. He had to control the pain, the shaking in his hands.

"Kelly will not make it through the night."

Asmodeus answered with a nod. He couldn't trust himself to speak. His species had been made with perfection in mind, built to be strong, both emotionally and physically ideal.

Yet now, with possibilities leaving him stricken with fear, he had never felt weaker or more inadequate.

"I'm trying to make her as comfortable as I can, but she's been trying to bite me. If she latches on I'm sure it will be hard to break free."

Asmodeus cleared his throat. "Desperation lends its hand to strength."

"That it does."

They were silent for a while. Asmodeus did his best to drag his thoughts away from Brianna. He should have thought about his actions before he took her to bed. It was his own damn fault for being weak.

"Where's Brianna?"

"At her bookstore." He'd sent Naberius with her. Searching for Leviathan would be useless. He could be anywhere, even a different realm if that was his choice. He had briefly thought about asking Brianna to summon Leviathan again, but decided against it. It was a bad idea on so many levels. If things went wrong she would be caught dead in the middle. They were stuck with waiting for his next strike. Forced into a defensive position. A weak position.

When Leviathan struck, he would be going for Kelly first. Without her, his carefully laid plan would fall to pieces. Without Asmodeus standing watch over Kelly he would have a damned good chance at apprehending her. Raum's and Naberius's powers were no match for his.

He cursed himself a fool. As diligent as he was being in protecting Brianna from Leviathan, he should have protected her from himself first. Instead he had possibly created a being that would one day die by his own hand.

Their child.

£

Leviathan couldn't flash himself into Raum's house. Asmodeus would sense him before he even finished materializing. He had been forced to break in like a common human.

It hadn't proven difficult to get past Asmodeus and his weak brother-in-arms. Asmodeus had seemed lost in thought, and Raum was nothing but a pathetic jackass.

He followed the stench of death and found Kelly curled in a corner of a back room. She was fading rapidly. The skin over her body was taut. Pale. She was shaking and mumbling spells to herself in a pitiable attempt to bust her ass out of Raum's.

Moving as swiftly as he was able, he ran across the room, placed a hand over her mouth and flashed them to Brianna's house.

Kelly didn't fight him. When he removed his hand she only kept mumbling to herself, as if he failed to exist.

Good. She was more animal than human, her eyes hungry and carnal. He waved a hand in front of her face to get her attention.

When she finally looked up at him she seemed not to recognize him. Her cold blue eyes were shiny and crazed. She launched herself at his throat with a low growl. He merely used his powers to keep her grounded to the floor as he attempted to sense Brianna's whereabouts. It was obvious she wasn't home. He had to be quick and find her before Asmodeus and Raum realized Kelly was missing. He had to keep Kelly here, which meant he would have to move fast. Taking Kelly to his house wasn't an option. Not when he'd burned the fucker to the ground.

His brush with the assassin had been close. He had to end this. He had to gain these powers or he would be dead.

Kelly was useless. Even if he asked her to summon Brianna, he doubted she would be able to do so. That left finding the bitch up to him.

From his association with Kelly, Leviathan was aware Brianna frequented two places—her home and her bookstore. If she wasn't with Asmodeus or Raum, she was more than likely with Naberius. After his attack they wouldn't leave her defenseless. He would check Naberius's house and her bookstore, and if he hadn't found her by then, Satan help them, because he'd be on the goddamned warpath.

He glanced down at Kelly's animalistic form, writhing on the floor, biting at the carpet, pulling out tufts of green-marbled insulation.

Fucking animal.

All he had to do was transport Brianna back here and Kelly would do the rest.

£

Brianna picked up another book out of one of the boxes Naberius had brought in. Tracy had done a perfect job with the finances while Brianna had been gone. Everything was neat and tidy, and there was a new aroma of pine needles and cinnamon from the potpourri Tracy had placed around the store.

She slid the book onto the four-dollar shelf. It was a classic. *Purgatorio* by Dante. Fitting, she thought, as she ran her finger along the cracked spine. She was saying goodbye to her store, goodbye to the life she would leave behind. The familiar smell of books, the ringing above the door when a customer walked in, a blast of fresh air mingling with the pine.

Naberius came around the corner with a bag. He set it by the box. "That's the last of the books."

She nodded, refusing to meet his eyes as a well of tears threatened to spill. A burning in her throat, carrying the raw emotion of failure, left her unable to say thank you.

The sun would set soon, and she would go back to her house only to pretend nothing was wrong. That was the hardest part. She didn't know if she was doing the right thing by keeping her mission from Asmodeus. What would he say? What would the angels do? Fear kept her from telling him what he deserved to know.

She cleared her throat. "I'll be ready in a few minutes."

"I'll lock the back door."

Suddenly she didn't want to linger in her store. She wanted out. Being reminded of what she was leaving behind...

She had called her lawyer, had Tracy's name placed on the deed for the bookstore. Tracy would take care of the place. She'd take care of the regulars who frequented.

As she dragged the bag of books to her side she heard Naberius grunt, which was quickly followed by the sound of something cracking.

She bounded from the floor and raced to the back of the store. She came up short when she saw Naberius and the demon Leviathan fighting. Leviathan had Naberius shoved up against the wall, his hand wrapped around his throat. A hot breeze swept through the room, causing books to fall from their displays. Naberius's eyes rolled back in his head.

Pivoting on her heel, she bolted for her cell to call Asmodeus. She instinctively knew she'd never make it. Rough arms grabbed her from behind. She struck out with her legs, kicking his shins as her feet left the floor. His arm came around her neck, a steel vise cutting off her air supply.

Her surroundings faded, the bookshelves replaced with the stark white paint of her living room walls. She was dropped unceremoniously to the floor, stars dancing in her line of vision. She tried taking in great breaths of air, which only made her nauseous.

Before she could regain her composure, a sharp pain

seemed to split her back in two. Snarling filled the air. Something was biting her.

The dog.

He had released his dog on her.

The growling and saliva from the bite put her into a panic, dredging up terrifying memories of the Nephilim attack. She tried to conjure up a spell, but terror had a hold of her. She could do nothing but flail around like a leaf in the wind.

Reaching around, she grabbed a hold of...hair. Short hair.

It wasn't a dog that had latched onto her.

Claws came around her throat, digging into her skin.

Not claws. Nails.

Kelly.

A strangled scream ripped through the air, a terrifying sound that didn't sound human.

It was her. The scream had come from somewhere deep inside of her. And she couldn't stop. She couldn't fight.

She was going to die.

Energy was being siphoned from her body. Her powers faded quickly. Her limbs were growing weak. Her head spun. Was this what bonding was? She recalled what Kelly said during their last encounter...

"You are doing exactly what he wants, Brianna. He wants me to bond with you, and the closer you come to me the less I am able to control myself."

Knowing the longer she allowed Kelly to take from her, the less chance she would have to fight her off, she forced clarity into her mind.

A spell. A spell. She needed a spell of protection. Fighting against the pull of energy Kelly was taking, she focused on the energy surrounding her. Energy from the rising moon and the setting sun.

"Fabric of life—"

Kelly growled, bit harder.

"—blood that ties, protect my flesh, from friend of mine."

The weight on her back was thrown from her, and a dizzying wind that carried the heat of the sun slid down her back. A roar of utter fury sliced through her home.

Leviathan was coming for her, and she lay powerless, spent. Her energy diminished, she could do nothing more than crawl away from the sounds of gurgling behind her. In the distance the dog clawed at the garage door, whining and barking.

She made it to the wall by her front closet and turned to see what was transpiring.

Kelly was only feet from her, blood coating her face, running down her chin, sliding down the bones above her chest. She was a skeleton. A wretched vision of death and decay, she sat and convulsed, spitting blood onto the carpet.

Leviathan grabbed Brianna by the hair and dragged her across the floor back to Kelly. Desperation mingled with terror as he brought her closer. Her nails dug into the carpet in a pathetic attempt to keep from getting closer to Kelly. As she started chanting another spell, he clocked her in the jaw. Pain shot up her head, down her ravaged back.

Kelly's eyelids peeled open, her convulsing coming to an end. Her eyes settled on Brianna once again. She looked stronger, as though the bonding was already having a positive effect on her ravaged body. Leviathan's hand was wrapped around her neck, immobilizing her.

As Kelly edged closer, Brianna tasted death.

She could only pray Asmodeus would be spared the sight of her lifeless body.

Chapter Eighteen

Asmodeus flashed himself to Brianna's bookstore, leaving Raum with Kelly. He had a compulsion to see her. The longer she was gone from his side, the more he felt a pull. Never having felt this way for someone, he didn't understand it.

The bookstore was silent as he materialized by the front desk, figuring they had already closed up for the night. Boxes lined the corner of the store, and books had toppled from tables. The open/closed sign faced the wrong way. He walked to the front door and tested it. It was unlocked.

When he slid the deadbolt in place he heard a moan come from the back of the store. He didn't run, he flashed himself to the back hall in attempt to reach the sound as quickly as possible.

Naberius was lying on his side on the floor, his eyes rolled back, showing only the whites. His back was arched as though he were trying to breathe, but not having the capability to do so.

Asmodeus bent down as breath rushed out of his lungs. He'd never seen Naberius in such a condition. His brother was strong. Powerful. It took a lot to take him out.

It would have to be another demon who contained powers from the first fall.

Leviathan.

Placing his hands on Naberius, Asmodeus healed him. The wounds that were making it difficult for his brother to breathe were on the inside of his body. Leviathan had not fought

Naberius with physical strength. He had fought with inherited power, searing Naberius's insides, likely infusing him with fire.

It took a moment before Naberius became coherent. His eyes were wild.

His voice was hoarse as he tried to speak. "I'm so sorry. I'm so—"

Asmodeus held his hand up for silence. "Leviathan?"

Naberius closed his eyes in defeat. "Yes."

Panic shook his body as he pulled his cell from the clip at his belt. Before he could dial out it rang. He flipped it open.

Raum was out of breath. "Kelly's gone."

"Flash yourself to Brianna's bookstore. Naberius is in need of assistance." Pain settled in his chest when he thought of Brianna in Leviathan's hands. He might not make it in time. It might be too late for Brianna.

That realization sent him into vicious action. His vision blurred as he flashed himself to Kelly's house. He'd no idea where to look for Brianna. Where would Leviathan take them? Surely not to Kelly or Brianna's house, though that would be the first places he would look. He had no other options at this point.

Scanning the premises with his senses, he could detect no one. He flashed himself to Brianna's, becoming dizzy from his rapid breathing. He palmed his sword as he materialized in Brianna's living room.

The sight of Brianna, Leviathan and Kelly on the floor, a tangle of legs and arms, made bile rise in his throat. More than shocked he had found them there, he roared as he raised his sword, aiming to flay the demon's head from his shoulders.

Leviathan let go of Brianna and jumped back, materializing his own sword. The dog Leviathan had left behind came out of nowhere and latched onto Asmodeus's leg. Leviathan must have materialized the dog out of the garage to aid him in the fight. Asmodeus grabbed it by the scruff of the neck and hurled it out of the way. The dog landed in a heap on the floor, where it lay motionless.

By fending off the dog he had opened himself up to Leviathan's attack.

Leviathan shouted an order. "Kelly. Demon. Now."

Kelly let go of Brianna, who crumpled to the floor. Kelly and Leviathan lunged at him simultaneously. He focused on the demon, allowing Kelly to latch onto his left arm as his right held his sword. He deflected blow after blow from the demon while Kelly tugged on his powers. He couldn't allow her to continue or he would be defenseless against Leviathan.

With his powers, Asmodeus sent Kelly flying. She bounded off the wall to his left, only to come running at him again, snarling. Leviathan's sword narrowly missed his chest as Kelly latched on once again.

The next thing that happened stopped his heart.

Brianna ran between him and the demon, barely dodging their swinging blades as she launched herself on Kelly, taking the witch down.

Asmodeus was now free to fight Leviathan, his faculties now his to command. He brought Leviathan down with a frigid wind, his sword a whisper in the air as he plunged it into the demon's chest. When he made contact a searing wave of fire threatened to consume him.

"Wrong tactic, Leviathan. The touch of fire is familiar to me."

The demon's eyes flashed fire at him, and he thrust his own sword. Asmodeus dodged it, and with another wave of his hand he sent the steel flying. Leviathan's sword clattered to the floor in the kitchen. Pulling his own sword out of the demon's flesh, he stepped back, swinging it in a deadly arc to decapitate him.

Leviathan was no more.

He swung around to help Brianna, only to see she had finished her own battle. Kelly lay on her back, her eyes closed and her breathing normal.

Before he could reach her, Brianna looked up at him. Tears fell from her eyes. Her neck was bloodied and bruised, her lip busted open. “She is healing. I used a spell to put her in a comfortable rest. She took some of my powers and I think it might help her.”

For Kelly what had just transpired would only be the beginning. To counteract what she had started with the *Demonic Book of Spells* she would need a bonding partner for life. This would only hold her over for a few short days. Hell, he wouldn’t tell Brianna now. He couldn’t. Not as hope bloomed on her face. He knelt down next to her and brought her close to his chest, his heart, crushing her. He closed his eyes and breathed in her scent as he flashed Leviathan’s body out of Brianna’s house.

He said three words that were a damned lie, but he couldn’t hold them back. “It is over.” It wasn’t over. Kelly would only start to deteriorate once their blood filtered through her system. Bonding was a continual process—a lifetime commitment.

He held Brianna as she sobbed against him. He healed her, a slight tingling in his core letting him know she had been badly injured.

Still she had fought for him. She had risked her life for his, unselfishly, without thought for her own well-being. In that moment he made a promise to himself that he would never let Brianna go. The feel of her tiny frame against his body felt right—even though their union went against natural law.

For the first time in centuries, since that terrible night so very long ago, tears fell.

A bright light flashed through the room. He didn’t turn to look at who had materialized. It was Raum and Naberius. Hands touched his shoulders, and he heard his friends kneel down. All four stayed in that position until the sky darkened to black.

£

Raum sat next to Kelly on the four-poster bed in his guestroom. She looked better now than she had since her deterioration had begun. Her cheeks were flushed pink, her breathing normal. She was still terribly thin, and would only get thinner. The blood she had consumed from Brianna and Asmodeus would wither away, leaving her in the same condition she had been in before she had consumed it.

The thoughts swirling around in his mind weren't worth thinking. She needed to bond with someone powerful. Someone who could sustain her and would promise to be there for as long as she needed it.

He had only heard of one other bonding that had worked. If one could consider it a success. A female witch had bonded with a demon, just the same as Kelly had done with Brianna and Asmodeus, and she'd had relapses. The longer she had gone without blood, the further the witch had depleted. It had been a constant tug-of-war to keep her alive. Sane. The feedings hadn't been constant. There had been times she needed to feed daily, other times a feeding once a week was enough. She couldn't be separated long from the demon she had bonded with.

Kelly had made a grave mistake when she had used the *Demonic Book of Spells.* But if anyone knew about mistakes, and atoning for them, it was he. Everyone deserved a second chance. Who was he to judge?

Her canines were gone for the moment, but like a vampire, they would elongate if offered a vein. The animalistic tendencies that now possessed her body would come alive at the prospect of a feeding. It was a survival mechanism.

He pulled the covers up to her chin when she shivered, tucking her into the soft comforter. Her head turned on the pillow, and for a second he thought she would open her eyes. Instead, she sighed and remained sleeping. Her features soft, her hair clean from her bath, she looked like a child. A helpless child.

Asmodeus and Naberius would not condone a decision to bond with her, if indeed that was what he wanted to do. It would weaken him, make her stronger. Fighting Nephilim would become more difficult, if not impossible, because he would be sharing his powers with her. He wasn't even sure how much power she would need to survive.

But how could he turn his back on her when she had only made a bad decision?

His conscience would never handle it.

Not when his past seemed dark and cold compared to her slip-up. There were things he had done that made her mistake look pathetic in comparison, yet he had been given another chance.

Who was he to deny her?

£

Brianna opened the sliding glass door and stepped onto her patio, allowing the cool breeze to brush over her skin. She inhaled deeply, enjoying every breath she took. Asmodeus thought their problems were over. Leviathan was dead, Kelly somewhat healed.

He had no idea that in only a few days the angels would come for them, and she doubted they would stop until both were imprisoned.

When she had witnessed Kelly's attack on Asmodeus, power had surged through her body, and she had defended him without thought. Leviathan she couldn't fight—Kelly, on the other hand, she could.

Her life had been empty before she had summoned Asmodeus. Her parents were in another state, her only friend had been Kelly and the occasional chat with Phillip at her store. She'd been unfulfilled and she hadn't even realized it until now.

The powers Kelly had taken from her were already trickling back. It was amazing she felt her powers now after so many years of denying them. Her lack of believing in herself had made her ineffective and clumsy when it came to spells.

She took a deep breath. She picked up the scent of honeysuckle in the air. She could hear a police siren in the distance.

The dog was resting at Naberius's house. Asmodeus had suggested they take it to the pound, but Naberius had offered to take it home. It was one less thing she had to worry about.

Asmodeus had loved her body for the past few hours. He was showering now. She had opted to get out of the confines of the house and gaze at the star-filled sky.

It was funny. She couldn't remember the last time she had taken the time to enjoy the beauty of the earth, yet she was always trying to wield its power. She only took, never gave anything back. Never cared.

As they had made love, promises spilled from Asmodeus. Promises of love. Of protection. She'd wept against him so many times, and he had assured her everything would work out. Why was everything going to be taken away now, when she was finally on the verge of contentment? Happiness.

She felt like a liar, and why shouldn't she? She was a liar. She claimed she loved him yet she kept a dark secret secured against her breast, terrified he would be taken away from her too soon. She kept knowledge of his future from him.

Suddenly the peace of the night gave way to an energy in the air, energy that had nothing to do with the energy the earth provided. Four angels materialized in front of her. She nearly stepped away from them, but caught herself in time. She had to show a strong front. She had only a few days left with Asmodeus, and she was not giving them up.

"You time has run out, Brianna."

She did recoil then. No, she hadn't miscalculated the days left to them. It had always been at the forefront of her thoughts. "No it hasn't."

"You have no intent to kill. We can sense it."

The angels before her were dressed for battle once again. Or was that what they always wore? Always prepared. Always ready. "I have gained his trust just as you asked of me. He professed to love me mere hours ago."

"You have no intention of killing him," the angel to the right repeated.

"I do. I was told I had a week." She used every power she had to keep her inner thoughts from surfacing. Could they read her that easily? Did they have access to her mind? Could they effectively read her thoughts?

"How do you plan to carry out your mission?"

"I will kill him while he sleeps." As the lie fell from her lips she felt like vomiting. She had no other course of action left to her. She had to convince them she still had intentions of carrying out her mission. She was desperate. "Give me the remainder of my week."

One of the angels smiled and she found she couldn't take her eyes from his face. He looked...evil. It was as though she had just done something that pleased him.

"You shall have until tomorrow night to complete your mission."

They disappeared.

Tension left her body in waves as she pulled a hand over her face. Lies. So many lies. Could she justify them? Yes. She wanted more time with Asmodeus before they took them away. Just a few more touches, a few more conversations. She didn't want to let him go.

She took a deep breath, glanced at the sky one last time and turned to go back in the house.

Asmodeus stood not ten feet from her. The sadness that registered on his face brought her to her knees. All she could think was how much her betrayal would hurt him. She wanted to tell him why she had said what she had. She wanted to run to him. Embrace him. But the pain in his eyes slowly dimmed to a dull stare. Then it melted into a look of hate.

No matter what he did, no matter what he said, she would not tell him the truth. She would give him one last night and day away from the Abyss and the torments that awaited him.

He deserved at least that.

She wished she could give him more.

His body went cold as he watched Brianna drop to her knees. A look of utter astonishment marred her features, and she brought a shaking hand to her throat. What did she think he would do? Unmercifully cut her down as she would have done to him? Apparently there were creatures prowling this earth that were far more conniving and evil than himself. Because he could *never* harm her. He could *never* touch her in anger.

Only she would never know that.

He materialized his sword. He waited for her to back away, to shield herself. Instead she only bowed her head as though she were a sacrifice.

And like a dumb bastard he loved her more.

She would never know that either.

"Even in sleep you wouldn't have taken me. Do you realize that, witch?"

She visibly flinched. "I understand."

So this was what she had hidden from him, and like a dumbass he hadn't detected her treachery. Or had he? Was he so hard up for companionship he had been willing to overlook obvious deceit?

Don't ask her. Don't do it. "Did I mean anything to you?" *Goddammit.* His voice sounded weak even to his own ears. He wanted to take the words back and cut her down where she kneeled. He had an overwhelming desire to attack her. Hurt her.

She kept her head lowered. "No."

"Very well." He should just let her kill him. The fact that moments before she admitted she felt nothing for him made him weak. Cold.

He had no purpose in this realm, yet for a short time he had felt wanted. Needed. Even now he wanted to go to her and hold her in his arms. Thankfully that need was stronger than the instinct to kill her, which was causing his body to shake from keeping himself from doing so.

"If you come near me for any reason, good or bad, I will cut you down without hesitation."

She gave no indication of having heard him.

"Are we clear, witch?"

She sniffed, her face lowered to the ground. "Yes."

He flashed himself from her house and onto the beach, in the exact spot they had lingered a few nights ago. That seemed so long ago. He remembered how beautiful she was, how sincere she had seemed when she admitted she had feelings for him. And like a fool he had believed her.

Even now he wanted to believe.

He lowered himself to the ground, clenching the wet sand in his palms, digging into the earth. He wanted to kill her. Love her. Heal her. Forgive her.

Goddammit. Get it together. He took deep breaths of cool ocean air. The salty breeze stung his face as he looked at the blackened sky. How many times would fate fuck with him? Someone had to be laughing their asses off at him.

Well, that was just fine. He'd survived much worse. He would survive this as well.

He got up from his pathetic display of self-pity. He still had things to do this night. Walking in the direction of Raum's house, he took the scenic route. He passed a few couples along the way, wishing them the happiness that was denied him. As soon as he wished them happiness, he wished them pain. Death.

Growling, he took off at a jog. Suddenly he wanted to be doing something. Anything but thinking about the witch.

His jog progressed into a run, and in no time he was at Raum's house. He climbed up the stairs in the back of the dwelling and let himself in. He needed to speak with someone. Needed to know why he hurt so badly, though the answer would never come.

When he walked by the guestroom he stopped and had to put a hand on the doorjamb to keep himself upright as he saw the unthinkable.

Kelly was feeding from Raum.

And he allowed it as he wrapped his body around hers. They looked like...old lovers. Her hands clutched him to her, as if she would never let go. He felt as though he were witnessing something private. Sacred.

He backed out of the room. Out of the house.

He let his self-pity hit a new high. He was alone. The feeling settled deep into his gut, making him want to retch.

Sometimes death was preferable. Welcomed.

God, he wanted to belong somewhere. It was a feeling, a weakness he couldn't afford.

And what of the possible offspring he had created with the witch? What would be done about that? She was a healthy female. Fertile. She was likely pregnant. In a few years he would be cutting down his own child. Again.

He barely made it to the edge of the deck. Holding onto the railing, he vomited, his muscles tightening painfully. His eyes swam, his head ached.

God, Brianna...

Yes, death was preferable.

Chapter Nineteen

Brianna had spent the night staring at the ceiling. She vaguely recalled coming in the house after Asmodeus had gone. Showering. Drinking Smirnoff. Lots of Smirnoff.

And lying in her bed. Thinking of nothing. Of everything. The sadness she had witnessed on Asmodeus's face, right before he replaced it with hate, had broken her. She didn't give a shit where she went tonight, or what happened to her. She just wished she could spare him the pain of what was coming. She'd already inflicted him with enough.

She got up, used the bathroom and brushed her teeth. The normalcy of what she was doing hit her suddenly, causing her to erupt in a fit of laughter. What, was she worried about cavities? Her next checkup?

She caught a glimpse of herself in the mirror and the shock of her reflection made her quit laughing. Jesus, she looked deranged. Her hair was straggly, she had dark circles under her eyes, and her skin was…yuck.

She jumped in the shower, feeling numb and dull. She thought about going to Naberius's, but Asmodeus had said he'd kill her if she came anywhere close to him. Dying by the hands of the man she loved had to be a downer, so she wasn't going there.

After she got out and towel dried the phone rang. Thinking it had to be her cousin Tracy, she picked it up. "Hello?"

"Brianna?"

Dear God, it was Kelly. Still, she had to ask, "Kelly?"

She was met with silence. Was this some cruel joke? "Kelly? Are you there?"

"I...I'm sorry about what I did, Brianna. I don't remember it, but Raum told me what happened. I'm so sorry."

Brianna sighed and sat on her bed. What could she say? How could Kelly form words? She had been an animal the last time Brianna had seen her. Past death's door. Had their blood done this much good? "Um...are you going to be all right?"

"I don't know."

Without confirmation, she knew Kelly was leaving something out. There was more to the situation, and Kelly wasn't about to tell her about it. Had things changed so drastically between them?

Yes, it had. She doubted she could trust Kelly again after she had lied to her about the spell book. The attack she could forgive, because that hadn't been her friend. "Well, I hope everything works out for you." God, had she just said goodbye?

"You too, Brianna."

Brianna heard a click. Kelly had hung up.

Brianna pressed end on the phone and lay back on her bed, tears forming. She'd been short with Kelly because she *was* saying goodbye. She was tying up loose ends. Looking over at her alarm clock, she read the blurry red numbers. Ten in the morning. She didn't have long now.

£

Asmodeus came awake as a sharp pain shot up his right side. He opened his eyes, squinting when he was met with bright light. Where the hell was he?

He sat up, glancing around. He heard the ocean before he saw it. Felt the cushioned beach chair he had curled up in. He was on Raum's back deck.

Raum walked into his line of vision. "Hey, brother, what are you doing? Why did you crash out here?"

Asmodeus wiped his eyes and pushed himself off the chair. Damn his back hurt. It was as though someone had nailed him in the side with a bat. Had Raum kicked him awake? He eyed his brother. "Must have fallen asleep."

Raum crossed his ankles as he leaned his back against the deck railing. His black silk robe flapped against his legs in the wind. "Oh. Well, you want some breakfast?"

No. He wanted a shower and a toothbrush. "How's Kelly?"

Raum's face remained impassive. "She seems to be doing pretty good, actually."

Surprise, surprise. He wasn't going to push him. Let the bastard do what he wanted with Kelly. It was his powers she would be taking, and it was no one's business if he wanted to allow a human to drain him of those powers every day. "I'll take some coffee."

"Where's Brianna?"

Asmodeus tried to keep the emotion off his face, but by the look Raum was giving him, he had failed. He turned away from him and opened the back door to the house.

He didn't mince words. Who the hell cared? What happened had happened. It was over. "She had been planning on killing me in my sleep."

He braced himself, figuring he would receive pity. Sorrow. Surprise. None of which he got.

Raum laughed.

Asmodeus stopped in the hallway and faced Raum. He felt like ripping the bastard's head off. "What the fuck is so funny about that?"

Raum's face lost its humor. His green eyes narrowed. "You're serious?"

"Fucking right, I'm serious."

Raum bent over with his hands on his thighs, falling apart in a fit of...giggles. The demon was giggling.

Asmodeus stood with his arms folded across his chest and

waited until Raum was finished. He'd never seen the demon giggle before, and frankly, it was disturbing. Especially since it was at his expense.

"I'm sorry," Raum said, wiping the tears off his face. "I need a moment."

"You've had nearly five."

Raum's laughter erupted again. After a few more moments he tugged his black robe together and ran a hand through his hair. He cleared his throat. "So, she said this to you?"

"I heard her speaking to the angels representing Destruction, Punishment, Vengeance and Death. Apparently they had struck a bargain between them. She agreed to kill me."

Raum's eyebrows came together as he realized the seriousness of the situation. "Why? Did they threaten her?"

Asmodeus went ramrod stiff. He hadn't thought of the why of it, he'd only focused on the fact that she had agreed to kill him. "I...I don't know why she agreed to do it."

"Sounds like they set her up. There's no way in hell, even with you sleeping, she could kill you."

Fear clutched Asmodeus's heart. He had said the very same thing to her last night. Truth was, she couldn't take him. Ever. "I heard it from her own mouth."

Raum's lips curled. "Asmoday, she could have killed you ten times over by now, or tried to, anyway. Haven't you been sleeping with her?"

He swallowed. Why was Raum making sense? No. No, Brianna was out to hurt him, to hand him over to those who would take him back to the Abyss. He wasn't going back to that torture. There was no way in hell... She couldn't have... "She lied to me. She told them she was gaining my trust by sleeping with me. She sounded convincing."

"Wouldn't you be if you were facing the angels of death?"

When Asmodeus began to say something, Raum held up his hand, cutting him off. "Listen, I'm not defending her, because I have no idea what the hell is going on. All I know is Brianna isn't like that. She's a little witch, pun intended, but she's not a whore and she's not a bad person. Certainly you can see that. I think there's more to this than you have allowed yourself to see." He paused, looking toward the guestroom. "What did she do when you confronted her?"

The vision had been burned into his memory forever. Her black hair lifted in the wind, her head lowered. "She fell to her knees as though she were offering herself as a sacrifice."

"That sounds more like Brianna to me, does it not to you?"

Asmodeus pivoted on his heel and stalked to the kitchen. The thought of going back to the Abyss took his breath away. The thought of Brianna sending him back to the Abyss took his soul away.

Could she be in trouble with the angels for summoning him? Why would they strike up a bargain with a twenty-four-year-old female who knew nothing about fighting or killing? There was something more here, but he couldn't pinpoint what it could be.

He yanked the coffeepot off the coffee maker and held it under the sink. As he filled it with water he turned over the events of the past forty-eight hours. She had come back to Naberius's after the Neph attack. She had tried to seduce him. She had recognized the angels in Tony's.

That all fit the bill that she had tried to gain his trust.

But the way she came apart in his arms. The trust she gave him as he made love to her. Had that been part of the seduction? When she arched her back and dug her nails into him, calling out his name, had she been playing a role?

She'd had plenty of opportunity to try and kill him.

He recalled when she had run a delicate finger over his sword back at Naberius's. The way his hair had stood on end and trepidation had hung in the air. Had she planned to use his own weapon on him? What about when he found her outside of Naberius's? She had talked of an insurance policy. She had clearly been up to something.

No. She had done her job, and had done it well. She had gained his trust.

Another thought occurred to him as he measured out the coffee. The angels knew he had overheard their conversation with her. One had looked directly at him. Why? They had intended him to hear it. They wouldn't have allowed it otherwise. They expected her to gain his trust, yet there he stood as the angels permitted him to witness her treachery.

He flipped the coffeepot on and walked to the window, running a hand through his hair. Something wasn't right with this situation.

Tread carefully, my fallen brother. The choices you make in the near future will not only affect you, they will determine the fates of others.

Jesus. Like the sharp ringing of a bell, the words of the angel washed over him, as though it were a reminder. What did it mean?

"What are you going to do?"

Asmodeus turned to see Raum leaning against the doorjamb. He looked tired, and well he should. He now shared his life force with Kelly. His powers.

"I'm going to leave it, Raum. She failed." For some sadistic reason, he wished she hadn't.

Raum seemed to regard him with pity and understanding. "Don't we all?"

Chapter Twenty

Brianna had been sitting at her kitchen table with the phone in her hand for hours. How did one say goodbye to parents who had no idea you were saying goodbye?

Time was ticking and all she could do was sit in her kitchen with her thumb up her ass. Questions were swirling in her mind at hurricane speed. Hadn't the angels known Asmodeus was standing behind her when they spoke to her? Wouldn't they have known he would hear?

Of course they would. But why would they do that? Something was going on and all she happened to be was a pawn in someone's sadistic game.

Screw it. What could she do about it?

A little voice in her head told her she could call Asmodeus. Tell him what was going down tonight. Somehow she doubted he would care. Another part of her figured he would bring in as many demons as he could muster, fight to the death.

She fingered the white phone, running her thumb over the gray buttons.

Bounding out of her chair, she went for her cell that lay on her bed in her room. Breathlessly, she scrolled down to his number. She could do nothing but stare at it until the light on her phone went off.

He wanted nothing to do with her, and rightly so. But she wanted everything to do with him. She wanted to see him, feel him...tell him that she loved him.

Michael's voice traveled through her mind, as if he were standing in the room with her.

The decisions he makes in the next few days will not only affect him, but those around him. His situation is precarious at best.

Yes, his situation was precarious, and so was hers. But she'd heard those words before. She had a small recollection of one of the angels saying that to Asmodeus the first night he had been in her house. Something about how a decision of his would affect him and those around him.

What decision? Could she merely sit here like a jackass and not call him? She had to warn him, whether or not he cared to hear her voice.

With trembling hands she dialed his number before she lost the nerve.

£

"Kelly?"

Raum shouldered his way through the guestroom door, closing it softly behind him. As his gaze found hers he breathed a sigh of relief. She looked better. Damn near like her old self. A possessive streak unexpectedly slammed through him. She was better because of him. He had done something good in this world.

He shook the emotion off. He was a selfish bastard, and fooling himself to think otherwise was a waste of time. "How are you feeling?"

Her gaze rested on the blue and gray comforter on the bed. "I'm feeling better. A little woozy."

Well, that was to be expected. She'd been through hell. "You'll be feeling like yourself shortly." Was he trying to convince her, or himself?

He slowly crossed the room and stood next to the bed.

"Mind if I sit down?"

She scooted her legs over.

As he sat next to her, he still couldn't believe what he had done. The utter selfless sacrifice he had made for her benefit. He'd never been like that. With anyone. He vaguely wondered if he could start liking the man he was once again. It had been so long.

Again, he pushed the thoughts away. Kelly had been right. When they argued the first time he had met her, she had told him he was a bad person. How could he not be? He was a demon. He had fallen from grace and no one had been beating down his door with an invitation welcoming him back.

"Is Asmodeus still here?" She closed the book she had been holding on her lap. No spell books for her. She was reading a romance novel.

"Yes. He's out on the porch."

"Still?"

"Yeah." And it was disturbing as all hell. Asmodeus acted like he was in mourning. He could understand how he would be rattled, given what he had heard Brianna say to the angels, but how could the bastard not realize something wasn't right with this scenario?

"Are you going to talk to him?"

"I already did. I think he needs his space now."

She nodded, looking down at the bedspread again, and in that moment he could sense exactly how she felt, as though she were useless. He glanced at the door, wishing he could help his fallen brother. But there was nothing to be done.

£

Asmodeus jumped when his cell phone rang. Raum had likely called Naberius and told him all the details of what transpired between himself and Brianna, and he really didn't want to listen to Naberius's shit at the moment.

Still, he found himself flipping the contraption open. "What?"

"Please don't hang up."

Asmodeus felt both rage and desire at the sound of Brianna's voice. A part of him wanted to ask her if she fared well, and the other wanted to tell her to go to hell. Being what he was, it was difficult for him to give his enemies his back, which was what he was doing by allowing her to live.

He didn't say anything. Didn't trust his voice to remain steady, or trust the correct words to come out of his mouth. He only waited for her to speak.

"What I'm about to tell you will likely start off a chain reaction of which I'll have no control over, and perhaps I should have told you earlier, but I just...couldn't."

He gritted his teeth. "I'm listening."

She sighed. "Okay. Well, you heard the mission the angels sent me on. And yes, I did accept their terms. It was the first day we met in the library..."

His body grew cold as she told him everything. She explained to him that she had been willing to kill him in the beginning, gave him her word that she had changed her mind, and told him the truth about the attack of the Nephilim she had instigated. He listened, and though he wanted to believe every word she said, his survival instinct told him to be cautious.

He chose his words carefully. "What do you gain by this call, Brianna?"

He had the overwhelming desire to flash to her house, hold her and tell her they could work things out.

But she was a human. Forbidden. And though he had already broken the rules, doing so again would be ignorant. Trusting her again went against everything he had learned in the Abyss.

"I just wanted you to be aware of the situation."

He laughed, feeling on the edge of a precipice he had no control over. "And you would have me do what? Are you calling me for protection?" *I would give it. Damn me, I would give it.*

Silence met his question. He waited as he battled the inner turmoil of his feelings. Battle plans were swirling in his mind. He wanted to gather a force, but he would not engage his brothers in his problem once again. If there was a fight coming, then it was his alone to face.

And Brianna's.

Dear God.

"Take care of yourself, Asmodeus."

The harsh sound of a dial tone met his ears, and he wanted to crush the phone with his hand. Yes, it had been too much to ask for more than a small reprieve.

The thought of going back to the Abyss made his blood run cold.

But the thought of Brianna there left him weak.

£

Brianna watched the sunset from her back porch. The purples, blues and pinks mingled together, giving her one last, beautiful glimpse of freedom.

A small part of her had thought Asmodeus would care enough to make an appearance before the angels arrived. It hurt to realize she had wounded him so badly that he didn't give a shit about their future. She could only pray he took what she said seriously and protected himself in whatever way he could.

A misplaced calm settled over her as she gazed at the sky and listened to the birds. The call to her mother had never happened. She hadn't the strength to say goodbye.

Michael had spoke of unconditional love. He had maintained that Asmodeus didn't know the meaning, nor was he capable of surrendering himself to such an emotion.

Michael was wrong. If she had more time, she might be

able to prove it, but time had run out.

She felt for the dagger she had slipped into her jeans. Still in its sheath, it was big and it dug into her thigh. She was going to keep it on her, just in case. It was just a feeling...an instinct that told her to keep Michael's dagger on her.

Getting up from her lawn chair, she made her way back into the house. Not long now. Surveying her living room, she was surprised to see what little belongings represented her time here on earth. Then again, material things had meant little to her. Books had been the most important part of her existence.

She could swear the angels were already there, as she felt another's presence. Seeing nothing out of the ordinary, she chalked it up to nerves.

The sun was nearly gone, the light casting an eerie orange glow throughout her living room. She turned on a lamp, and just as she did so, a bright light filled her home.

So soon. Time was up.

Straightening, she turned to the four angels who now stood in her living room. Dressed in their battle gear, they reminded her of old Roman warriors, not the angelic beings they were.

"You have failed your assigned mission."

She kept her eyes locked with his obsidian stare. During her first encounter with the angels she had been a different person. Selfish and unfulfilled. She was stronger as a person now, and she was confident in her capabilities. "Did I? I don't believe I did."

The angel stepped forward, his white robe settling around him. "You did not kill him, as his soul remains in this realm."

"Which is exactly where it should be." She clasped her hands behind her back so the angels would not see her shaking. "I summoned Michael yesterday, and I explained to him I felt Asmodeus had been punished enough. I made my own mission after I spoke to him. I was not going to be a part of his apprehending, because I don't agree with it and I do not think it is right."

"That is not your decision to make."

"And yet I made it."

Silence fell on the room. She stood as straight as the trembling in her body would allow her.

She wanted to weep as he unrolled a scroll. "Brianna Claxton, as the individual who summoned Asmodeus, leader of the Second Angelic Revolt, out of the Abyss, you are hereby sentenced to one century in the second tier, of which you will report to immediately. Your compliance in this matter—"

"I will go willingly if you recant that order."

Brianna went bone-chilling numb when her gaze settled on Asmodeus. He wore the brown robe he'd had on the first night, as if he were humbling himself. He didn't look at her, but he didn't have to. His warmth surrounded her, and she closed her eyes, relishing the feel of him.

Within seconds she collected herself enough to react to his presence in the one way Michael had taught her. She had to prove he was capable of unconditional love, the type of love that could redeem a man of his past sins. She would not let him sacrifice himself for her while she stood and did nothing.

She took Michael's dagger out of her jeans and held it out to the angels. "I would summon Michael and obtain audience with him once more."

"That is not an option available to you."

Keeping her attention on the angels, she brought the blade across her palm as she had done yesterday. Confident in her abilities, she recalled the correct spell and once again summoned the archangel.

As before, bright light settled into the room and collected together to form Michael.

She prayed this would work.

Trying not to concentrate on the pain in her palm and the fact that Michael and Asmodeus were in the same room together, she laid it on the line. "Asmodeus is capable of caring for others, and capable of love and selfless acts. I am proof he deserves another chance."

Michael's eyes bore into hers. "You are not saving the

demon with your words, Brianna. I warn you now you are condemning him."

She shook her head. Didn't he see where she was going with this? "You told me, those who are capable of love deserve redemption. He *is* capable of love."

"You believe he loves you?"

Finally Michael began to catch her meaning. Hoping against hope it was true, she nodded. "I do."

The light in Michael's eyes faded. It suddenly occurred to her she had said the one thing that would damn the very man she was trying to save. "Demons are not permitted to lie with humans. Asmodeus, as part of the Holy Watchers, was given the job of watching over this realm. Having protected humans for centuries, he was subject to the way in which they lived as he watched over them. He envied them. He fell for them. He condemned himself then with his coveting with them, and he condemns himself now by planting his seed within you."

Asmodeus stepped forward. "Then take me. I will go willingly. Brianna did not know the spell she was casting when she summoned me, and she was not aware of the repercussions. Her fault lies in her ignorance, not in treachery."

Michael faced Asmodeus. "For this arrangement I will require your sentence to be doubled."

"No!" she screamed, slicing the dagger through the air. How had she made the situation worse? "You cannot—"

"Silence." Michael pinned her with his powerful stare. "The decision is up to him. You both report to the Abyss, you for a century, and he for another millennium, or he goes willingly to his imprisonment with two millennia in the Abyss and you will remain here. There will be no other choice given."

Before she could respond, Asmodeus stepped forward once again. "I accept."

Michael bowed his head. "It is done."

Someone started screaming "*No!*" over and over again as she fell to her knees. She dropped the dagger in front of her as the angels and Asmodeus disappeared from the room. The screaming was deafening, yet there was no one else left in the room.

It was then she realized it was her.

She was the one screaming.

Chapter Twenty-One

The devastation on Brianna's face took his breath away. Asmodeus closed his eyes as her guttural cry cut though the room. It seemed as though everyone he became close to suffered because of their association with him.

At least she would not be suffering in the Abyss. Two millennia in the Abyss. By the time he served his sentence Brianna would be a forgotten memory in her realm, having passed so many years before.

When he opened his eyes he was faced with a white office. Michael sat behind a desk and pulled a hand over his face. Odd after all of his years of planning Michael's demise he contained none of that hatred now. The angel looked as drained as he felt.

"Sit."

Asmodeus sank into the chair to the side of the desk. He felt like closing his eyes and never waking.

"You have a request. State it."

Yes, he did have a request, didn't he? "Two requests, actually." He waited for Michael's acknowledgment, which he did with a nod. "I request Brianna will be taken care of."

Michael pulled a tan file from his dresser. "In what way? You know I require specifics."

He was drained of emotion. What he was doing now proved how tired he was. He lacked the emotion to make any of this real. He had to make sure Brianna was safe, and then he would proceed to his fate. "Monetarily. I also want her protected."

"From?"

Asmodeus pushed the pain down. "From the child she carries."

Michael set the file on the desk and flipped it open. "So you admit the child she carries is yours."

He had been guessing, but the validity of Michael's statement only brought on more of the numbness he was experiencing. "I do not deny it."

"You request I destroy it?"

It. Such a callous description for a child. "I..."

Michael leaned back in his chair. "Do you recall Gabriel's fall?"

"No."

"That's right. You were in the Abyss. Well, long story short, he fell from grace when he took a human woman. No child was born of the union, though he had clearly disgraced the Holy Watchers with his conduct. Fact of the matter is he was reinstated."

Reinstated into the Holy Watchers? Christ, he had never heard of that happening. How did one go from being a demon to being an archangel once again? "How?"

Michael shrugged. "He wanted to come back. Begged to come back. So he was tested."

Asmodeus's heart felt like lead in his chest. "And?"

"He passed the test."

Understanding dawned on him. Energy seemed to seep back into his core. He sat forward in his chair. "This was a test?"

"You were given a second chance through Brianna. We chose her specifically. Gabriel headed the assignment, making sure Leviathan got his greedy hands on the book. Gabriel used his powers to mentally convince Brianna to say the spell which summoned you from the Abyss. You didn't really think a human could effectively summon you from the Abyss before your time was up, did you?"

Hell yeah he had. "But my time wasn't up."

"To us it was."

Asmodeus pushed himself from the chair, pacing the confines of the office. "You knew damn well I was going to come after you."

"You didn't."

"Because of Brianna. She's the only reason—"

"That's why we chose her. If we had chosen someone like Kelly, she wouldn't have fought you, and she would have summoned me. Brianna is a good person, and she has shown you the light."

And he had shown her the darkness. Himself. "And now? She's to suffer because of her contact with me?"

"Absolutely not. She was never to face such a sentence. In offering yourself you have shown the one thing that connects us to the humans. The very thing you fell for."

"Unconditional love." He stopped pacing and faced Michael. Anger built inside of him. "I have already felt unconditional love. For my sons I would have done anything."

"It's easy to love those of your own flesh and blood. Just as it's easy to pray for a friend. How many souls pray for their enemies? Is it not taught in the scriptures you should pray for those who persecute you? And forgiveness? Do you carry it in your heart?"

He stood staring at Michael. Duty. He had only been doing his duty when he sent out the order demanding death of the Nephilim. He'd only been protecting the humans. He had never once considered what that had done to Michael. He had never forgiven him of his actions that night, but he had never thought about Michael's pain.

True, he had been forced to end the lives of his children, one who was a Neph, the other soon to change. But he was not the only one forced to carry out an order that night. Michael had been doing his duty, not carrying out his wishes.

The depth of sorrow reflected in Michael's eyes spoke of pain. "It was not my finest hour, my fallen brother."

Asmodeus turned away from him. Forgiveness would not come on this day. “What are the choices given to me?”

“I can reinstate you as a Holy Watcher, and you can reign with myself, Gabriel, Uriel and Raphael.”

Four of the original Holy Watchers. Michael offered forgiveness from the echelon. Redemption. He was offering him a purpose. “Or?”

“Brianna.”

There it was. The ultimate choice. He couldn’t have everything he wanted.

He remained silent. On one hand, he would have everything he’d been willing to fall for. The love of a woman. A child. A home. Yet he would still contain darkness. If he chose to be reinstated he would be whole once again, in body and spirit. But not in heart.

“There’s one question you must ask yourself.”

Asmodeus gripped the back of the chair, leaning his weight against it. “And that is?”

“You were willing to face the fires for her, but are you willing to give up Heaven?”

This was just another trick. Another test. “By natural law I cannot be with Brianna. You just got through reminding me. Humans and demons are not to coexist.”

“No, they can’t.”

“Then why do you tempt me with what I cannot have?”

“Because in a few weeks’ time Brianna will no longer be human.”

Chapter Twenty-Two

Brianna wasn't listening to Raum blather on about the baby, or Naberius's insistence they call some vampire named Ambrose. She didn't care that Ambrose was the first vampire, or that he had once been a mighty Warrior Angel. They were talking crazy, so she had tuned them out a while ago. It was nearly two in the morning, and she was too tired to care.

It had been two days since Asmodeus had been taken to the Abyss, and all she could think about was the pain he must be in. The agony. She had failed. Replaying the events that had transpired, she was certain she could have done things differently that would have ensured a better outcome. She should have told him about the angels. Her mission. By working together they might have avoided this horrendous outcome. Perhaps if she had spoken to Michael once—

"Brianna."

She brought her head up and rolled her eyes. "Yeah, sure. Whatever you say." She was so tired of listening to their bullshit. Didn't they care about Asmodeus? Why didn't they show any concern for their friend?

They had come to her house when they felt Asmodeus's absence, and had found her on the floor. She didn't remember much of what happened after that, only that she had woken up in Naberius's house, in the same bed she had shared with Asmodeus. Over the past few days they had talked to her about her possible pregnancy. She had finally taken a pregnancy test, even though Naberius and Raum had been convinced it wouldn't work.

Apparently it had. It came back positive.

"So you're willing to give it a try?"

Guess she'd missed something important. Did it really matter? "Sure."

"I'll call him now."

Naberius left the kitchen table and she went back to playing with the blue silk napkin in her lap. She had tried summoning Michael again and again. He had finally appeared, and when he did he was pissed.

He'd taken her powers from her, telling her, "I'm sick and tired of your constant pull. Now I won't be bothered by you."

So now she was without Asmodeus, her powers or her sanity.

"Brianna?"

Annoyance thrummed up her spine. "*What?*" Christ, she was tired of talking to them.

Raum cocked his right eyebrow. "You realize you won't be able to go out in the daytime for a long while."

She scrunched her face. "What are you talking about?"

"You weren't even listening, were you?"

She sighed. Not really. Not when they were discussing turning her into a vampire. For God's sake, a vampire? Why? So she could string her depressed ass along for centuries?

Did Xanax work for the undead?

Naberius walked back into the kitchen. He held a cordless phone out to her.

She didn't take it. "What?"

"Ambrose wants to speak with you." He thrust the phone in her hand and whispered, "Remind him of your powers. Your psychic powers are going to be a huge selling point to Ambrose."

She damn near growled. Michael had taken her powers, and she wasn't sure if, or when, she would ever get them back. What was the point of this nonsense? Nothing could be done. If they were sure turning her into a vampire would save the child she carried from turning into a Nephilim, she would do it in a heartbeat. But the truth was this had never been done before. What if they made another form of creature? Some fanged, undead, drooling baby?

Hallmark didn't make cards for that occasion.

She gritted her teeth and brought the phone to her ear. "Hello?"

"Hello, Brianna. My name is Ambrose. How are you feeling?"

Was he serious? She felt like choking the stranger with his own soft, Scottish brogue. "Just cheeky. Couldn't be better. How about you?"

"There's no need to make smart-ass comments. I don't like this any more than you do."

"Really? You get a blood bank for a day and I get to play Russian roulette with an embryo. What's not to like?" She felt bad for snapping at him just as soon as the words left her mouth. Raum and Naberius were only trying to help, as was the man on the phone, but all she wanted to do was sleep. Possibly never wake up.

"I'm leaving this decision up to you. I'm not sure what the outcome will be, since nothing like this has been done before. But the alternative is just as disturbing, isn't it?"

The vision of the Neph that attacked her flooded her mind, and she started tearing up. She got up from the chair and slammed the phone down on the kitchen table.

Panic attack, here I come...

She stomped into the living room and bumped into Valencia.

Valencia laid a hand on her arm. "Whoa. I... What happened?"

She couldn't speak; she merely shook her head. Valencia wrapped her in a hug.

They had become closer in the past few days. Naberius had demanded she move in so she wouldn't be alone throughout her pregnancy. Valencia had stood up for her, saying it was

Brianna's decision. Valencia was the only one to realize more change would only push her further over the edge. She wished she were home that very second so she could mourn in private. All the talk of vampires, babies and the Abyss were too much.

She held on to Valencia for a few minutes before she finally spoke. "They want to turn me into a vampire." A laugh escaped her. "A vampire. Can you believe that?"

Valencia pulled away, holding her by the shoulders. "Did they call Ambrose?"

She knew him? "Uh...yeah."

Valencia glanced toward the kitchen, and then met her eyes in a conspiratorial manner. "I used to have the biggest crush on him."

"On a vampire? Are you serious?"

Valencia tilted her head to the side and studied her.

The look on Valencia's face gave her a bad feeling. "What?"

"I'm a vampire. Didn't you know?"

Brianna pulled away, seeing Valencia in a whole new light. Just when she was feeling comfortable...

"It's not as though I'm going to bite you. What did you think I was?"

Brianna made an attempt to regain her composure, something she found herself doing a lot of lately. "I thought you were a demon like the rest of them."

"There are no women demons that I'm aware of. Women are smart like that. When we know we have it good we're less likely to throw it away."

Oh, like she was supposed to know that. It wasn't like CNN did special news reports on shit like that.

She made a wide circle around Valencia and settled on the couch. If only Asmodeus were here, she would ask him what he thought of the proposal. What if she gave birth to a monster? A hybrid VampNeph with demonic powers? Good grief.

"Brianna, if Ambrose agrees to turn you, you should do it. He's a former Warrior Angel who fell from grace. He's the first vampire. The only vampire with the ability to turn someone without taking too much away from them."

She'd heard all of this before, except for the last part. She really didn't want to ask, but found herself trudging ahead like a good little girl scout. "Take what away?"

Valencia sat next to her on the couch. "Let me put it to you this way. If I were to turn you, you would become a vampire, but the transformation would be risky. My blood isn't strong enough. Those who are made by Ambrose are just as they were before they were turned, only they drink blood to survive. In the beginning you can't go into the light, but within a century or two, the light will no longer bother you."

A century or two? She'd said it in such a nonchalant manner, as if living that long were completely normal. "So vampires are immortal?"

"Yes. I was born in the tenth century."

The age didn't surprise her much, as she had thought Valencia much older than that. Brianna's original assumption was that Valencia was a demon, and angels had existed from the beginning of time. "And who do you drink from? Humans?"

"I drink from Naberius. Demon blood is thicker, and can sustain me longer. I'm sure he wouldn't mind if you drank from him."

She figured if she wanted to vomit just from the thought of drinking Naberius's blood, actually doing so could pose a problem. "Gee, thanks. Why don't we just do a threesome?"

"If you're into that kind of thing."

Oh. My. God. This day was getting better and better. The image that surfaced was just... She cleared her throat. "Um, no. Thanks."

Valencia put a hand on her shoulder. The faint sound of the doorbell rang. "In all seriousness, if I were you I'd give it a try. You have more to lose if you don't."

Valencia left the room to get the door and Brianna took that time to sort through everything she had learned. No one had said being a vampire was a bad thing. There seemed to be no downside to the transition.

Except for the whole blood-drinking thing. *Disgusting.*

Ah, damn. What choice did she really have?

A slew of feminine voices came from the hallway. She looked up to see the three fanged sluts walk into the living room.

Great.

"So Ambrose is going to, like, turn you? You're going to love it."

All three were still dressed like sluts, but the threatening vibe was gone. She guessed they were just protecting their territory the other night. Had it really only been a few days?

The girl with the long blonde hair sat next to her, and the redhead sat on her other side. The one with the pixie cut plopped into a sitting position on the floor in front of her.

She was trapped.

"I'm Carrie," the blonde said, holding her hand out. Brianna shook it. "And this is Trish and Nadine."

Trish was the one with the pixie cut. She smiled and Brianna saw her fangs. "Raum told us to come and talk to you. What do you want to know?"

Brianna scooted back into the couch. How thoughtful of Raum. Actually, where else could she get answers from such blunt vampires? "I don't know. I guess...what's it like?"

"So awesome—"

"—senses are amplified—"

"Sex is insane."

Brianna closed her eyes and shook her head. "Whoa, whoa, whoa. Let's start off with Pixie. What is so awesome about being a vampire?"

Pixie perked up. "Pixie. I love the name." She ran a hand back and forth over her hair, causing it to look messy. "Well, I like being a vamp because I'll never age."

"That is such a plus."

"Oh yeah, no wrinkles!"

"No Depends for us."

Brianna turned to the blonde, rolling her eyes at the Depends comment. "Why is sex better?"

"I knew that'd get your interest." She winked at her. "All of your senses are heightened. Sense of smell, touch, hearing. You can move faster...get it? Faster. Harder."

"I get it." She wasn't so worried about her sexual appetite. Not when the man she wanted was currently being tortured for the next two millennia. At least she would still be alive when Asmodeus was released—not that she expected him to be happy to see her. "So you don't regret changing? How did it happen?"

The redhead spoke up. "Last year we went on a trip to Scotland. We got snatched up by a class D vamp. He nearly killed us. Class D vamps are the dumbest vampires. Ambrose turned us, since we would have died. He didn't want to, 'cause he generally doesn't like making more vampires, but he felt it his honor-bound duty. I guess he thinks all of the vampire's evil deeds reflect on him, because he was the first."

"Yeah, he's such a bleeding heart. But he's hot, so that's cool."

When they started talking about how they'd like to bang the ancient vampire, she quietly excused herself. When she walked into the kitchen Raum and Naberius were waiting for her. She fought past the lump in her throat. Becoming a vampire didn't seem all that bad. Not when she looked at the big picture. And it did give her hope for her child.

"All right, let's do it."

"Yeah, well, you're calling Ambrose back," Naberius said as he slid the phone across the table at her. He took a drag off his cigarette. "Slamming the phone down on him pissed him off and he's not someone you want to piss off. Especially since he's only trying to help."

Okay. Now she had to call the vampire and beg him to sink his fangs into her flesh. Piece of cake.

Next, please?

£

Michael dropped Asmodeus in the third tier of the Abyss after explaining he had to go back and retrieve the *Demonic Book of Spells* from Raum. The book would remain safe in his office. He'd also mentioned that Brianna had summoned him to speak to him about Asmodeus.

The thought of Brianna fighting for him gave him high hopes of their future together. The only thing that hung in the air was that Michael would not expand on what he meant by Brianna not being human by the time he got back to her realm.

As he settled on the mist he inhaled the invigorating air. He was used to smells and wind, not the void that currently surrounded him. Michael's office contained material things—chairs, desk, files. The third tier of the Abyss resembled Heaven. A virtual space of light and mist.

Zagzagel, the Angel of Wisdom, took his place at the front of the vast gathering area. Asmodeus could sense others, but as was the rules, he could not see them. He was not permitted to be distracted in this area of the Abyss; he was to learn.

He focused on the angel and willed his thoughts away. Three weeks of learning and he would be free.

£

Kelly set the romance novel down and put her head in her hands. Powers she had always dreamt of having were now hers to control, yet she couldn't effectively harness them. It was all foreign to her, as these powers didn't come from the energy of the earth. They were just...there.

She picked her book back up and flipped to the page she had been on. She had to quit thinking about the powers. It was going to make her lightheaded, as it had so many times in the past few days.

She sat upright as a man walked into the room. His aura was bright—blinding.

He was an angel.

And he held the *Demonic Book of Spells* in his hands. She felt the pull instantly, surprised the book still had a hold on her.

"This is not the last time you will see the book. I am taking it with me. Weigh your actions carefully when you see this book again."

He disappeared, leaving her to stare in wonder.

£

"Brianna, hold still."

Fuck this. "I changed my mind."

Ambrose sighed and moved away from her, resting his back against the headboard of the bed. For the umpteenth time he pinched the bridge of his nose.

He was a scary bastard, and she was having a hard time getting past that. He reminded her of Naberius. Long black hair, angular jaw, and a look that screamed, "Don't fuck with me or I'll dismember you."

And his eyes. *Ack.*

When he first came into the room his eyes had been a very light blue. When it came time to go all vamp on her, his eyes had gone completely white. No pupils, no color, just white. The only other time she had seen that had been at Raum's house, and it was just as disturbing now as it had been then. Actually, it was more disturbing since she was expected to just let him latch on to her.

"Just give me a minute," she said as she paced the room.

"I've given you two *hours*."

Okay. This wasn't sexual. He was married for Pete's sake. It was just a bite. He had to drain her, and he assured her when it came time for her to bite him she wouldn't get sick. It would feel necessary. Natural in a way.

Whatever.

Okay. Okay. She sat back on the bed, laying herself out like a sacrifice. "Okay. Just do it and get it over with."

"This time I'm not letting you up."

Her heart stopped. She looked up to see him leaning over her. His eyes white, his jaw set, she decided going this route was total crap. "Never mind. I don't—"

True to his word, he didn't give her a chance to change her mind. He bent down, held her by the arms and bit her neck.

Chapter Twenty-Three

Asmodeus flashed himself to Naberius's after he had already checked Brianna's house and her bookstore. She was either running errands or some such thing. He needed a cell phone to call her and he had left his cell at Raum's. Not wanting to run into Raum and Kelly, he opted to use Naberius's phone.

"Naberius?"

The house seemed quiet, but there was a small pocket of energy coming from upstairs. He took the stairs two at a time, just wanting a cell to call Brianna. Having to endure three weeks of the third tier of the Abyss made him antsy.

When he reached the top of the stairs he caught Naberius and Raum pacing. Valencia sat against the wall, and even she seemed unnerved. The three vamps he'd met at Raum's place sat next to Valencia.

"Hey."

Naberius's eyes bugged out of his head. "Asmoday? I thought I'd sensed you but I—"

"What the fuck?" Raum actually backed away from him.

Why were they all convened like some paranormal boy scout troop? He ignored their strange behavior. "Long story. Can I borrow your cell? I can't find Brianna."

Both fell silent. Naberius looked as though he were going to be sick.

A coldness settled in his stomach. He recalled Michael's

words.

"Because in a few weeks' time Brianna will no longer be human."

"What is it? What's going on?"

Raum stuttered. "I... Uh..."

Naberius stepped forward and held his hands out. "Now, don't get alarmed. Everything's being handled."

Asmodeus took a step toward Naberius, his heart pounding. "What is being handled? Does this have anything to do with Brianna? So help me God, if you—"

"We all agreed it was in her and the baby's best interest."

"Naberius—"

He heard gagging coming from the room everyone seemed to be huddled around. He took a step toward the door and Raum and Naberius stepped in front of him, as if to head him off. Even Valencia and the three vamps straightened to stand in front of him.

"Brianna's in there?"

All stayed in front of him, creating a virtual brick wall.

He heard more gagging, followed by a fit of coughing.

What the hell was happening in that room? Better yet, what were they *allowing* to happen in that room? *She will no longer be human...*

"Get the hell out of my way. Now."

"Asmodeus—"

He shoved all six of them to the side and shouldered his way through the door.

What he saw stopped him cold.

Brianna sat up on the large bed holding a man's wrist to her mouth. Every now and again she would let go of his wrist and gag.

The man turned to see who had come into the room. Ambrose. A Warrior Angel. The first vampire.

She will no longer be human...

"What in the hell are you doing?" Ambrose barked.

Brianna finally looked up at him. She looked stricken and sick to her stomach. But then recognition dawned. "Asmodeus?" She sounded as though her throat were raw. She tried getting off the bed, but Ambrose stopped her by holding her arm.

"Enough," Ambrose said, turning back to Brianna. "Finish or you won't live throughout the day."

She kept her eyes locked on his. When she opened her mouth to speak, he saw two fangs.

Jesus Christ! "Get off her!"

Asmodeus went for Ambrose's throat, and Raum and Naberius grabbed him from behind as Valencia placed herself between him and Ambrose. He fought against their hold, wanting to launch them across the room.

Ambrose pushed himself off the bed and stood to face him. "She has to finish. She's in a transition state right now. Get him the hell out of here."

He broke Raum's hold and was about to launch Naberius against the wall when Brianna shook her head, still looking shocked he was even there. "It's done, Asmodeus. Let me finish. It hurts."

"She's not finished feeding. If she doesn't continue her pain will only become more severe." Ambrose looked back at Brianna as if checking on her.

Asmodeus held up his hands, telling them without words he wasn't going to fight them any longer. Jesus, they had turned her into a vampire. "Finish then. But I stay."

She looked like she wanted to argue, but didn't have the strength. The dark blue eyes he loved so much were much lighter. Almost white. She nodded as Ambrose settled back on the bed.

When he held out his wrist she blanched. She looked as though she didn't want to feed. That must have been her gagging. He could see the two small pinpricks on her neck where Ambrose had drained her.

Ambrose put his wrist closer to her mouth. "You haven't

taken enough."

She looked at his wrist as though it were a snake. "I thought you said this would seem natural to me."

Asmodeus slowly walked to the bed and sat on the other side of her. He would demand explanations later. Right now she needed to finish her transition. He had to touch her. Know that she truly was there...in the room. This was real.

He held her hand and squeezed.

As she squeezed back she lowered her head to Ambrose's wrist. She stayed on his wrist for the duration of the transition, falling asleep sitting up.

Asmodeus gently laid her back against the pillows.

"She'll sleep for a few days as her body adjusts."

"Explain to me the reason for this decision."

As Ambrose spoke of the reason for the change he felt hope rise in his chest. Had he found his redemption in Brianna and their child? Could they be saved with the blood of a vampire running through her veins?

£

Brianna came in and out of consciousness for the next few days. Ambrose had left, telling him he could supply the blood she would need now. She also had to be kept out of the sunlight at all costs.

Brianna hadn't taken any blood from him yet. She acted as though she would retch from the mere thought of it.

The sun was just now setting. She would be waking in a few short minutes. It was uncanny the way her body responded to the onset of twilight. Her eyes would open the second the sun was gone from the sky, an instinctual habit Ambrose had said was common in newly formed vampires.

Right on time, her eyes fluttered open and she smiled when she saw him, showing off her tiny fangs. "Good evening."

She thought it funny to say *guud eeevning* the way Dracula did in some obnoxious movie about vampires.

"Sleep well?"

"Like the dead."

Her way of coping with the transition had been humor. She was dealing with her new life quite well. Except for the blood-drinking aspect. "Ambrose said you should feed today."

All humor faded from her face. "Maybe later."

"I think now would be a good time."

"I don't think anytime is a good time to drink someone else's blood."

He smiled at the look on her face. Who would have thought? His little vampire didn't like drinking blood. "I hear when done right, the process can be very stimulating."

She sat up against the pillows, her interest obviously overshadowing her disgust on the subject. "What do you mean?"

"Sexually stimulating."

He watched as the hunger surfaced on her face. Whether it was bloodlust, or sexual in nature, he couldn't decide. She was likely hungry for both. So he hoped.

"I...I don't know."

In all his long life he hadn't thought he would try to convince a vampire to take from him. He'd heard of them in the fifties, when he had a brief stint in this realm, but until recently he had never seen one up close. Not until he met Valencia. She seemed decent enough.

He gently pulled her off the pillows, then settled himself on top of her. Perhaps in the throes of passion...

It didn't take long. She wrapped her arms around his neck and gently sank her fangs into his flesh. Bringing her leg over his hip, she ground against him.

This bonding was...sensual. Just the knowledge that he was sustaining her, providing for her, touched something deep inside of him. He had a purpose. Brianna and his child. He finally belonged somewhere and knew he was needed.

Before long she retracted her fangs. It was obvious she was still getting used to this way of surviving.

"Thank you."

"Do not ever thank me for this."

"Not for this. With Michael. When you—"

"I would do anything for you, Brianna." He vanished the clothes he had put on her earlier. He needed to feel her, skin to skin.

"I should have told you about the angels."

Damn she was beautiful. Her cheeks were flushed after her feeding. She looked like a vision. "What angels?"

She rolled her eyes. "The angels who gave me my mission. I meant to tell you, but I was afraid the second I told you they would come and take us both away. So I thought it best to keep it to myself. I just wanted more time with you."

"Everything worked out." Couldn't they talk about this later? He didn't want to talk. He wanted to taste. He lowered his head to do just that...

"Asmodeus."

Sighing, he brought his head up and looked down at her.

"I love you."

Her whispered declaration took his breath. He lightly kissed her on the lips. "I love you, Brianna."

"Okay. Get back to what you were doing," she said with a mischievous grin and a wiggle of her hips.

Chapter Twenty-Four

She waited as his gaze settled on her gift. Her heart beat painfully and her hands fidgeted on the seam of her shirt. He was either going to love this or hate her for bringing up the pain of his past.

She could hear the others by the bonfire, singing and laughing. The light from the moon and the stars shone down on them, and she could feel the power and energy they provided her. She missed the sun something fierce, and she was unable to run her bookstore, but she was content. Happy. Tracy had taken the management position before she had even finished pitching the idea to her. All was well.

Except for the pounding of her heart as she waited for Asmodeus's reaction to her present.

When he finally turned to her, he had tears in his eyes. *Oh great. Oh shit.* She had only meant to honor his sons...

Without saying a word he took her in his arms and buried his face in her neck. "You will never know what this gesture means to me."

She let her gaze wander to the gravestones. Both stones were made of marble, and each of Asmodeus's sons' names had been etched into the smooth surfaces. She hadn't been aware of the dates of their life and death, so she had simply put, "Beloved son of Asmodeus. Cherished and loved."

She leaned into his strength and nestled into his arms. "I just thought that they deserved a resting place. Even if...even if they aren't really..."

"I understand." He pulled away and put his palms on her face. "I can come here when I think of them and remember my time spent with them."

She nodded, grateful that he had understood her meaning.

His strength and powers still astounded her. She was just now getting used to her own. Though she could only be out at night, being a vampire definitely had its advantages. Coupled with her own powers, of which she was no longer denied, and Asmodeus's blood, she could feel the power as it surged through her.

"Come on, guys. The steaks are almost done. Brianna, we made yours super rare, because us creatures of the night like it like that."

Pixie, who loved her new nickname, went skipping back to the others who were relaxed on Naberius's back lawn. Raum, Kelly, Valencia, Nadine, Carrie and Naberius were waiting for them. She was thankful they had respected her privacy, though privacy was something she would likely experience very little of in the house from now on.

All but Raum and Kelly were going to be living with Naberius. It was decided that until Asmodeus figured out what he was going to do for a job—now *that* should prove interesting—they would stay with Naberius. Carrie, Pixie and Nadine weren't too happy about living with Kelly, who was, as they put it, "constantly sucking on Raum," so they opted to take Valencia's invitation to stay with them for the time being.

"I have a present for you as well."

"Really?" She couldn't imagine what he had for her. There wasn't anything else she wanted.

"I spoke to Michael earlier this afternoon while you were asleep."

Just hearing his name annoyed her, but she'd forgiven the archangel after he gave her back her powers. "And?"

"I point-blank asked him about our child."

"Wh-What did he say?" She'd been trying to summon him again, but hadn't wanted to push it too far. She liked her new powers right where they were.

"He said he'd start saving for college if he were in our shoes. That shit can get expensive."

She grabbed his arm. "No, seriously. What did he say?"

"I just told you."

"So...the baby..."

"Actually, he did slip up and say one other thing."

She squeezed his arm. "Asmodeus..."

"He mentioned that you had promised your firstborn to him. But he said he'll just settle on us naming the baby after him."

"It's...it's a boy?" She wasn't going to be able to go to a regular doctor, so she hadn't expected to know the sex of the baby.

"It's a boy."

She leaned into him as he wrapped his arms around her.

"Come on, guys. The food's getting cold."

She pulled back to look at the people gathered around the bonfire. Demons and vampires. Who would have thought? Reading the ancient texts was one thing. Learning from those who lived it was another. In some weird twist of fate everything had fallen into place. Even the dog, now named Hunter, pounced happily from person to person, tail wagging.

She walked hand in hand with Asmodeus to the bonfire, thankful for the turn her life had taken.

Oh, and there was one thing she learned that was absolutely true about vampires.

The sex really *was* better.

About the Author

I grew up in the city of Sacramento, California. I decided I wanted to see the world, so I enlisted in the Navy right out of school. Shortly after joining the Navy I was stationed in Italy where I met my husband—a Marine who guarded the building I worked in. No one can convince me that love at first sight does not exist. We have two beautiful daughters and now reside in his home state of Michigan.

To learn more about me, please visit www.dawnmcclure.com. Send me an email at dawn@dawnmcclure.com.

CPSIA information can be obtained at www.ICGtesting.com
Printed in the USA
BVOW042238180313

315871BV00001B/56/P

9 781605 044330